13

Tsutomu Sato

Illustration **Kana Ishida**

Illustration assistants
**Jimmy Stone,
Yasuko Suenaga**

Design **BEE-PEE**

The
Irregular
at
MagicHigh
School

Azusa Nakajou

Became student council president in place of Mayumi. Nervous, withdrawn personality.

"I can't believe they'd change the events like this!"

"Fortunately, we still have time..."

Kei Isori

Senior. Former student council treasurer. Top magic theory grades in his class. Engaged to Kanon Chiyoda.

Yakumo Kokonoe

A user of the ancient magic *ninjutsu*. Tatsuya's martial arts master.

"Thanks."

"Miyuki, I'm counting on you."

"Of course, Brother."

Tatsuya Shiba

The older brother of the Shiba siblings. In Class 2-E of the National Magic University First Affiliated High School. Sees right to the core of everything. His sister Miyuki's Guardian.

Miyuki Shiba

Class 2-A. Tatsuya's younger sister. Honors student who was the class representative last year. Cooling magic is her specialty. Adores her brother. A severe case of brother complex.

Masaki Ichijou

Junior at Third High. Entering the Nine School Competition for the second year in a row. Next head of the Ichijou family, one of the Ten Master Clans.

"Complaining about something that's already decided won't get us anywhere."

"I guess not..."

Shinkurou Kichijouji

Junior at Third High. Entering the Nine School Competition for the second year in a row. Known by the nickname Cardinal George.

"We'll performance test the Parasidolls at the Nines."

"Would you welcome these Taoist priests as your esteemed house-guests?"

Gongjin Zhou

A young man with handsome features who guided Chen and Lu to Yokohama. A mysterious figure who prowls Chinatown.

Retsu Kudou

One of the strongest magicians in the world. Called the Old Master out of respect.

Kanon Chiyoda

A senior. Became the disciplinary committee chairman after Mari stepped down. Engaged to Kei Isori.

"No need to push yourselves too hard, everyone!"

Ayako Kuroba

A girl who is Tatsuya's and Miyuki's second cousin. Has a younger twin brother named Fumiya.

"Victory is mine!"

Fumiya Kuroba

A boy who is a candidate for next head of the Yotsuba family. Tatsuya and Miyuki's second cousin. Has an older twin sister named Ayako.

"Phantom Blow!"

"Guh...!!"

Takuma Shippou

The freshman representative this year. Eldest son of the Shippou, one of the Eighteen Support Clans with strong magicians.

"ᵒᵒᵒᵒᵒᵒ"

The Prime Four

Mysterious combat gynoids who barged in during the new Nines event, the Cross-Country Steeplechase. Their code name refers to how they are the first four specimens of this type.

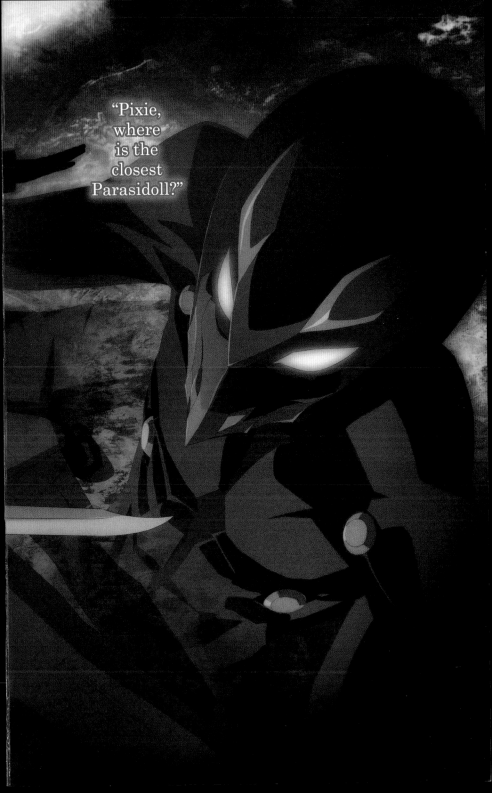

Magic Technician Development Institutes

Laboratories for the purpose of magician development that the Japanese government established one after another in response to the geopolitical climate, which had become strained prior to World War III in the 2030s. Their objectives were not to develop magic but specifically to develop magicians, researching various methods to give birth to human specimens who were most suitable for areas of magic that were considered important, including, but not limited to, genetic engineering.

Ten magic technician development institutes were established, numbered as such, and even today, five are still in operation.

The details of each institute's research are described below.

Magic Technician Development Institute One

Established in Kanazawa in 2031. Currently shut down.

Its research focus, revolving around close combat, was the development of magic that directly manipulated biological organisms. The vaporization spell Burst is derived from this facility's research. Notably, magic that could control a human body's movements was forbidden as it enabled puppet terrorism (suicide attacks using victims that had been turned into puppets).

Magic Technician Development Institute Two

Established on Awaji Island in 2031. Currently in operation.

Develops opposite magic to that of Lab One: magic that can manipulate inorganic objects, especially absorption-type spells related to oxidation-reduction reactions.

Magic Technician Development Institute Three

Established in Atsugi in 2032. Currently in operation.

With its goal of developing magicians who can react to a variety of situations when operating independently, this facility is the main driver behind the research on multicasting. In particular, it tests the limits of how many spells are possible during simultaneous casting and continual casting and develops magicians who can simultaneously cast multiple spells.

Magic Technician Development Institute Four

Details unknown. Its location is speculated to be near the old prefectural border between Tokyo and Yamanashi. Its establishment is believed to have occurred in 2033. It is assumed to be shut down, but the truth of that matter is unknown. Lab Four is rumored to be the only magic research facility that was established not only with government support but also investment from private sponsors who held strong influence over the nation; it is currently operating without government oversight and being managed directly by those sponsors. Rumors also say that those sponsors actually took over control of the facility before the 2020s.

It is said their goal is to use mental interference magic to strengthen the very wellspring of the talent called magic, which exists in a magician's unconscious—the magic calculation region itself.

Magic Technician Development Institute Five

Established in Uwajima, Shikoku, in 2035. Currently in operation.

Researches magic that can manipulate various forms of matter. Its main focus, fluid control, is not technically difficult, but it has also succeeded in manipulating various solid forms. The fruits of its research include Bahamut, a spell jointly developed with the USNA. Along with the fluid-manipulation spell Abyss, it is known internationally as a magic research facility that developed two strategic-class spells.

Magic Technician Development Institute Six

Established in Sendai in 2035. Currently in operation.

Researches magical heat control. Along with Lab Eight, it gives the impression of being a facility more for basic research than military purposes. However, it is said that they conducted the most genetic manipulation experiments out of all the magic technician development institutes, aside from Lab Four. (Though, of course, the full accounting of Lab Four's situation is not possible.)

Magic Technician Development Institute Seven

Established in Tokyo in 2036. Currently shut down.

Developed magic with an emphasis on anti-group combat. It successfully created colony control magic. Contrary to Lab Six, which was largely a nonmilitary organization, Lab Seven was established as a magician development research facility that could be relied on for assistance in defending the capital in case of an emergency.

Magic Technician Development Institute Eight

Established in Kitakyushu in 2037. Currently in operation.

Researches magical control of gravitational force, electromagnetic force, strong force, and weak force. It is a pure research institute to a greater extent than even Lab Six. However, unlike Lab Six, its relationship to the JDF is steadfast. This is because Lab Eight's research focus can be easily linked to nuclear weapons development, (though they currently avoid such connotations thanks to the JDF's seal of approval).

Magic Technician Development Institute Nine

Established in Nara in 2037. Currently shut down.

This facility tried to solve several problems modern magic struggled with, such as fuzzy spell manipulation, through a fusion of modern and ancient magic, integrating ancient know-how into modern magic.

Magic Technician Development Institute Ten

Established in Tokyo in 2039. Currently shut down.

Like Lab Seven, doubled as capital defense, researching area magic that could create virtual structures in space as a means of defending against high-firepower attacks. It resulted in a myriad of anti-physical barrier spells.

Lab Ten also aimed to raise magic abilities through different means from Lab Four. In precise terms, rather than enhancing the magic calculation region itself, they grappled with developing magicians who responded as needed by temporarily overclocking their magic calculation regions to use powerful magic. Whether their research was successful has not been made public.

Aside from these ten institutes, other laboratories with the goal of developing Elements were operational from the 2010s to the 2020s, but they are currently all shut down. In addition, the JDF possesses a secret research facility directly under the Ground Defense Force's General Headquarters' jurisdiction, established in 2002, which is still carrying on its research. Retsu Kudou underwent enhancement operations at this institution before moving to Lab Nine.

The Irregular at Magic High School

STEEPLECHASE ARC

13

Tsutomu Sato

Illustration Kana Ishida

YEN ON

NEW YORK

THE IRREGULAR AT MAGIC HIGH SCHOOL
TSUTOMU SATO

Translation by Andrew Prowse
Cover art by Kana Ishida

MAHOUKA KOUKOU NO RETTOUSEI Vol. 13
©TSUTOMU SATO 2014
First published in Japan in 2014 by KADOKAWA CORPORATION, Tokyo.
English translation rights arranged with KADOKAWA CORPORATION, Tokyo, through Tuttle-Mori Agency, Inc., Tokyo.

Yen On
150 West 30th Street, 19th Floor
New York, NY 10001

Visit us at yenpress.com
facebook.com/yenpress
twitter.com/yenpress
yenpress.tumblr.com
instagram.com/yenpress

First Yen On Edition: October 2019

Yen On is an imprint of Yen Press, LLC.
The Yen On name and logo are trademarks of Yen Press, LLC.

Library of Congress Cataloging-in-Publication Data
Names: Satou, Tsutomu. | Ishida, Kana, illustrator.
Title: The irregular at Magic High School / Tsutomu Satou ; Illustrations by Kana Ishida.
Other titles: Mahōka kōkō no rettosei. English
Description: First Yen On edition. | New York, NY : Yen On, 2016–
Identifiers: LCCN 2015042401 | ISBN 9780316348805 (v 1 : pbk.) | ISBN 9780316390293 (v. 2 : pbk.) |
    ISBN 9780316390309 (v. 3 : pbk.) | ISBN 9780316390316 (v. 4 : pbk.) |
    ISBN 9780316390323 (v. 5 : pbk.) | ISBN 9780316390330 (v. 6 : pbk.) |
    ISBN 9781975300074 (v. 7 : pbk.) | ISBN 9781975327125 (v. 8 : pbk.) |
    ISBN 9781975327149 (v. 9 : pbk.) | ISBN 9781975327163 (v. 10 : pbk.) |
    ISBN 9781975327187 (v. 11 : pbk.) | ISBN 9781975327200 (v. 12 : pbk.) |
    ISBN 9781975332327 (v. 13 : pbk.)
Subjects: CYAC: Brothers and sisters—Fiction. | Magic—Fiction. | High schools—Fiction. |
    Schools—Fiction. | Japan—Fiction. | Science fiction.
Classification: LCC PZ7.1.S265 Ir 2016 | DDC [Fic]—dc23
LC record available at http://lccn.loc.gov/2015042401

ISBNs: 978-1-9753-3232-7 (paperback)
        978-1-9753-3246-4 (ebook)

10 9 8 7 6 5 4 3 2 1

LSC-C

Printed in the United States of America

The Irregular at MagicHigh School

STEEPLECHASE ARC

An irregular older brother with a certain flaw.
An honor roll younger sister who is perfectly flawless.

When the two siblings enrolled in Magic High School,
a dramatic life unfolded—

Character

Tatsuya Shiba

Class 2-E. Advanced to the newly established magic engineering course. Sees right to the core of everything. His sister Miyuki's Guardian.

Miyuki Shiba

Class 2-A. Tatsuya's younger sister; enrolled as the top student last year. Specializes in freezing magic. Dotes on her older brother.

Leonhard Saijou

Class 2-F. Tatsuya's friend. Course 2 student. Specializes in hardening magic. Has a bright personality.

Erika Chiba

Class 2-F. Tatsuya's friend. Course 2 student. A charming troublemaker.

Mizuki Shibata

Class 2-E. In Tatsuya's class again this year. Has pushion radiation sensitivity. Serious and a bit of an airhead.

Mikihiko Yoshida

Class 2-B. This year he became a Course 1 student. From a famous family that uses ancient magic. Has known Erika since they were children.

Honoka Mitsui

Class 2-A. Miyuki's classmate. Specializes in light-wave vibration magic. Impulsive when emotional.

Shizuku Kitayama

Class 2-A. Miyuki's classmate. Specializes in vibration and acceleration magic. Doesn't show emotional ups and downs very much.

Subaru Satomi

Class 2-D. Frequently mistaken for a pretty boy. Cheerful and easy to get along with.

Eimi Akechi

Class 2-B. A quarter-blood. Full name is Amelia Eimi Akechi Goldie.

Akaha Sakurakouji

Class 2-B. Friends with Subaru and Amy. Wears gothic lolita clothes and loves theme parks.

Shun Morisaki

Class 2-A. Miyuki's classmate. Specializes in CAD quick-draw. Takes great pride in being a Course 1 student.

Hagane Tomitsuka

Class 2-E. A magic martial arts user with the nickname "Range Zero." Uses magic martial arts.

Mayumi Saegusa

An alum and former student council president. Has advanced to the Magic University. Has a devilish personality.

Azusa Nakajou

A senior. Student council president after Mayumi stepped down. Shy and has trouble expressing herself.

Suzune Ichihara

An alum and former student council treasurer. Calm, collected, and book smart. Mayumi's right hand.

Hanzou Gyoubu-Shoujou Hattori

A senior. Former student council vice president. Head of the club committee after Katsuto stepped down.

Mari Watanabe

An alum and former chairwoman of the disciplinary committee. Mayumi's good friend. Good all around and likes a sporting fight.

Katsuto Juumonji

An alum and former head of the club committee. Has advanced to Magic University. "A boulder-like person," according to Tatsuya.

Midori Sawaki

A senior. Member of the disciplinary committee. Has a complex about his girlish name.

Koutarou Tatsumi

An alum and former member of the disciplinary committee. Has a heroic and dynamic personality.

Isao Sekimoto

An alum and former member of the disciplinary committee. Lost the school election. Committed acts of spying.

Kei Isori

A senior. Student council treasurer. Top grades in his class in magical theory. Engaged to Kanon Chiyoda.

Kanon Chiyoda

A senior. Chairwoman of the disciplinary committee after Mari stepped down. Engaged to Kei Isori.

Takeaki Kirihara

A senior. Member of the *kenjutsu* club. Junior High Kanto Kenjutsu Tournament champion.

Kasumi Saegusa

A new student who enrolled at Magic High School this year. Mayumi Saegusa's younger sister. Izumi's older twin sister. Energetic and lighthearted personality.

Sayaka Mibu

A senior. Member of the kendo club. Placed second in the nation at the girls' junior high kendo tournament.

Izumi Saegusa

A new student who enrolled at Magic High School this year. Mayumi Saegusa's younger sister. Kasumi's younger twin sister. Meek and gentle personality.

Takuma Shippou

The head of this year's new students. Course 1. Eldest son of the Shippou, one of the Eighteen, families with excellent magicians.

Minami Sakurai

A new student who enrolled at Magic High School this year. In the position of Tatsuya and Miyuki's cousin. A Guardian candidate for Miyuki.

Kento Sumisu

Class 1-G. A Caucasian boy whose parents are naturalized Japanese citizens from the USNA.

Koharu Hirakawa

An alum and engineer during the Nine School Competition. Withdrew from the Thesis Competi-tion.

Chiaki Hirakawa

Class 2-E. Holds enmity toward Tatsuya.

Tomoko Chikura

A senior. Competitor in the women's solo Shields Down, a Nine School Competition event.

Satomi Asuka

First High nurse. Gentle, calm, and warm. Smile popular among male students.

Kazuo Tsuzura

First High teacher. Main field is magic geometry. Manager of the Thesis Competition team.

Jennifer Smith

A Caucasian naturalized as a Japanese citizen. Instructor for Tatsuya's class and for magic engineering classes.

Haruka Ono

A general counselor of Class 1-E. Tends to get bullied, but has another face.

Masaki Ichijou

A junior at Third High. Participating in the Nine School Competition this year as well. Direct heir to the Ichijou family, one of the Ten Master Clans.

Shinkurou Kichijouji

A junior at Third High. Participating in the Nine School Competition this year as well. Also known as Cardinal George.

Gouki Ichijou

Masaki's father. Current head of the Ichijou, one of the Ten Master Clans.

Midori Ichijou

Masaki's mother. Warm and good at cooking.

Akane Ichijou

Eldest daughter of the Ichijou. Masaki's younger sister. Enrolled in an elite private middle school this year. Likes Shinkurou.

Ruri Ichijou

Second daughter of the Ichijou. Masaki's younger sister. Stable and does things her own way.

Harumi Naruse

Shizuku's elder brother-in-law. Student at National Magic University Fourth Affiliated High School.

Yakumo Kokonoe

A user of an ancient magic called *ninjutsu*. Tatsuya's martial arts master.

Gongjin Zhou

A handsome young man who brought Lu and Chen from the Great Asian Alliance to Yokohama. A mysterious figure who hangs out in Chinatown.

Retsu Kudou

Renowned as the strongest magician in the world. Given the honorary title of Sage.

Makoto Kudou

Son of Retsu Kudou, elder of Japan's magic world, and current head of the Kudou family.

Rin

A girl Morisaki saved. Her full name is Meiling Sun. The new leader of the Hong Kong-based international crime syndicate No-Head Dragon.

Minoru Kudou

Makoto's son. Freshman at National Magic University Second Affiliated High School, but hardly attends due to frequent illness. Also Kyouko Fujibayashi's younger brother by a different father.

Xiangshan Chen

Leader of the Great Asian Alliance Army's Special Covert Forces. Has a heartless personality.

Mamoru Kuki

One of the Eighteen Support Clans. Follows the Kudou family. Calls Retsu Kudou "Sensei" out of respect.

Ganghu Lu

The ace magician of the Great Asian Alliance Army's Special Covert Forces. Also known as the "Man-Eating Tiger."

Toshikazu Chiba

Erika Chiba's oldest brother. Has a career in the Ministry of Police. A playboy at first glance.

Anna Rosen Katori

Erika's mother. Half Japanese and half German, was the mistress of Erika's father, the current leader of the Chiba.

Naotsugu Chiba

Erika Chiba's second-oldest brother. Possesses full mastery of the Chiba (thousand blades) style of *kenjutsu*. Nicknamed "Kirin Child of the Chiba."

Inagaki

A police sergeant with the Ministry of Police. Toshikazu Chiba's subordinate.

Hiromi Saeki

Brigadier general of the Japan Ground Defense Force's 101st Brigade. Ranked major general. Superior officer to Harunobu Kazama, commanding officer of the Independent Magic Battalion.

Harunobu Kazama

Commanding officer of the 101st Brigade's Independent Magic Battalion. Ranked major.

Muraji Yanagi

Executive officer of the 101st Brigade's Independent Magic Battalion. Ranked captain.

Shigeru Sanada

Executive officer of the 101st Brigade's Independent Magic Battalion. Ranked captain.

Kousuke Yamanaka

Executive officer of the 101st Brigade's Independent Magic Battalion. Physician ranked major. First-rate healing magician.

Kyouko Fujibayashi

Female officer serving as Kazama's aide. Ranked second lieutenant.

Ushio Kitayama

Shizuku's father. Big shot in the business world. His business name is Ushio Kitagata.

Sakai

Belongs to the Japan Ground Defense Force's general headquarters. Ranked colonel. Seen as staunchly anti–Great Asian Alliance.

Benio Kitayama

Shizuku's mother. Once an A-rank magician known for her oscillation magic.

Kouichi Saegusa

Mayumi's father and the current leader of the Saegusa. Also a top-top-class magician.

Wataru Kitayama

Shizuku's younger brother. Sixth grade. Dearly loves his older sister. Aims to be a magic engineer.

Maki Sawamura

An actress who has been nominated for best female actress in a leading role at various distinguished movie awards. Acknowledged not only for her beauty but also her acting skills.

Miya Shiba

Tatsuya and Miyuki's actual mother. Deceased. The only magician skilled in mental construction interference magic.

Honami Sakurai

Miya's Guardian. Deceased. Part of the first generation of the Sakura series, engineered magicians with strengthened magical capacity through genetic modification.

Sayuri Shiba

Tatsuya and Miyuki's stepmother. Dislikes them.

Ushiyama

Manager of Four Leaves Technology's CAD R & D Section 3. A person in whom Tatsuya places his trust.

Ernst Rosen

A prominent CAD manufacturer. President of Rosen Magicraft's Japanese branch.

Pixie

A home helper robot belonging to Magic High School. Official name 3H (Humanoid Home Helper: a human-shaped chore-assisting robot) Type P94.

Maya Yotsuba

Tatsuya and Miyuki's aunt. Miya's younger twin sister. The current head of the Yotsuba.

Hayama

An elderly butler employed by Maya.

Mitsugu Kuroba

Miya Shiba and Maya Yotsuba's cousin. Father of Ayako and Fumiya.

Ayako Kuroba

Tatsuya and Miyuki's second cousin. Has a younger twin brother named Fumiya. Student at Fourth High.

Fumiya Kuroba

A candidate for next head of the Yotsuba. Tatsuya and Miyuki's second cousin. Has an older twin sister named Ayako. Student at Fourth High.

Angelina Kudou Shields

Commander of the USNA's magician unit, the Stars. Rank is major. Nickname is Lina. Also one of the Thirteen Apostles, strategic magicians.

Virginia Balance

The USNA Joint Chiefs of Staff Information Bureau Internal Inspection Office's first deputy commissioner. Ranked colonel. Came to Japan in order to support Lina.

Silvia Mercury First

A planet-class magician in the USNA's magician unit, the Stars. Rank is warrant officer. Her nickname is Silvia, and Mercury First is her codename. During their mission in Japan, she serves as Major Sirius's aide.

Benjamin Canopus

Number two in the USNA's magician unit, the Stars. Rank is major. Takes command when Major Sirius is absent.

Mikaela Hongou

An agent sent into Japan by the USNA (although her real job is magic scientist for the Department of Defense). Nicknamed Mia.

Claire

Hunter Q—a female soldier in the magician unit Stardust for those who couldn't be Stars. Q refers to the 17th of the pursuit unit.

Alfred Fomalhaut

A first-degree star magician in the USNA's magician unit, the Stars. Rank is first lieutenant. Nicknamed Freddie.

Rachel

Hunter R—a female soldier in the magician unit Stardust for those who couldn't be Stars. R refers to the 18th of the pursuit unit.

Charles Sullivan

A satellite-class magician in the USNA's magician unit, the Stars. Called by the codename Deimos Second.

Raymond S. Clark

A student at the high school in Berkeley, USNA that Shizuku studies abroad at. A Caucasian boy who wastes no time making advances on Shizuku. Is secretly one of the Seven Sages.

Gu Jie

One of the Seven Sages. Also known as Gide Hague. A survivor of a Dahanese military's mage unit.

Glossary

Course 1 student emblem

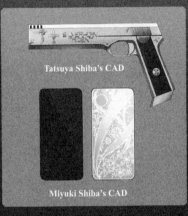

Tatsuya Shiba's CAD

Miyuki Shiba's CAD

Magic High School

Nickname for high schools affiliated with the National Magic University. There are nine schools throughout the nation. Of them, First High through Third High adopt a system of Course 1 and Course 2 students to split up its two hundred incoming freshmen.

Blooms, Weeds

Slang terms used at First High to display the gap between Course 1 and Course 2 students. Course 1 student uniforms feature an eight-petaled emblem embroidered on the left breast, but Course 2 student uniforms do not.

CAD (Casting Assistant Device)

A device that simplifies magic casting. Magical programming is recorded within. There are many types and forms, some specialized and others multipurpose.

Four Leaves Technology (FLT)

A domestic CAD manufacturer. Originally more famous for magical-product engineering than for developing finished products, the development of the Silver model has made them much more widely known as a maker of CADs.

Taurus Silver

A genius engineer said to have advanced specialized CAD software by a decade in just a single year.

Eidos (individual information bodies)

Originally a term from Greek philosophy. In modern magic, *eidos* refers to the information bodies that accompany events. They form a so-called record of those events existing in the world, and can be considered the footprints of an object's state of being in the universe, be that active or passive. The definition of *magic* in its modern form is that of a technology that alters events by altering the information bodies composing them.

Idea (information body dimension)

Originally a term from Greek philosophy; pronounced "ee-dee-ah." In modern magic, *Idea* refers to the *platform* upon which information bodies are recorded—a spell, object, or energy's *dimension*. Magic is primarily a technology that outputs a magic program (a spell sequence) to affect the Idea (the dimension), which then rewrites the eidos (the individual bodies) recorded there.

Activation Sequence

The blueprints of magic, and the programming that constructs it. Activation sequences are stored in a compressed format in CADs. The magician sends a psionic wave into the CAD, which then expands the data and uses it to convert the activation sequence into a signal. This signal returns to the magician with the unpacked magic program.

Psions (thought particles)

Massless particles belonging to the dimension of spirit phenomena. These information particles record awareness and thought results. Eidos are considered the theoretical basis for modern magic, while activation sequences and magic programs are the technology forming its practical basis. All of these are bodies of information made up of psions.

Pushions (spirit particles)

Massless particles belonging to the dimension of spirit phenomena. Their existence has been confirmed, but their true form and function have yet to be elucidated. In general, magicians are only able to sense energized pushions. The technical term for them is *psycheons*.

Magician

An abbreviation of *magic technician*. *Magic technician* is the term for those with the skills to use magic at a practical level.

Magic program

An information body used to temporarily alter information attached to events. Constructed from psions possessed by the magician. Sometimes shortened to *magigram*.

Magic-calculation region

A mental region that constructs magic programs. The essential core of the talent of magic. Exists within the magician's unconscious regions, and though he or she can normally consciously use the magic-calculation region, they cannot perceive the processing happening within. The magic-calculation region may be called a black box, even for the magician performing the task.

Magic program output process

❶ Transmit an activation sequence to a CAD. This is called "reading in an activation sequence."
❷ Add variables to the activation sequence and send them to the magic-calculation region.
❸ Construct a magic program from the activation sequence and its variables.
❹ Send the constructed magic program along the "route"—between the lowest part of the conscious mind and highest part of the unconscious mind—then send it out the "gate" between conscious and unconscious, to output it onto the Idea.
❺ The magic program outputted onto the Idea interferes with the eidos at designated coordinates and overwrites them.

With a single-type, single-process spell, this five-stage process can be completed in under half a second. This is the bar for practical-level use with magicians.

Magic evaluation standards

The speed with which one constructs psionic information bodies is one's magical throughput, or processing speed. The scale and scope of the information bodies one can construct is one's magical capacity. The strength with which one can overwrite eidos with magic programs is one's influence. These three together are referred to as a person's magical power.

Cardinal Code hypothesis

A school of thought claiming that within the four families and eight types of magic, there exist foundational "plus" and "minus" magic programs that number sixteen in total, and that by combining these sixteen, one can construct every possible typed spell.

Typed magic

Any magic belonging to the four families and eight types.

Exotyped magic

A term for spells that control mental phenomena rather than physical ones. Encompasses many fields, from divine magic and spirit magic—which employs spiritual presences—to mind reading, astral form separation, and consciousness control.

Ten Master Clans

The most powerful magician organization in Japan. The ten families are chosen every four years from among twenty-eight: Ichijou, Ichinokura, Isshiki, Futatsugi, Nikaidou, Nihei, Mitsuya, Mikazuki, Yotsuba, Itsuwa, Gotou, Itsumi, Mutsuzuka, Rokkaku, Rokugou, Roppongi, Saegusa, Shippou, Tanabata, Nanase, Yatsushiro, Hassaku, Hachiman, Kudou, Kuki, Kuzumi, Juumonji, and Tooyama.

Numbers

Just like the Ten Master Clans contain a number from one to ten in their surname, well-known families in the Hundred Families use numbers eleven or greater, such as Chiyoda (thousand), Isori (fifty), and Chiba (thousand). The value isn't an indicator of strength, but the fact that it is present in the surname is one measure to broadly judge the capacity of a magic family by their bloodline.

Non-numbers

Also called Extra Numbers, or simply Extras. Magician families who have been stripped of their number. Once, when magicians were weapons and experimental samples, this was a stigma between the success cases, who were given numbers, and the failure cases, who didn't display good enough results.

Various Spells

• Cocytus

Outer magic that freezes the mind. A frozen mind cannot order the flesh to die, so anyone subject to this magic enters a state of mental stasis, causing their body to stop. Partial crystallization of the flesh is sometimes observed because of the interaction between mind and body.

• Rumbling

An old spell that vibrates the ground as a medium for a spirit, an independent information body.

• Program Dispersion

A spell that dismantles a magic program, the main component of a spell, into a group of psionic particles with no meaningful structure. Since magic programs affect the information bodies associated with events, it is necessary for the information structure to be exposed, leaving no way to prevent interference against the magic program itself.

• Program Demolition

A typeless spell that rams a mass of compressed psionic particles directly into an object without going through the Idea, causing it to explode and blow away the psion information bodies recorded in magic, such as activation sequences and magic programs. It may be called magic, but because it is a psionic bullet without any structure as a magic program for altering events, it isn't affected by Information Boost or Area Interference. The pressure of the bullet itself will also repel any Cast Jamming effects. Because it has zero physical effect, no obstacle can block it.

• Mine Origin

A magic that imparts strong vibrations to anything with a connotation of "ground"—such as dirt, crag, sand, or concrete—regardless of material.

• Fissure

A spell that uses spirits, independent information bodies, as a medium to push a line into the ground, creating the appearance of a fissure opening in the earth.

• Dry Blizzard

A spell that gathers carbon dioxide from the air, creates dry-ice particles, then converts the extra heat energy from the freezing process to kinetic energy to launch the dry-ice particles at a high speed.

• Slithering Thunders

In addition to condensing the water vapor from Dry Blizzard's dry-ice evaporation and creating a highly conductive mist with the evaporated carbon dioxide in it, this spell creates static electricity with vibration-type magic and emission-type magic. A combination spell, it also fires an electric attack at an enemy using the carbon gas-filled mist and water droplets as a conductor.

• Niflheim

A vibration- and deceleration-type area-of-effect spell. It chills a large volume of air, then moves it to freeze a wide range. In blunt terms, it creates a super-large refrigerator. The white mist that appears upon activation is the particles of frozen ice and dry ice, but at higher levels, a mist of frozen liquid nitrogen occurs.

• Burst

A dispersion-type spell that vaporizes the liquid inside a target object. When used on a creature, the spell will vaporize bodily fluids and cause the body to rupture. When used on a machine powered by internal combustion, the spell vaporizes the fuel and makes it explode. Fuel cells see the same result, and even if no burnable fuel is on board, there is no machine that does not contain some liquid, such as battery fluid, hydraulic fluid, coolant, or lubricant; once Burst activates, virtually any machine will be destroyed.

• Disheveled Hair

An old spell that, instead of specifying a direction and changing the wind's direction to that, uses air current control to bring about the vague result of "tangling" it, causing currents along the ground that entangle an opponent's feet in the grass. Only usable on plains with grass of a certain height.

Magic Swords

Aside from fighting techniques that use magic itself as a weapon, another method of magical combat involves techniques for using magic to strengthen and control weapons. The majority of these spells combine magic with projectile weapons such as guns and bows, but the art of the sword, known as *kenjutsu*, has developed in Japan as well as a way to link magic with sword techniques. This has led to magic technicians formulating personal-use magic techniques known as magic swords, which can be said to be both modern magic and old magic.

1. High-Frequency Blade

A spell that locally liquefies a solid body and cleaves it by causing a blade to vibrate at a high speed, then propagate the vibration that exceeds the molecular cohesive force of matter it comes in contact with. Used as a set with a spell to prevent the blade from breaking.

2. Pressure Cut

A spell that generates left-right perpendicular repulsive force relative to the angle of a slashing blade edge, causing the blade to force apart any object it touches and thereby cleave it. The size of the repulsive field is less than a millimeter, but it has the strength to interfere with light, so when seen from the front, the blade edge becomes a black line.

3. Douji-Giri (Simultaneous Cut)

An old-magic spell passed down as a secret sword art of the Genji. It is a magic sword technique wherein the user remotely manipulates two blades through a third in their hands in order to have the swords surround an opponent and slash simultaneously. *Douji* is the Japanese pronunciation for both "simultaneous" and "child," so this ambiguity was used to keep the inherited nature of the technique a secret.

4. Zantetsu (Iron Cleaver)

A secret sword art of the Chiba clan. Rather than defining a katana as a hulk of steel and iron, this movement spell defines it as a single concept, then the spell moves the katana along a slashing path set by the magic program. The result is that the katana is defined as a mono-molecular blade, never breaking, bending, or chipping as it slices through any objects in its path.

5. Jinrai Zantetsu (Lightning Iron Cleaver)

An expanded version of Zantetsu that makes use of the Ikazuchi-Maru, a personal-armament device. By defining the katana and its wielder as one collective concept, the spell executes the entire series of actions, from enemy contact to slash, incredibly quickly and with faultless precision.

6. Mountain Tsunami

A secret sword art of the Chiba clan that makes use of the Orochi-Maru, a giant personal weapon six feet long. The user minimizes their own inertia and that of their katana while approaching an enemy at a high speed and, at the moment of impact, adds the neutralized inertia to the blade's inertia and slams the target with it. The longer the approach run, the greater the false inertial mass, reaching a maximum of ten tons.

7. Usuba Kagerou (Antlion)

A spell that uses hardening magic to anchor a five-nanometer-thick sheet of woven carbon nanotube to a perfect surface and make it a blade. The blade that Usuba Kagerou creates is sharper than any sword or razor, but the spell contains no functions to support moving the blade, demanding technical sword skill and ability from the user.

Strategic Magicians: The Thirteen Apostles

Because modern magic was born into a highly technological world, only a few nations were able to develop strong magic for military purposes. As a result, only a handful were able to develop "strategic magic," which rivaled weapons of mass destruction.

However, these nations shared the magic they developed with their allies, and certain magicians of allied nations with high aptitudes for strategic magic came to be known as strategic magicians.

As of April 2095, there are thirteen magicians publicly recognized as strategic magicians by their nations. They are called the Thirteen Apostles and are seen as important factors in the world's military balance. The Thirteen Apostles' nations, names, and strategic spell names are listed below.

USNA

Angie Sirius: Heavy Metal Burst
Elliott Miller: Leviathan
Laurent Barthes: Leviathan
* The only one belonging to the Stars is Angie Sirius. Elliott Miller is stationed at Alaska Base, and Laurent Barthes outside the country at Gibraltar Base, and for the most part, they don't move.

New Soviet Union

Igor Andreivich Bezobrazov: Tuman Bomba
Leonid Kondratenko: Zemlja Armija
* As Kondratenko is of advanced age, he generally stays at the Black Sea Base.

Great Asian Alliance

Yunde Liu: Pilita (Thunderclap Tower)
* Yunde Liu died in the October 31, 2095, battle against Japan.

Indo-Persian Federation

Barat Chandra Khan: Agni Downburst

Japan

Mio Itsuwa: Abyss

Brazil

Miguel Diez: Synchroliner Fusion
* This magic program was named by the USNA.

England

William MacLeod: Ozone Circle

Germany

Karla Schmidt: Ozone Circle
* Ozone Circle is based on a spell co-developed by nations in the EU before its split as a means to fix the hole in the ozone layer. The magic program was perfected by England and then publicized to the old EU through a convention.

Turkey

Ali Sahin: Bahamut
* This magic program was developed in cooperation with the USNA and Japan, then provided to Turkey by Japan.

Thailand

Somchai Bunnag: Agni Downburst
* This magic program was provided by Indo-Persia.

The International Situation
State of the World in 2096

West EU and East EU are allied states, but nations are independent

New Soviet Union

Japan, Mongolia, and Kazakhstan are in an alliance

Japan

USNA (United States of North America)

Indo-Persian Federation

Great Asian Alliance

Taiwan is an independent nation

Arab Alliance

Southeast Asian Alliance (includes Taiwan, the Philippines, and New Guinea)

African Continent (southwestern portions are mostly lawless)

Brazil

Other nations have broken into regional local governments

World War III, also called the Twenty Years' Global War Outbreak, was directly triggered by global cooling, and it fundamentally redrew the world map.

The USA annexed Canada and the countries from Mexico to Panama to form the United States of North America, or the USNA.

Russia reabsorbed Ukraine and Belarus to form the New Soviet Union.

China conquered northern Burma, northern Vietnam, northern Laos, and the Korean Peninsula to form the Great Asian Alliance, or GAA.

India and Iran absorbed several central Asian countries (Turkmenistan, Uzbekistan, Tajikistan, and Afghanistan) and South Asian countries (Pakistan, Nepal, Bhutan, Bangladesh, and Sri Lanka) to form the Indo-Persian Federation.

The other Asian and Arab countries formed regional military alliances to resist the three superpowers: the New Soviet Union, GAA, and the Indo-Persian Federation.

Australia chose national isolation.

The EU failed to unify and split into an eastern and a western section bordered by Germany and France. These east-west groupings also failed to form unions and now are actually weaker than they were before unification.

Africa saw half its nations destroyed altogether, with the surviving ones barely managing to retain urban control.

South America, excluding Brazil, fell into small, isolated states administered on a local government level.

The Irregular at Magic High School

New Rules of the Nine School Competition

* For old rules and events, please refer to print Volumes 3 and 4.

Number of Entrants

Twelve each for men's and women's rosters in the main competition; nine each for men's and women's rosters in the rookie competition.

■ Ice Pillars Break	3 entrants (1 in solo match, 2 in pair match); rookie competition is pair only.
■ Rower and Gunner	3 entrants (1 in solo match, 2 in pair match); rookie competition is pair only.
■ Shields Down	3 entrants (1 in solo match, 2 in pair match); rookie competition is pair only.
■ Mirage Bat	3 entrants (individual event).
■ Monolith Code	3 entrants (team event).
■ Cross-Country Steeplechase	Anyone second-year or above can enter.

* Previous rules stated that one person may enter any two events, but this year each person may only enter the Cross-Country Steeplechase and one other event.

Event Methods

■ Ice Pillars Break ■ Shields Down	Three teams are assigned to each group to play qualifier matches. This applies to both solo and pair teams. The teams that place first in each group move on to the finals.
■ Rower and Gunner	Time trial for each competitor or team. Single lap. One lap is allowed for practice.
■ Mirage Bat	Two venues, six qualifying matches with four or five entrants in each (based on a lottery). First place in each match moves to a final match with six entrants. Three periods, with each period being 15 minutes. Five-minute break between periods. One match is one hour. Qualifier starting times are 8:00, 9:30, and 11:00. The finals will be at 19:00.
■ Monolith Code	Round-robin. Time limit for one match is one hour. Draws will be treated as a loss for both teams. Match starting times are 9:00, 10:30, 13:00, 14:30, and 16:00.
■ Cross-Country Steeplechase	Twelve entrants from each school run at the same time for a total of 108 entrants each for men's and women's.

Event Scoring

■ Ice Pillars Break	1st – 50 points, 2nd – 30 points, 3rd – 20 points
■ Shields Down ■ Rower and Gunner	1st – 60 points, 2nd – 40 points, 3rd – 20 points
■ Mirage Bat	1st – 50 points, 2nd – 30 points, 3rd – 20 points, 4th – 10 points
■ Monolith Code	1st – 100 points, 2nd – 60 points, 3rd – 40 points
■ Cross-Country Steeplechase	1st – 50 points, 2nd – 30 points, 3rd – 20 points, 4th–6th – 5 points, all other entrants 7th and below that reach the goal within one hour – 1 point.

Nine School Competition New Events

Rower and Gunner

Players compete by trying to complete a water course as quickly as possible while destroying targets. In the pair event, one pilots the boat, while the other handles the targets. In the solo event, one person does both. The waterway uses the Battle Board course. Targets are set up next to the waterway and overhead, with miniature boat targets running back and forth atop the water.

This is not a competition where multiple competitors (or pairs) run the course at once. The event is completely done in a time trial format where one person (or pair) attempts the course at a time.

To remove advantages and disadvantages of rowing order, the first lap is designated as a practice run, while the second lap is the real thing.

Each destroyed target subtracts a proportional amount of time from the course completion time. The team with the shortest overall time wins.

Shields Down

Players hold shields or affix them to their arms and attack the opponent's shields. Shields can be equipped anywhere on the body as long as it is at shoulder level or below.

Whoever disqualifies the opponent first wins. In pair matches, whichever team disqualifies both players in the enemy team first wins.

Disqualification occurs when shields break, players fall out of the ring, or players break the rules. Each player must have only one shield. However, attaching up to two handles is permitted.

There are no restrictions on shield shape. Curved surfaces are allowed. However, the curve cannot end up pointing outward. Hemispherical surfaces are permitted, but wavelike ones are not.

Shields must be at least 0.5 square meters for men and 0.3 square meters for women, with no limits on weight or thickness. However, injecting resin or other supportive materials into a shield is forbidden. Compression without injecting supportive materials is allowed. Magical strengthening is also allowed. A shield is considered broken when at least 30 percent of it has been destroyed.

Cross-Country Steeplechase

A cross-country event on a woodland course with obstacles. The course utilizes the Mount Fuji eastern artificial training woods, whose construction began in the 2040s.

Obstacles range from typical things such as rock walls, pitfalls, and mud to event-specific ones for JDF magicians like equipment that shoots automatically, devices that fire net-loaded bullets.

The course is an area four kilometers wide and four kilometers long, and players may take any route they wish so long as they stay within that area. The starting and goal lines are both four kilometers long, so runners can enter anywhere and finish anywhere within that area. Runners are fitted with a transmitter that works in tandem with a WPS, or wide-area positioning system, which relies on stratospheric platforms. By tracing these signals, judges can keep track of each runner's position.

Leaving the course at any point is grounds for disqualification. Jumping higher than the height of the trees is against the rules as well and is grounds for disqualification.

Many nets are strung up between the trees, so if a runner carelessly jumps to avoid an obstacle, they'll hit the net, take damage, get tangled in the net, and/or lose time.

Point distribution for both men's and women's events is 50 points for 1st, 30 for 2nd, 20 for 3rd, and 5 for 4th through 6th. In addition, all runners who complete the course in under an hour receive 1 point. All competitors (12 each for men and women) are permitted to enter this event. At most, men and women's events can earn 121 points each, making this final event more likely to create turnabout victories than Monolith Code.

As an event first adopted for the 2096 Nine School Competition, nobody has any proven traversal techniques yet, but schools are separated into those who move as a team in order to eliminate obstacles and those who move alone or in pairs to disperse the risk of encountering highly difficult obstacles.

Rule Change: Mirage Bat

Flight magic cannot be used for more than one minute at a time. Players are required to land within one minute.

[0]

Each of the ten magician development institutes founded in Japan had its own unique research theme.

For example, the theme of Lab One, the first established institute, was the practical implementation of biological-manipulation magic to create the most efficient weapon of all: directly interfering with a target's natural biological processes.

Lab Four used mental interference magic to aim for the strengthening of the magic calculation region itself, which exists in the magician's unconscious and is the wellspring of this strange ability dubbed "magic."

Lab Seven's goal was the development of magic that placed emphasis on combat against groups. Its fruit was colony-control magic.

And the theme of Lab Nine, built in Nara and inviting large numbers of ancient magicians, was to integrate ancient magic into modern.

By joining Lab Nine, these ancient magicians had hoped to improve upon the old magic passed down to them and, by scientific means, create new and more powerful spells. However, Lab Nine's only goal was to develop strong modern magic that used *elements* from ancient magic—the production of talented magicians as *weapons*.

As a result, the ancient magicians gained nothing, their work taken advantage of and their secrets stolen. They could never be satisfied with this course of events, of course; one could call it inevitable that they'd harbor enmity toward magicians crowned with the character for "nine."

This antagonism was still deep-rooted even now in 2096 AD.

Monday, June 25, 2096 AD. Retsu Kudou, in two capacities—as senior member of Japan's magic world and retired Japan Ground Defense Force major general—was paying a visit to the old Magician Development Institute Nine with Makoto Kudou, his eldest son and current head of the Kudou family.

Lab Nine, as a national institution, had been shut down not long after World War III's conclusion, but it still maintained its functions as a laboratory. Currently, as a *civilian* research company and joint investment of the Kudou, Kuki, and Kuzumi families, it researched perception-type magic—a field struggling to make advancements compared to the more active, applied types of magic.

At least, that was supposed to be the case. While Lab Nine did present itself to the world this way, that wasn't its *main* research topic at the moment.

Retsu and Makoto had been led deep within the laboratory to a room where lines of life-sized human puppets stood.

Four rows and four columns, for a total of sixteen. The puppets, fixed to slender pillars, were female-type robots called gynoids.

If this had been a development lab for 3Hs—Humanoid Home Helpers—the sight might not have been that unusual. A few research facilities developed humanoid machines for other purposes, too, like military ones.

But gynoids stuck out in a magical laboratory—from an average, commonsense viewpoint.

"How is the progress?" asked Makoto.

The head researcher, the man who had guided them here, responded with a proud look. "The parasite cultivation is going smoothly, sir. Our proficiency at installing them in the gynoids has reached a success rate of sixty percent, too. As you can no doubt see, we have a total of sixteen Parasidoll prototypes."

"You've met the original quota, then."

"Yes, sir."

The scientist's attitude seemed conceited, but neither Makoto nor Retsu cared. The results his team had produced were worth bragging about.

The head researcher must have sensed their permissiveness—his silver tongue grew smoother by the minute.

"The cultivated parasites are currently in a complete sleep state inside the gynoids thanks to the effects of a loyalty spell. We're also no longer observing the resistance they originally exhibited. The loyalty spell was the greatest obstacle to getting the Parasidolls into a usable state—and allow me to say we have perfected it. Should you give the order, we can immediately begin performance tests."

The head researcher's anticipation-laden words exceeded Makoto's expectations. He'd assumed it would still take some time before they could conduct field testing; he hadn't mentally prepared a process for it in his head yet.

"It's too early for combat trials. You may have integrated the loyalty spell, but you have to test it more before letting them take any autonomous action."

The answer to the researcher's proposition came not from Makoto but from Retsu.

"We also don't know how much demon-power they can stably use outside of test conditions."

"Yes, sir, and like I said, the tests for that—" persisted the head scientist, unconvinced, before Retsu waved his hand to stop him.

"You're aware that in August every year, there is a competition among the magic high schools? This year, they've decided to adopt a cross-country event called the Steeplechase. It is a long-distance obstacle course where competitors have to overcome both physical and magical interference."

The researcher immediately understood Retsu's intent. "You'd like to use the Parasidolls as its obstacles in the event, sir?"

"Even the JDF likely doesn't have enough people to spare for a high school competition. Using the Parasidolls means that any retaliation from the students won't harm military magicians, and if we set a cap on their spirit power with the loyalty spell, we won't have to worry about students sustaining major injuries. It's the perfect chance to get them out of the testing rooms and conduct their first field tests."

"Father, will the administrative committee agree to that? Considering what the public's reaction will be if news of this experiment leaks, I don't think they would simply nod and agree."

Makoto hadn't been informed of Retsu's plan; he was merely expressing concern about how the public would treat the competition's administrative committee if high school students were being used as guinea pigs.

However, Retsu didn't waver. "No, the committee will nod and agree. They've already submitted to JDF intervention during this year's event selection. They don't have the backbone left to refuse our requests at this point."

However, Retsu didn't mention what they'd do if information got out. It was clear he had no intention of personally shouldering that responsibility.

And neither he nor Makoto pointed out the worst-case scenario—a Parasidoll losing control and harming a student.

Leaving the detailed procedures of the Parasidolls' performance testing to his son, Retsu returned to the main Kudou estate in Ikoma. As soon as he arrived, he headed for his grandson Minoru's room.

Minoru Kudou was a freshman at the National Magic University Second Affiliated High School and Makoto's youngest child. He would be turning sixteen this year. Normally, he would have still been at school at this time, but he was home sick for the day—*again*.

"Minoru, it's me."

Retsu knocked and announced himself, and after a somewhat hurried series of sounds, the room's door opened. A skinny, pale-skinned boy's face appeared from behind it. His features were gentle and delicate, but none would ever mistake him for a girl. He was a textbook pretty boy, should that sort of expression be permissible. He was also wearing rumpled pajamas.

"Grandfather, I apologize for my appearance."

His young and bright voice, a good match for his face, formed words of apology.

"No need to worry about things like that. Are you all right? Shouldn't you be resting?"

This wasn't false concern. Worry and heartfelt consideration for his pajama-clad grandson's health was clear in Retsu's expression.

Minoru tried to respond with a smile. "I'm okay. My fever's gone down already, so—"

But just as he was about to continue his sentence, a fit of severe coughing struck him, preventing him from accomplishing even that modest goal. His body had betrayed his heart. For Minoru, who didn't want his grandfather to worry, all he could do now was not cry in front of his family's esteemed patriarch.

"Minoru, lie down," prompted Retsu, rubbing his grandson's heaving back until the attack passed.

"Grandfather, I... All right."

Minoru was about to say he was fine again, but he stopped. He knew what state his own body was in, and he couldn't put on a brave face. He obediently returned to bed, knowing that was the right course of action to keep his grandfather from worrying any further.

After his grandson pulled the covers up to his neck, Retsu drew a chair closer and sat down. "Minoru, there's no need to rush things just because of how many absences you have," he explained in a gently admonishing tone.

Though he had said it to cheer Minoru up, it was also an honest assessment. "Your magic power stands at the top of your generation," he went on. "Almost no students can rival you—not even the ones entering the Nine School Competition."

It wasn't familial bias, either. Minoru possessed magic power worthy of the grandson of Retsu Kudou.

"Thank you, Grandfather."

Minoru knew his grandfather recognized his talents. The sorrow clouding his face cleared up; Retsu's words had succeeded in encouraging him.

At the same time, they'd been a little thoughtless.

"The Nines... I kind of wanted to enter it." Minoru sighed longingly.

Retsu Kudou felt like he'd been punched in the chest. "Minoru..."

By his magic power alone, Minoru would have 100 percent been chosen as a representative at the Nines for his school, Second High. But he'd spent a quarter of the year sick in bed; even if he had received an invitation, he would have had to turn it down so he wouldn't become a liability for his school's team.

"Don't look like that, Grandfather. The Nines isn't the only stage where I can display my power."

"That's right. You're bright, too. You'll have plenty of opportunities in the future to shine as a magician or as a magical engineer."

Retsu grinned at his smiling grandson while pushing down his own pain, which welled up in him.

Retsu distinctly understood that Minoru earnestly wanted to enter the competition and demonstrate the full extent of his natural talents where others would be watching. Retsu also knew that his grandson believed that opportunity would never come.

If he'd been healthy, he wouldn't have needed to give up on that future.

If he'd been powerless, he never would've harbored such a wish in the first place.

Minoru's abilities were incredible, and that was exactly why he suffered. Retsu thought it was terribly unfair.

Worse, it hadn't been any god or devil, some immaterial being, who had visited that unfairness upon him.

——The one who had engraved this miserable fate upon him was his own father.

——And the one who hadn't been able to stop it was his grandfather.

Self-loathing began to gnaw at his heart.

"By the way, Kyouko came to visit me today. She said she wanted to see you, too."

"Is that so? I'm glad to hear it, Minoru."

"Yep."

Among Retsu's grandchildren, Minoru and Kyouko Fujibayashi were especially friendly with each other. Minoru seemed genuinely happy as he talked about her visit.

His grandson was finally smiling for real—but that made him seem even more pitiful. Retsu began to find it difficult to be there. He placed his hand on his grandson's cheek to check that his fever wasn't too high, then stood.

"Why don't you rest for a while, Minoru? If you do, your fever should go down."

"I will, Grandfather."

After hearing his grandson's obedient reply, Retsu struggled to show him a smile in response before leaving Minoru's room.

In his study, Retsu sank deep into his favorite seat, a soft, over-stuffed leather armchair that he could imagine sinking into forever. The bottle of Armagnac on his sideboard beckoned to him, and he fetched it with just two steps; one there and one back.

And yet, he felt that escaping through alcohol would be intolerable right now.

How did it come to this? He knew that was a silly question. His story wasn't very unusual; it was egotism, pure and simple—shrugging off the ails of others as inevitable facts of life but worrying for hours upon hours when they befell his loved ones... Retsu tried to think about it that way, but no matter how much he ridiculed or berated himself, the anguish wouldn't go away. And he knew it wouldn't.

Minoru's frailty was a side effect of genetic manipulation. He was an engineered magician—a genetically modified human with an enhanced magic factor.

The reckless genetic manipulation of his own son was something Makoto had done because of his complex toward his father—Retsu. Ever since he was young, Makoto always felt inferior, because his magic power would never come close to matching his father's. His children were also merely average among the Ten Master Clans, possessing talent only slightly above his own, and he had despaired at not being able to grant them more.

Objectively speaking, Makoto and his children all had fairly strong magic power. Retsu was simply a poor measure to compare against. There was only one difference: Retsu had survived the acquired-strength program, which had a survival rate of 10 percent; Makoto displayed laudable abilities even without taking a similar risk. Retsu had told his son and heir as much, at every opportunity. But nothing he said was ever enough to convince Makoto.

When the disappointment inside him changed into an obsession with power, a madness began to take root within Makoto. He was imprisoned by the fallacious idea that if he couldn't *naturally* have an heir with high magic power, he'd simply create one artificially.

He'd further enhanced the Kudou genes, created by planned crossbreeding via artificial fertilization and synthetic womb technology, then used the genetic material to create the strongest magician.

Minoru was the result. Publicly, the story was that Minoru had been born after Makoto and his wife opted for in vitro fertilization. However, the truth was not nearly so *decent*.

Minoru's genetic father was Makoto Kudou.

His genetic mother was Makoto's youngest sister, who had married into the Fujibayashi family.

In other words, Minoru was Kyouko's half brother by a different father—a child born between siblings.

He was not a child born of incest, however. There had been no sexual relations between Makoto and his younger sister. They'd only provided the raw genetic material. However, there was no mistaking the fact that he was a child born to blood-related parents.

No one knew if Minoru's health condition was because of faulty genetic modification or an effect of the inbreeding. However, there was no doubt that this unique conception had cursed him.

From a magic-power reinforcing point of view, the engineering had been a success.

Minoru had some of the highest latent magical ability among modern magicians. His magic power could rival both Miyuki Shiba's and Angelina Sirius's.

But because of his extremely frail constitution, Minoru couldn't consistently display that magic power. He hadn't descended into infirmity like Mio Itsuwa, so he could use magic however he wanted when he wasn't sick. But as someone whose condition would leave him bed-ridden for even the smallest things, chances to flex his talent as a magician were limited.

Not only was Retsu's grandson unable to live a full-fledged magician's life, he couldn't even serve as a biological weapon, the role he'd been born to fulfill as an engineered magician. And after over ten years of agony, Retsu had come to one conclusion: It was the corruption of modern magic research, hell bent on turning magicians into living weapons, that had cast a terrible curse upon Minoru.

* * *

We must stop seeing magicians as weapons.

We must not create any more children like Minoru.

For the hundredth time, perhaps for the thousandth time, Retsu hardened his resolve.

[1]

After school, during the final week of June—despite regular examinations looming on the horizon—the National Magic University First Affiliated High School's student council room was abuzz with the clicking of keys, beeps, and occasional hushed voices going back and forth to ask questions, give replies, deliver reports, and discuss matters.

Their last afternoon class had ended about an hour ago. That meant the students hadn't been there for very long, but at that point, Tatsuya stood up and walked over to Azusa.

"President, I've organized all the reports and proposals from the autonomous committee and disciplinary committee in the directory called *Waiting for Decision*, so please go over them before tomorrow."

"I will… Um, I really wouldn't mind if you handled them all the way through, you know."

"That won't do, President."

Either Azusa trusted in his abilities or simply considered it a pain to handle. Tatsuya tersely shook his head, refusing her attempt to leave the work with him.

"Now if you'll excuse me."

"Thank you."

Closing time was still some ways away. The other members all continued their work without getting up. Despite that, Azusa very naturally accepted Tatsuya declaring that he'd be escaping, thanking him before he left.

Tatsuya was actually leaving early because of Azusa's instructions— or rather, her pleading.

Currently, the student council members numbered one president, two vice presidents, one accountant, and two secretaries, totaling six people. That was one more person than they had at this point last year. The amount of work each person was assigned had already decreased, but with Tatsuya involved, the situation had improved *too much*.

In short, Tatsuya had gone through his work too fast.

The student council was entrusted with multiple jobs necessary for the school's *operations*. This wasn't unique to magic high schools—it was considered standard for most schools at the end of the twenty-first century.

However, this didn't mean important matters that would affect the school's *management* were left up to students. Cases that ballooned out of proportion like the Blanche incident, which had happened the previous April, were rare. The student council's jobs mostly involved making simple decisions, overseeing adjustments that took quite a long while to deal with, and miscellaneous office work that was even more time-consuming.

And if Tatsuya put his processing power to full use, he could single-handedly finish all the decision-making and the office work with time to spare. That would leave the other members without work to do, which meant they'd lose opportunities to build experience.

At most, student council members were only in office for two and a half years. If Tatsuya did every little thing himself, his juniors would never learn, his classmates would forget how to do the work, and even his seniors would lose track of their progress. If he was ever absent for an extended time, the student council wouldn't get any work done; the school could even stop functioning.

That was a one-in-a-thousand risk, but the mere possibility was extremely bad. That was the conclusion the student president Azusa and the secretary Isori had made after the single month of April had gone by. Still, neither of them, especially not Azusa, had the nerve to directly ask him to take it easy. So, as a desperate last resort, they'd recommended that he leave early instead.

This was convenient for Tatsuya, too. From the beginning, all he'd wanted to do was browse the literature available only in Magic University–related facilities, which included the magic high schools, and use it to train. He hadn't volunteered for his positions (and the work that came with them) in the disciplinary committee and the student council. If they told him it was okay to stop working early, well, he had plenty of other ways to use the leftover time.

"Miyuki?"

"Yes, I'll be waiting for you."

They'd repeated this exchange so many times he no longer needed to say, "I'll come back to get you."

As Tatsuya left the student council room, Honoka, one of the secretaries, watched him restlessly.

As Tatsuya left the student council room, Izumi, the other secretary, glared after him coldly, as if to berate him for his laziness—but she did so discreetly, so that Miyuki wouldn't notice.

It was an awkward time of day to head to club activities. Thus, the changing room was empty; after changing into outdoors training gear, Tatsuya put the bag containing his uniform into his classroom locker before heading out to the practice woods behind the school.

The man-made forest was not only for magical training—it was created to meet the needs of students who aspired to be soldiers, police officers, rescue squad members, and the like. To facilitate their physical training, the planners had calculated the ideal tree density, as well as the rise and fall of the ground; they'd also placed ponds, sandy areas, waterways, and trails throughout the field; a variety of fixtures and devices had been installed in it, too. Because of its design, magic competition clubs weren't the only ones who used it as their main practice location. Clubs involving purely physical outdoors activities had their own assigned usage days, too.

Tatsuya was about to visit one of those nonmagic competitive clubs.

"Yo, Tatsuya," called his friend Leo before Tatsuya could offer his own greeting.

"Big Brother Tatsuya." Minami, having realized he had shown up, turned to him and bowed, a large teakettle in her hands.

"Thanks for letting me join, Leo. Minami, it looks like you're working hard, too." Tatsuya raised a hand in response. "By the way, where's Agata?" he asked, inquiring about their supervisor's whereabouts.

"Right here."

The answer to Tatsuya's question came from the man himself. Someone appeared from the thick underbrush in the woods, rather than from a running trail that cut between the trees: Kenshirou Agata, president of the mountaineering club that Leo belonged to.

To reach Agata, Tatsuya had to slip past the male first- and second-year club members lying on the ground moaning. Tatsuya bowed. "Thank you for giving me permission to be here again today."

"Sure thing. Take it easy. You can go ahead and put the freshmen through the wringer if you want."

Half the living corpses flinched at the remark, but none of the club members could get up to run away.

"All right. Maybe after I take a run around the course."

"After a run around the course? Is *that* all...?" Agata grinned. "And meanwhile, the rest of you..." Here he took a pitiful look around at the club members, who still couldn't get to their feet. "It was only a ten-kilometer run through the woods, you lazy bums! Look at Saijou—he's all ready to go."

"...Please don't compare us to with Leo," one of the juniors squeaked out. He'd recovered enough to speak, but he didn't seem able to get up yet.

"Enough complaining. The seniors are taking an extra lap around already. How long is this nap gonna take? I know none of you are dead yet."

Tired laughs went up here and there, and the juniors rallied their strength one by one to get themselves up. They didn't seem to appreciate him accusing them of playing dead.

However, the juniors were the only ones who got up. The freshmen didn't even have the strength left to be stubborn.

"What am I gonna do with you...? Sakurai!"

Minami, who had been waiting patiently until then, answered Agata with a "yes," picked up the teakettle she had left at her feet, then trotted up next to her nearest classmate.

"Do it."

"All right."

At Agata's instruction, Minami tilted the teakettle in her hands.

"Ow, hot!"

The liquid poured from the teakettle into a freshman's face. He rolled away from Minami's feet, then rose and scrambled away on wobbling legs.

"Boiling water...?" muttered Tatsuya unintentionally.

Leo, who had come up next to him, laughed and shook his head. "Nope. It's only one hundred thirteen, one hundred fourteen degrees at most. That's not enough to burn you."

The female members sitting in the shade only let out accidental smiles; they didn't seem to be worried. It seemed to be nothing major, certainly, but Tatsuya still thought it was rather violent.

"They say a century ago, people would douse rugby players who ·fell during a game with water from a kettle to raise their spirits," mentioned Agata upon overhearing their conversation, offering a bit of trivia.

"Was using hot water instead of cool water your idea, President?"

"Well, it *is* summer. The cold water felt so good for one guy that he fell asleep," explained Agata, revealing some insider information. And as they watched, Minami went from one male classmate to the next, baptizing each in hot water.

Several ropes were drawn across a pond, with slender logs suspended from them. As Tatsuya grabbed the logs to propel himself forward through the air, Leo, his face equally cool, spoke up from beside him.

"Hey, Tatsuya, how come Sakurai joined our club?"

"You're only asking now?"

"I mean, I was curious about it before, but…"

As Leo said, Minami was an official member of the mountaineering club. In contrast, Tatsuya was an outsider; he was just borrowing their space… Incidentally, he had gotten permission to participate in their activities on the condition that he tune the club members' CADs. Some of the second-years called him things like "honorary member."

All that aside…

"She's got all that magic power," said Leo. "Weren't a bunch of clubs trying to get her to join them?"

The question was a natural one. After the stellar reactor experiment in April, the entire school knew about Minami's magic power. But even further back during recruitment week, a lot of clubs had had their eyes on Minami for her high scores on the entrance exams. Most expected that she would have joined a magic competition club by now.

"She said she wanted to train her body," replied Tatsuya half truthfully—with no strain in his voice, even after they made it to the opposite shore and began hopping across small footholds. He didn't seem to find this any more difficult than running across flattened ground.

"I kinda feel like, if a freshman girl can move around the way she can, she doesn't need to do more training," pointed out Leo.

Leo had a point. For starters, Minami had been raised as a combat magician in the Yotsuba family; it was only natural for her to possess high physical abilities.

Maybe her physical abilities were more than sufficient for a high schooler—but so was her magic power. Honing that in a club was even more pointless.

"I'm sure Minami has her reasons."

She wasn't just part of the mountaineering club but the cooking club as well. Her number one motive for participating in club activities was to kill time so that she could go home with Tatsuya and Miyuki, who worked in the student council—more specifically, it was to wait for Miyuki, who was Minami's master. Tatsuya refrained from revealing that other half of the truth, though.

For magic high schools that put great stock in practical skills, the Nine School Competition—the National Magic High School Goodwill Magic Competition Tournament—was an extremely important event. Not only for the schools themselves but for their students as well. After all, it wasn't rare for their achievements in the competition to affect their career paths directly. Perhaps it was inevitable some students would devote more of their efforts to the competition than to their periodic exams.

Azusa Nakajou, the ever-judicious First High student president, had gotten started on preparing for the competition a month earlier than previous years, lest she waste the students' passion. And her efforts had been rewarded: She was on track to finish the prep work with time to spare and without having to cram for her exams to boot.

At least, until today, Monday, July 2, 2096 AD, when an unexpected piece of news arrived.

Tatsuya and Miyuki headed for the student council room that day after school like they always did. Their testing period was next week, but their student council work wouldn't pause for that. Still, for aforementioned reasons, the burden on the student council members was actually lighter compared to previous years... And even if that hadn't been the case, the Shiba siblings hadn't pulled an all-nighter a day in their lives, preventing the buildup of irritation or discontent.

Nevertheless, as soon as Tatsuya opened the student council room door like usual...

In spite of himself, he stopped walking. The mood in the room was *heavy*.

"Brother? What's the ma—?"

It wasn't only Tatsuya who thought that, either. After peeking into the room from behind him, Miyuki froze as well, unable to finish her question. Inside, they saw Azusa, head in her hands, emanating such despair that it wouldn't have been strange if she suspected the world was ending.

"Oh. Thanks for coming, both of you," said Isori, standing in front of the student president's desk at a loss.

That gave Tatsuya the chance to finally commit himself to setting foot into the glum atmosphere. "Thanks for holding the fort, Isori. What on earth happened?" he asked, bypassing Azusa herself, whose face was still buried—Tatsuya always cut to the chase after making up his mind to get involved.

"Well, you see..."

"The Nines' administrative committee just sent us this year's overview of events," answered Azusa, face still hidden, cutting off Isori's vague half-reply.

"Ah, right. It's that time of year already."

"They said the details will go up on their official website tomorrow, too."

"I see. What's the problem, then?"

Tatsuya could tell there was an issue in the overview that had left Azusa at her wit's end. But what could have possibly gotten her this upset? Tatsuya didn't have the choice of not asking.

"Everything!"

Azusa could have been waiting for this very question; her head shot up, and she began to rattle off complaints that almost sounded like curses.

"The message said the events would be changing!"

"...What's different this year?"

That was indeed bad news. First High's student council had been preparing for the competition under the assumption that its basic rules and conditions would be the same as last year. Still, there was no rule that stated events couldn't change just because they had remained the same in recent years. The committee always reported the chosen events to each school one month before the competition, so giving notice that the rules were changing was nothing more than a formality to uphold regulations.

"Three events are changing!" cried Azusa.

Still, Tatsuya couldn't help but be surprised at that answer.

"They took out Speed Shooting, Cloudball, and Battle Board, then they added Rower and Gunner, Shields Down, and the Cross-Country Steeplechase!"

Six events in all—and half had been switched out. Moreover, the abilities and types of magic needed for the new events were very different from the old ones. Everyone would probably have to rethink their player selection.

But it was too early to draw that conclusion. Azusa wasn't finished yet.

"And the only choice people have for a second event is the Steeplechase! On top of that, they're splitting Pillar Break, Rower and Gunner, and Shields Down into solo and pair events!"

Azusa slapped her hands on the desk as she emphasized that. At this point, Tatsuya felt a strange sense of the pieces fitting together. These revisions would force each school to make dramatic changes to how they approached the competition. They'd have to go back and rethink everything, from which students they'd pick to their strategy and tactics.

In other words, all the early prep work they'd done had been for nothing. Their careful planning had backfired. He couldn't blame Azusa for feeling depressed. In fact, he realized she was actually taking it quite well, considering how she hadn't fallen into a hysterical panic.

"Brother?"

As Tatsuya wondered what words he should use to soothe the wheezing student president, Miyuki addressed him hesitantly from behind.

"Rower and Gunner? Shields Down? And Cross-Country Steeplechase...? What kind of events are those?"

Miyuki would probably end up entering Pillar Break; the chances of her taking part in Rower and Gunner or Shields Down were pretty much zero. But she would most likely enter the Steeplechase, since it was the only additional event competitors were allowed to enter, and she must have been interested about the other two as an athlete participating in the games. It was a natural curiosity.

"Well, they won't necessarily use the rules I'm familiar with, but..." Tatsuya prefaced, deciding to answer his sister's question for that reason. "Rower and Gunner is an event where a pair, one rowing and one shooting, pilot a small, powerless boat and shoot down targets, some of which are set up next to the waterway and others that will move around on the water's surface. Teams get points based on how long it takes them to reach the finish line and how many targets they hit. If there's a solo version, it'll probably be a single person handling both rowing and shooting. The event originates from amphibious-assault support training the USNA's Marines do."

After making sure Miyuki didn't have any questions, Tatsuya moved on to his explanation for the next event.

"Shields Down is a close combat event involving shields. It typically takes place on a raised surface above the ground or the floor. You win by destroying your opponent's shield, stealing it, or causing them to fall outside the arena. They don't allow physical attacks against your opponent, but you can target their shield. In other words, you either have to use magic or your own body to attack your opponent's shield or use magic to knock them outside the arena."

"That means you can ram your shield against your opponent's and win by ring out, right?"

"Yes, of course."

"This time, the rules say even if you don't steal the opponent's shield, if they aren't in possession of it for over five seconds, you'll win," added Isori after Tatsuya responded to Miyuki's question. Tatsuya paused for a moment, but no further info or corrections seemed to be forthcoming, so he moved on to the next thing.

"The Cross-Country Steeplechase is just what it sounds like. A steeplechase is like an obstacle course, and this event is combined with cross-country. Everyone competes to be the first to make it through a forest filled with obstacles. It's a kind of military exercise that ground forces do for mountain and forest training. Aside from physical items, both natural and man-made, they use everything from automatic gun emplacements to magical obstructions."

"That sounds quite severe…" said Miyuki quietly.

Tatsuya frowned and nodded. "Rower and Gunner and Shields Down are one thing, but the Cross-Country Steeplechase isn't the kind of event they should be making high school students do. What could the administrative committee possibly be thinking?" he muttered darkly.

"And both sexes are allowed to enter Steeplechase as long as they're a junior or senior," Isori added. "Essentially, anyone but freshmen can compete in it."

"…If we don't draw up some very detailed plans for it, we'll have a lot of dropouts."

When Tatsuya said *dropouts*, he didn't mean people dropping out of the event—he meant people becoming unable to live their lives as magicians entirely. The others must not have considered the possibility.

"But that's…!"

With a despair-filled groan, Azusa's head flopped back down to the desk.

The student council had more on their plate than preparing for the Nine School Competition. Not only magic high schools but also nearly all high schools these days delegated much of their operational business to the student council. If that work was left undone, it would hinder the school's operation. That meant the members of a school's student council always needed to do at least the bare minimum of work, even in situations like this, so by the time Honoka, who had been on an errand, and Izumi, whose practical skills class had run late, showed up in the student council room, both Tatsuya and Miyuki had already gotten started on their work.

…Azusa, though, still had her face buried on the desk.

…Isori, however, was fighting hard to get her head back above water.

"What's done is done—we'll just have to rethink who we pick for our players."

"…"

"Fortunately, we still have time! And it's not like *all* the preparations we did were for nothing!"

"…"

"And I'm sure we'll figure something out for Steeplechase! So come on, Nakajou. For now—"

Isori circled behind Azusa, beginning to gently rub her shoulders in an attempt to at least coax her out of her own world, when…

"Kei?"

…a cold voice from behind froze him.

"…Kanon?"

With clunky motions, Isori turned to the staircase that led to the disciplinary committee HQ. As expected, his fiancée was standing there—smiling, veins visible on her temples.

"Keeeeiiii," she said slowly, stretching out the word. "What might you be up to?"

"Eh? Wait, what do you mean by—?"

"I see you hovering over Nakajou. What were you planning on doing exactly, hmm?"

The completely fake smile that was stuck on her face like a sticker made Kanon's state of mind incredibly obvious.

"You're misunderstanding! You got it all wrong!"

As Isori shook his head desperately, Azusa retreated to a corner of the room. She'd evidently chosen to respond to the carnage about to unfold before her instead of the coming competition. As for the other members' reactions—Izumi, for example, looked at Isori in annoyance as he desperately tried to make excuses, but then, as if tired and fed up with it all, she turned to her work display, or rather, to Miyuki, who was reading the report on the desk.

For Izumi, Miyuki was like an oasis of the mind. Whenever she was tired of the work or was faced with a difficult problem, or when her nerves were fraying from irritation, simply keeping Miyuki in her field of vision made her heart feel enriched. At the moment, her enthusiasm for this squabble that nobody wanted to touch with a ten-foot pole had hit rock bottom. Steal a glance at Miyuki was (by Izumi's logic) a necessary, indispensable method for her to recharge her motivation.

However, by some coincidence—Izumi, who had turned around, and Miyuki, who had looked up, locked eyes perfectly. As Izumi panicked and began to think of an excuse, Miyuki offered a somewhat worried smile, then shifted her gaze to Kanon and Isori. And then she turned back around to examine Izumi.

Izumi, guessing how the "big sister" she adored was feeling, used her eyes to ask what they should do. Or at least, to show she was paying attention.

Miyuki gave one slight shake of her head as if to say there was nothing to be done, then flashed a troubled smile once again.

*   *   *

Once again, Tatsuya and the others stopped by their regular café, Einebrise, like they often did after school. The group consisted of Tatsuya and the usual other seven juniors, and Minami, the only freshman. Izumi, who had been with them part of the way, had seemed like she wanted to mingle, but her older twin sister Kasumi didn't have the slightest intention of following suit, so she apparently had no choice but to go straight home. Minami seemed quite uncomfortable being surrounded by upperclassmen, but her loyalty to her duties left her no other option.

Mikihiko had been the one to suggest an after-school coffee break this time. Most would say it was rare for him to be proactive; it felt like he wanted to bring up something specific.

As expected, as soon as they put in their orders, Mikihiko asked Tatsuya a question.

"Tatsuya, is it true they changed up the events in the Nines?"

"You caught wind of that pretty quickly," affirmed Tatsuya with a sharp wryness. "Who did you hear from?"

"The chairwoman and Isori were talking about it."

This revelation came not from Mikihiko but from Shizuku. But that in and of itself gave Tatsuya an answer: They were both disciplinary committee members. In other words, they'd been eavesdropping from their HQ.

"We don't know the details, though," said Mikihiko, needlessly adding an excuse.

Erika perked up. "Wait, the events are changing? Which ones?"

"We got a notification addressed to the student council today. They're taking out Speed Shooting, Cloudball, and Battle Board and adding Rower and Gunner, Shields Down, and the Cross-Country Steeplechase."

"What kind of events are those?" Erika wondered.

After Tatsuya gave her the same explanation he'd given Miyuki, Erika grinned.

"Huh... That sounds fun. Especially Shields Down," she said, a slight spring to her voice.

"Wait, really...? It seems kind of scary," Mizuki countered quietly.

"Yeah... All the events they chose up until last year didn't involve directly fighting opponents," remarked Honoka.

"Even Monolith Code was like that, too," Mizuki agreed immediately.

"But it sounds like the most dangerous one among them is the Steeplechase, despite what Shields Down sounds like on paper," Shizuku added.

Miyuki nodded. "Yes. Brother said that as well."

"If there aren't any trails in the forest, even just moving around can be dangerous. If they're adding physical obstacles and magical interference, too, it'll be stranger if nobody gets hurt."

"Yeah. Even if you were running where there *were* mountain trails, you'd need a really experienced person in the lead. Competing for speed in a forest you've never been in is far too reckless."

Leo and Mikihiko's respective opinions were also critical—or rather, completely negative—and they came from personal experience.

"Hey, Tatsuya, it kind of feels to me like the events they added are all awfully military."

Leo's comment was something everyone present sensed one way or another.

"They do."

This hunch was undeniably correct. Tatsuya could only nod and agree. "Probably because of the Yokohama Incident last year. People related to the JDF realized again how beneficial magic military power is, so maybe they're trying to bring our martial education up to scratch."

"Just like the anti-magic media incited them to," Erika ribbed with a mean-spirited grin.

Tatsuya couldn't smile away her cynical interruption. "Yeah. *Bad timing* is all you can call it. Why would they make such a transparent change now…? I don't think there's any need to rush things, given the current international situation."

Honoka and Mizuki's expressions clouded with anxiety at the thought.

"…That aside, we're about to get very busy," he continued, almost as though he was deliberately acting annoyed in an attempt to change the mood.

But it wasn't completely an act, either. What had happened today would, after all, force him to hang up his *pleasant after-school experience* for a while, at least until the competition was concluded.

First High students weren't the only ones dissatisfied over the competition changing. At the estate of the Ichijou, one of the Ten Master Clans, a Third High student was complaining to his classmate.

"It's just so sudden… I can't believe it."

"Yeah."

"Maybe they *are* following proper procedure… But if they were going to make such sweeping changes, they could have told us earlier."

"You're not wrong."

"We started practicing for the events they took out long ago and, at this point, were even fine-tuning the activation sequences we'd use… Now all the work we did was pointless."

"Got that right."

"We have to rethink everything, starting with what competitors to select… Hey, Masaki, are you listening?!"

Kichijouji, who had been whining about the administrative committee's notice, clearly felt like Masaki, who was repeatedly giving him only short replies and nods, was blowing him off and flared up.

"Of course I am. I'm hurt you'd think I was ignoring you."

But Masaki wasn't in a very peaceable state of mind, either, and his remark came off fairly sharp.

"...Sorry, I was just venting."

"No, that was my fault. No point in taking it out on you, George."

Once they'd gotten their respective feelings off their chests, their heads cooled. The thorny mood quickly dissipated, and their wasted efforts seemed to fill the space between them.

"Anyway, complaining about something that's already decided won't get us anywhere."

"I guess not." Kichijouji sighed, resignation filtering into his voice. "We'll have to revise our rep selection first, hrmm..."

"Yeah, but... It all depends on how you look at things, George."

The next words that left Masaki's mouth were filled with an energy that made it seem like it wasn't just an empty consolation.

"What do you mean?" returned Kichijouji, his own expression growing serious, albeit dubious.

"All the events they swapped in are heavy on practical combat skills. We should have the upper hand against First High."

"I see now... First High focuses improving its students' ranking in international grading standards. Combat abilities aren't directly linked to magical capacity, so they probably don't concentrate as much on them."

"There are exceptions, like Sawaki—the magic martial arts guy—and *you-know-who*. But if you take their school as a whole, we have better magic for actual combat than them. Even if we only compare competition entrants, the odds should still favor us."

"Yeah... Right, but..." Kichijouji agreed, albeit conditionally. "Winning in the Nines isn't about average ranking of the participants. It's about total points, which are decided by ranks in each event. After all, the rules this year state we can only field one solo player and one pair for each event, aside from Mirage Bat. The key will be figuring out who to bring out as solo competitors and who to put into the pairs."

"I get it. Now that you mention it, they limited multiple entries this year. You're right—splitting the solo entrants from the pairs will probably end up deciding a lot. For example, if we wanted certain victory, the best thing to do would be pair up you and me. But—"

Masaki broke off suddenly and looked toward the door. Nobody had knocked. But his senses were undeniable.

"Hello, Shinkurou!"

A moment later, Masaki's sister (and the oldest daughter of the Ichijou family), Akane, entered the room with a sprightly greeting.

"Come on... I keep telling you to knock first before coming in."

Ignoring her older brother's scolding—it was routine at this point—Akane took an iced tea and a packet of gum syrup off a tray and placed them in front of Kichijouji.

"Here you are, Shinkurou. You like one packet of gum syrup, right?"

"Uh, thanks, Akane."

"You're welcome. You don't need any, right, Masaki? You wouldn't want a drink from a boorish sister who comes in without knocking," Akane shot off, her expression composed.

The target of her words answered with a sour face. "...Leave it here."

Obviously, Akane had been joking. Smiling, she offered some iced coffee to her brother. The fact that she didn't continue flinging unneeded sarcasm or insults at this point spoke to how *good* her personality and upbringing were.

This kind of exchange was a regular event for these siblings.

"Akane, did you just get back?"

Therefore, Kichijouji didn't mind it anymore, either. He found Akane's clothes more curious.

"Mm-hmm."

After nodding casually, Akane's face lit up, as though she'd just realized what he meant by it.

"Oh! This is the first time you're seeing me in summer clothes."

Still holding the empty tray, she did a little spin in place. Her pleated skirt and sailor collar, made of thin summery fabric, fluttered as she twirled.

"What do you think? Do I look good?"

Akane's sweet smile was surprisingly girlish. Seeing his friend's younger sister make a rapid transition from a little kid to a girl had been startling Kichijouji for some time now. Though he had thought he understood, Akane's spur-of-the-moment act made his heart leap.

"Y-yeah. That looks good on you," managed Kichijouji, an empty compliment.

"Really? Thanks! I'm so happy to hear it." Akane smiled gently in sincere happiness. Not a half a year ago, she would have been so overjoyed she would've clapped. Even in this minor act, her charm showed through.

A short-sleeved, cool-looking sailor uniform of white and aqua. The elite private middle school's uniform, in highly traditional colors, made her look even more dazzling, and Kichijouji unconsciously watched her intently... Then suddenly, he felt a gaze on him from the side, both criticizing and somewhat sympathetic.

"I thought so, George..." Masaki muttered.

"You're wrong!"

Kichijouji reflexively denied the suspicion. Had they been alone, his reaction might not have caused an issue. But with all three involved parties present, it hadn't been wise.

"Hmm..." Akane leered. "Masaki, are you jealous?"

Anyone would be hurt if someone they liked immediately claimed to not have any feelings for them. Age didn't have anything to do with it. Especially with someone like Akane, who was aware of her own romantic feelings.

But directing her frustrations at Masaki instead of Kichijouji himself was a childlike way of venting—or perhaps it was out of a womanly sentiment of not wanting the man she liked to hate her.

"Don't be dumb."

Whichever it was, all Masaki could do was bluntly deny it. He didn't feel like dealing with her seriously, but he knew treating her too much like a kid would only make her start pouting and invite even more trouble.

"Hmph. Always dodging the question."

Until now, the banter was relatively common. Normally after reaching this point, Akane would spit out a "I'm not giving Shinkurou to you!" after which Kichijouji would start mediating between them.

"I hear things, you know."

But today, the winds blew in a slightly different direction.

"Like what?" retorted Masaki.

Akane wore a smug smile. "About how you asked for Shinkurou to be your dance partner!"

"What?!"

"Huh?!"

Not only Masaki but Kichijouji as well couldn't help but be shocked. Especially because neither of them had any recollection of this.

"You were just saying how you and Kichijouji pairing up would be the best, weren't you?"

"Hey, were you eavesdrop—"

"That's so indecent."

Akane cut off Masaki's words and leveled a look of scorn on him.

"Men pairing up would be unproductive."

"Hey, wait a second, Akane! You're misunderstanding—that's not what he meant!"

Burned by a middle school girl's vitriol, Kichijouji began to mount a defense like his life depended on it. In his mind, it *did* actually depend on it—his social life anyway.

While Masaki, owner of this room in the Ichijou residence, turned to ice for two literal hours, Kichijouji's impassioned *excuses* continued to ring out.

[2]

It was the morning of Tuesday, July 3, one sunset and sunrise after the surprise notification that had thrown all the magic high schools into a vortex of confusion and chaos: In the JGDF 101st Brigade command room, located in Tsuchiura in old Ibaraki Prefecture, the brigade's leader, Major General Hiromi Saeki, had summoned the chief of the Independent Magic Battalion, Major Harunobu Kazama.

Major General Saeki was a female officer who would be turning fifty-nine this year. She was a genius who had always walked the path of a staff officer, and due to her entirely white hair—which looked silver in certain light—people secretly called her names like the Silver Fox. Despite that moniker, at a glance her features were those of a kind elementary school principal more than anything else.

She was also known for leaning far to the right in her stance toward the Ten Master Clans within the JDF. Even so, she didn't harbor any emotional aversion or instinctual hatred against magicians. For some time, she had been ringing the warning bells: Their national defense relied heavily on the Ten Master Clans, which were a private entity. Because of that, there was a tendency for people to treat Saeki as a political rival to Retsu Kudou, but she, at least, didn't feel that way at all.

She and Kazama went all the way back to the Dai Viet conflict.

During that war, which had seen the Great Asian Alliance moving southward with the aim of conquering the Indochinese Peninsula, Kazama had directly intervened in the fighting against the wishes of military command. The guerrilla warfare he'd engaged in stalled the GAA invasion, attracted USNA and New Soviet Union intervention, and ultimately caused the GAA to retreat without accomplishing its objective.

Kazama's actions at that time earned him the title of global expert on forest warfare. But he had only been able to achieve those results because Saeki, then an intelligence staff officer with the Defense Army General Headquarters, had supported him with both intel and planning when he was almost completely isolated (mostly by allies) during the fighting.

Through his maverick actions during the Dai Viet conflict—Kazama's assigned mission at the time was to secretly obstruct the GAA's southward movements, and though he'd disobeyed the "secretly" part, the "maverick" part was probably a false accusation—Kazama would have ordinarily been cut off from the path to promotion. Saeki, however, was not censured for having supported him, either in public or in private. She was too talented for even military command to treat her poorly.

And so, four years later, right after the Defense of Okinawa, they'd adopted her plan to establish the 101st Brigade and instated her as its first commanding officer. Saeki had called up Kazama, who had been stuck at the rank of company officer, and along with promoting him to major, she'd given him command of the Independent Magic Battalion.

In light of that, though the two of them had little time to exchange words since then, their relationship ran deep. They were also compatible in terms of personality, and now they were a tried and true superior and subordinate who could talk about how they *really* felt. Even if they hadn't been, the Independent Magic Battalion's mission was the testing of new magical gear and magical tactics. The 101st Brigade's founding principle was to form a magical force that didn't depend on the Ten Master Clans, and the team Kazama was entrusted with were essentially just that. Saeki and Kazama becoming close was something that had happened naturally.

In this command room, the two of them discussed many shady topics that they couldn't talk about publicly with others.

"Major Kazama, did you know there have been major changes to the events in this year's National Magic High School Goodwill Magic Competition Tournament—the Nine School Competition?"

And what Saeki wanted to talk about this morning began with that question.

"Yes, ma'am, but only that they were considering them. Have they officially made the decision?"

As he asked his question in return, Kazama felt a sense of surprise. Saeki had minor magical talent, but she wasn't a magician. She possessed knowledge few others in the JDF had regarding strategic planning that integrated magical factors as well as the implementation of magical combat forces on a tactical level, but he hadn't thought she had much interest in magic competitions that weren't directly related to combat.

"I must say you seem rather slow on the uptake, Major. An official notification addressed to the magic high schools went out yesterday."

Saying that, Saeki, who had remained seated, held out a stack of papers to Kazama, who was standing at ease in front of her desk. She'd taken the time to print them on paper to avoid the possibility of leaking the information through the digital network. It was a peculiarity of hers, one removed from practicality.

For a short while, the only sound in the command room was that of pages turning. After reaching the end of the documents at a fairly high speed, Kazama looked up and asked with his eyes what she needed.

"What are your thoughts?"

But it seemed they hadn't yet arrived at the main idea. It would be ineffective to rush someone like Saeki, so Kazama decided to patiently go along with her process.

"This is a military training program, ma'am."

"...I might not have said it so bluntly myself, but my opinion is essentially the same."

As though she had only just remembered, Saeki pressed a button on the edge of her desk. A folded-up chair emerged from the wall and moved behind Kazama. She gestured for him to sit.

This was a signal that the conversation would take a while. Kazama saluted, then unfolded the seat and sat down facing her.

"These event changes were affected by the Yokohama Incident. A result of the JDF reaffirming the efficacy of magicians as components of combat strength and attempting to draw out the relevant abilities."

"I believe anyone would interpret it that way, ma'am, even if they didn't know the truth."

Nodding once at Kazama's remark, Saeki added, "The Magic Association only opposed the JDF's request as a formality."

Kazama looked dubious. "You mean to say that even *he* didn't resist it, ma'am?"

Saeki offered a hint of a smile at that. "His Excellency Kudou did not oppose it."

But then Saeki's smile disappeared, and she changed topics suddenly.

"The JGDF General Headquarters wants to know how this brigade would feel about assisting this year's Nines."

"They want to know, ma'am? They didn't order us?"

Kazama's comment was less of a true request for confirmation and more of a way to keep the conversation going.

"Correct. But we must also consider what it means for them to have come straight to our brigade with this—or more specifically, to me."

"I follow."

It was well-known throughout General HQ that Saeki was critical about how the Ten Master Clans dominated the current Japanese magic world. Bringing a request for assistance in this competition to the brigade she headed up was likely a kind of harassment—against both Saeki and the Magic Association, which hosted the event.

"Our superiors do not seem pleased that the Magic Association is gaining leverage with the JDF."

"At long last, then, ma'am?"

On the surface, Saeki's remarks sounded like complaints. But Kazama was easily able to understand what she was truly saying: Their superiors, too, had finally begun to perceive a danger in their dependence on the Clans. Saeki directed a satisfied expression at her subordinate, proof he was correct.

"I plan to answer their call," she said.

Kazama mentally readied himself for the marching orders sure to follow.

"However, I will not use the Independent Magic Battalion. Major, I order you and your battalion to remain on standby for the duration of the Nines."

Saeki's command, however, was to hold fast.

"…Understood, ma'am. The Independent Magic Battalion will remain on standby until we receive orders stating otherwise."

Because the instructions he received were so completely unexpected, Kazama's response came a moment late. Nevertheless, he repeated his orders quickly enough that it wasn't considered a breach of discipline.

"As we were discussing earlier…"

Instructing Kazama, who had risen and saluted, to sit back down, Saeki once again changed the topic.

"Not only has His Excellency Kudou refrained from opposing the change in events, he actually seems to have adopted a proactive stance toward them."

Except it wasn't really a change in topic as much as it was simply returning to talking about Retsu Kudou's reaction to the competition's event revisions.

"Of the new events, the retired general has apparently displayed a strong interest in the Cross-Country Steeplechase. And if word is to be believed, he is the one who proposed the event be changed to allow all athletes to participate. I also hear the course itself was made longer and broader according to his wishes."

"I find that quite surprising, ma'am."

The Cross-Country Steeplechase was a harsh training routine that could regularly bring even regular military magicians to their knees. The broader and longer the area, the more difficult it was to complete the course. And it proportionally increased the risk of a magician losing their way of life. Kazama already knew the elder's true feelings on the matter: He didn't want to see young magicians sacrificed for the sake of the military. That only made this inside story Saeki was telling all the more surprising.

"As His Excellency Kudou has always urged that we should stop treating magicians as weapons, this incident paints him in a treacherous light. Things are never so simple, however, when it comes to him."

"You believe he has an ulterior motive, ma'am?"

"You think so yourself, don't you?"

He'd asked the question without thinking, but a moment of thought revealed the answer to be self-evident. Retsu Kudou didn't want to make military sacrifices of magicians or treat them as mere weapons—he would never have cooperated so easily.

"I have one more piece of information that may come as bad news to you, Major."

Kazama's attention, taken up by his own thoughts, immediately pulled back to the conversation with Saeki's ominous preface.

"With regards to this Steeplechase incident, the Fujibayashi family appears to be hand in hand with the Kudou family in some plot."

"Is that why we're on standby, ma'am?"

Kyouko Fujibayashi, Kazama's aide, was a Fujibayashi by blood. He didn't think she was under suspicion, but her extant relationship to them alone was enough reason to keep him out of the incident.

"Correct."

Saeki made no attempts to deny Kazama's deduction.

"This might go without saying, but depending on how the situation plays out, I may have your team participate as well. In case that happens, I want you to remain ever attentive to Second Lieutenant Fujibayashi's movements."

Not only did she not deny it—she specifically ordered him to keep Fujibayashi under observation.

"Yes, ma'am."

Kazama's feathers weren't ruffled. Trusting in someone's character and preparing for unanticipated events were different issues—to him, at least.

As Kazama left the command room, he wasn't thinking about the female officer working as his aide but about the irregular officer who was technically his subordinate, Specialist Ryuuya Ooguro—in other words, Tatsuya.

He was sure to take part in the competition turned experiment. Was it all right not to inform him of this? Saeki hadn't mentioned anything about dispatching Specialist Ooguro, so maybe he shouldn't reveal anything just yet. As long as nobody gave him marching orders, the specialist was no more than a civilian.

But his sister would also enter the event in question. If it seemed that the young woman who so blindly adored him might be harmed, even if danger was ultimately averted...

Kazama couldn't help but feel that considering the tragedy—no, the *catastrophe*—that would doubtlessly occur, was keeping what he knew to himself not a gravely foolish decision?

◇ ◇ ◇

As expected, the Nine School Competition event changes threw First High into chaos. After the details were announced on the official competition website, a large number of students from clubs related to the events were either overjoyed or heartbroken.

Even so, it affected the student council the most.

First, they had to visit the clubs with students who had planned to enter the dead events and explain the situation to them. Their current competitor selections were still no more than informal decisions, so they didn't tell those students about it; but if they'd be going to the competition, they'd need to prioritize it over club practice. Which meant they had to let the clubs the participants belonged to know that in advance. Their head start on previous years had ended up being overeager thanks to the extensive event changes. Azusa felt like bees had come to sting her when she was already crying.

They'd have to start from square one choosing the competitors. They certainly had to rethink the representatives for events that weren't switched out, too. In some cases, someone they'd assigned before was more suitable for one of the new events. Plus, they had to consider the new rule that participants couldn't double up on any event except the Steeplechase. Choosing the athletes was left mainly to the student council, but they still couldn't ignore the opinions of related clubs, and so they'd need to parley both with individual clubs and the club committee just to get that done.

They also had to prepare the necessary items for the new events. This was purely office work, but they'd first have to read over all the competition rules for Rower and Gunner, Shields Down, and the Cross-Country Steeplechase to find out what sort of equipment was needed and what was permitted and what wasn't. By the time the student council members left the school gates today, their faces were all drooping with exhaustion. Tatsuya and Miyuki were no exception.

* * *

Despite their youth, this exhaustion was not something they'd easily recover from. After returning home and finishing dinner, Miyuki was standing in the kitchen, clearly dragging along the lethargy from when they'd left school. But even so, at this time and in this place, she didn't try to leave this role to Minami. If one was to speak of her unabashed feelings, she considered it her natural right and sacred duty to give up her own relaxation time to Tatsuya. Her mannerisms politer than normal, she made coffee and then, with a smile that didn't even so much as hint at her fatigue, placed a cup of it in front of him.

"Thanks, Miyuki."

Tatsuya gave her a smile, looking his sister straight in the eyes, gratitude filling his gaze.

"No, I... You're welcome."

Even Miyuki was accustomed to the casual thoughtfulness Tatsuya displayed enough to not blush every single time. No matter how impassive he looked normally, no matter how cold and brutal he looked when facing an enemy, Miyuki thought of her brother as a deeply kind person. Still, the abrupt affection directed at her did cause her eyes to redden slightly, a response—an emotional excitement—she couldn't avoid.

"You must be tired after today. Come here."

Tatsuya, sitting not in the usual one-seater armchair but the three-person sofa, patted the place next to him.

"...Okay!"

Miyuki's eyes widened for a moment, but then she sat down happily next to her brother. Minami stood in front of them, unable to completely conceal her displeasure with having been given the role of waitress, but either Miyuki had forgotten or just didn't care; she was practically glued to him.

But even if Miyuki didn't care, Minami had to. She wasn't that used to this yet, and she was a world away from enlightenment. She

wanted to look away from them, even though it would violate maid etiquette. Just as she was unable to resist the desire any longer, the incoming e-mail tone went off.

Springing at the chance, Minami headed over to the console. Rather than the main display taking up the living room wall, she peered at the smaller monitor attached to a console.

When she turned back around, her face was brimming with confusion.

"Lord Tatsuya."

She seemed honestly perturbed—she'd forgotten her promise to call him "Big Brother."

"An e-mail has arrived. It…doesn't have a sender."

Her confusion was well earned.

"It doesn't?"

Tatsuya's reply was also filled with uncertainty. Regardless of how things were before the war, modern e-mail systems defined very strict data formats. With advanced network technology, a person may have been able to fake their e-mail's origin, but having a sender name was essential. Leaving it blank should have been impossible.

Conversely, however, if you did have technology to send data into the network that was defective according to the specifications, it would be easier to disguise your origin. Maybe he could interpret this e-mail as the unknown sender trying to convey their identity by showing off their advanced technology.

If that was true, he could only think of so many people. Out of everyone he knew, it would have to be someone who had a command of networking on an incredibly advanced level…

No, it's too early to draw conclusions.

Tatsuya denied the convenient idea rearing its head in his mind. The possibility that *she* had sent this e-mail—or that someone had sent it on her instructions—was not zero. In fact, he considered it to be over 50 percent. But as for the little bit under 50 percent remaining, it could have actually been malware sent by someone who meant him harm.

I'll have to check what it says first.

On an unconnected console in his hands, rather than open the e-mail he'd considered to be possibly malware, he brought up the raw data right on the screen. Sequences of characters, stripped of their execution privileges, filled his display to the brim. Tatsuya was able to get a sense for their unique structure.

He booted up a decoder and fed the displayed characters into it. The type of encryption was a common one the JGDF used. The 101st Brigade used a different encryption format, but he couldn't say for sure this electronic message *hadn't* been sent from the Independent Magic Battalion.

In modern times, communication technology that only allowed authentication of data when received on specific hardware was in practical use. (In fact, it was to intercept such data that the Echelon system had been upgraded from II to III.) The most important security depended on this, and it was possible the e-mail data itself was purposely using a common encryption.

In any case, he couldn't determine from the encryption format alone whether it had come from an ally or an enemy. He'd have to read the contents for that. Without a word, he waited for the decoding to finish.

"That can't be…"

But the contents of the decrypted e-mail were enough to sideline the sender's identity for now. The information was so awful that Miyuki, who had left a small space between her and Tatsuya, lest she get in the way, murmured in disbelief without meaning to.

"New weapon testing… I'd take it with a grain of salt, but I suppose I can't deny it outright."

The suspicious e-mail detailed three things: how this year's Nine School Competition event changes were due to JDF pressure, that the Kudou family was taking advantage of it to performance test secretly developed weapons, and that the location for the testing would be the Cross-Country Steeplechase.

"The JDF's involvement is probably true. But the anonymity makes the message shady, and standard practice says to mix in plausible lies with truth…"

As Tatsuya thought about it, Miyuki brought herself close to him again. This time it wasn't to fawn; she was worried for him.

"Brother… What will you do?"

It bothered Miyuki not to have a single thoughtful comment to offer. It may have been self-satisfaction, but even if listening to what he had to say was all she could do, she wanted to at least be able to share his burden.

But her fears were groundless.

"Hmm. Well, I can ask Master tomorrow morning."

Tatsuya's answer was an extremely plain one. While he didn't want to hand Yakumo the ball and leave, he did seem totally willing to push much of the work onto him. Relieved at her brother's usual poor attitude, she relaxed.

"Brother, would you like me to bring you some more coffee?"

"Sure, thanks."

"Right away. Please wait a moment."

Miyuki, shifting gears—she'd go with him to speak to Yakumo, so she could leave it for tomorrow—disappeared into the kitchen. Because of that, she missed the next thing Tatsuya said.

"Minami, could you forward this e-mail to Hayama?"

"Yes, Lord Tatsuya."

"Using the strongest encryption."

"Of course."

While some people were like Tatsuya and wanted to get involved in as little trouble as possible, others decided they wanted to proactively cause it. Some especially diligent ones would even peel their eyes and strain their ears to goings-on across the sea, constantly searching for seeds of chaos.

Gongjin Zhou's master was precisely one of those people.

"Gongjin."

A stuffed human body, moved by a necromantic technique, spoke the kneeling man's name.

"We've learned that in this so-called Nine School Competition taking place in August, the Japanese military will be secretly conducting tests of new weapons."

The one speaking to him through the corpse's mouth and from across the Pacific Ocean was one of the Seven Sages, Gide Hague, also known as Gu Jie, a survivor of the Dahanese military's immortalist unit.

"New weapons, Master?"

As he repeated the phrase respectfully, in his mind he was saying *again?* Not in regard to the new weapons, however—but that they'd be interfering with that competition again. No-Head Dragon, Hague's former precious playing piece, had become useless after their sabotage attempts during the last summer's competition.

He was of the opinion that meddling with a high school competition was mostly risk and little reward. But it seemed his master saw things differently, he thought with a private sigh.

"They're being referred to with the code name P-Weapon. We haven't obtained any solid evidence, but based on the situation, there is little doubt they are attempting to seal parasites into automatic dolls and use their power."

Zhou was honestly impressed after hearing that deduction. Not at Hague's information network but at the Japanese military's technological level. He was no expert, but even he, as someone who had studied the Taoist immortalist arts himself, had heard the difficulty of arts for sealing fairies—not the European sort but the mystical energy at the core of supernatural beasts—and utilizing them.

To replicate what the Yellow Turban Strongman did—the Japanese are quite capable...

"Do they think they can control things of that nature? They are not transcendents. And it is truly foolish that they are attempting to test their capabilities using high school students."

But Hague's impression differed from Zhou's. Or maybe he just didn't want to acknowledge it.

"Should we not simply interfere with their tests?"

I've prepared a spell to drive them mad. It's a Norman shaman spell, but I've adjusted it to be compatible with the immortalist framework, so it should be serviceable as your tool as well."

"Understood, sir. I will make arrangements to embed this lunacy spell into the P-Weapons."

Building a process in his head, one that made use of defectors from the GAA, Zhou suddenly thought of something and asked it.

"Would it be fine to only threaten them?"

We don't need to hold back from hurting anyone, but we also don't need to kill them. Stealing the Japanese military's magic technology is enough to weaken them. It will be more painful to linger on as incompetents than dying now."

Hague's plans seemed to involve making them suffer as long as possible. It was a very insidious—and naive—idea.

"At once, Master Hague."

As he scorned the old man in his mind, Zhou prostrated himself, respectful only in form.

Before going to school the next morning, Tatsuya paid a visit to Yakumo with Miyuki in tow.

Tatsuya was in his usual training wear. Miyuki, in contrast, had a perfectly summery sportswear outfit on, consisting of a short-sleeved

T-shirt, anti-UV-ray arm covers, a sun visor, shorts, and UV-blocking tights. She also sported inline skates with detachable wheels on her feet. A belt pouch was tied around her waist, holding her CAD and other small items.

Both of them had come dressed for morning practice, but last night, they'd actually sent a message in advance that they wanted to hold off on this morning's training because there was something they wanted to talk about. However, the moment they passed through the temple gates, a throng of pupils attacked Tatsuya.

But given Tatsuya's expression as he fought them off, he wasn't particularly displeased at the development; in fact, he'd predicted something like this would happen. That was why he'd come dressed the same as he always did. However, it did certainly seem like he was rushing it. The topic he wanted to discuss wasn't the sort where they'd reach a conclusion very easily. As a result, he beat Yakumo's disciples down in the shortest time possible—meaning he had no mercy on them.

Yakumo had taken a seat on the staircase to the priests' quarters to watch them. Attended by Miyuki behind him, Tatsuya walked over in front of him.

"Good morning, Master."

"Good morning, Sensei."

Miyuki, too, perhaps in consideration for her brother's feelings, offered her greeting with grace and didn't criticize his prank.

"Hey, morning."

Meanwhile, virtually no sense of guilt could be gleaned from Yakumo's face, either, despite being the one who had pulled the prank. Maybe he didn't think of loosing his disciples on Tatsuya as any more than a greeting.

Still, that didn't matter today, either. Filing the memory of what had just happened away into the corner of his mind as a debt to be repaid one day when the opportunity arose, Tatsuya decided to cut to the chase.

"Shall we talk inside?"

But whether by contrivance or coincidence, Yakumo took the initiative. Getting up from the stair he'd been sitting on, he proceeded into the priests' quarters. Tatsuya followed, looking slightly disheartened.

When Miyuki entered after Tatsuya, the door automatically closed behind them. Tatsuya couldn't see any traces of psionic activity, so it must have actually been an automatic door, despite its appearance. Or maybe it ran on human power—like a disciple shutting it outside.

The windows were all shut tightly as well, leading the priests' quarters to feel more claustrophobic than they'd otherwise thought. In the pitch-black room, the candles along one wall lit up. A strong scent wafted over—the aroma of perfumed oil, likely kneaded into the candles. Neither Tatsuya nor Miyuki was surprised at the flames lighting themselves: Yakumo had used magic; the fact was as clear to them as if they'd physically witnessed it.

Three candles in a candlestick wouldn't be enough to light the whole room, but with this many, the candles should have provided at least some dim illumination. But to Tatsuya's eyes, when the candles lit, the priests' quarters seemed to grow even darker.

But it wasn't because of the fire, he reasoned...it was because of the scent of the oil filling the room.

What he'd felt was a decrease in psionic light.

"Is this a bounded field?"

Tatsuya knew secondhand that psionic information bodies—spirits, *shikigami*, and so forth—disliked certain odors; it appeared this scent enveloping them was one of those.

"We wouldn't want any of this getting out, right?"

Tatsuya's opinion was that no caster, no spell existed that could infiltrate this temple without Yakumo knowing, including in the Yotsuba family. But the owner considered it a necessary precaution, and as someone who had come to ask for assistance, he had plenty of reason to help him.

"Miyuki, would you mind?"

"Of course, Brother."

Miyuki immediately picked up on her brother's idea, constructing a barrier that would completely block all electromagnetic and sound waves.

"Thanks."

Yakumo gave a somewhat wry grin at this response. It seemed like this bounded barrier was more of a habitual thing whenever he had to talk in private. Still, considering the discussion that Tatsuya was about to have with him, they couldn't be too cautious. Tatsuya got to the point.

"Master, I apologize for bringing a troubling matter to you today."

As Tatsuya lowered his head, Miyuki offered a polite bow of her own. It was an apology assuming Yakumo would be providing assistance.

Though this visit had started with a preemptive attack right out of the gate, once Yakumo had heard the general story, even he was keen to help them out. The details weren't something he could personally ignore.

"I have to give it to Kudou—that's a pretty dangerous idea he's got."

But instead of wasting time with banter like always, Yakumo cut straight to the heart of the issue.

"I'm sure I don't have to tell you this, but the Steeplechase is already a dangerous event."

"I see you think so as well, Sensei," remarked Miyuki politely, though her voice was trembling faintly. Her tone was like magma rumbling deep underground, thick with an intense anger.

Even events chosen in the past, such as Mirage Bat, Monolith Code, and Battle Board, carried a risk of accidents that could lead to participants' losing their magical capabilities. As with everything, it was a spectrum—but the Steeplechase's level of danger was incomparably higher than those.

"He wants to use a dangerous event like that to conduct performance testing on new weapons? It's enough to make me start doubting his sanity."

Coming from Yakumo's mouth, that comment held a lot of weight. An ancient magic practitioner who performed rigorous acts of asceticism on a daily basis saying that was a sign it bordered on genuine madness.

"Were you already aware of the tests the Kudou family is planning, Master?"

Tatsuya had called him on the phone last night after eight. He asked because he felt like even Yakumo couldn't have looked into it that fast.

"Would you happen to know what the new weapons are?"

Eventually, Yakumo said reluctantly, "I only know a code name: P-Weapons. Unfortunately, I'm not clear on any details."

"Even you don't know, Sensei?" Miyuki probed, half-doubtful. It was very hard for her to believe Yakumo *couldn't find something out even after investigating*... True, he hadn't ascertained the siblings' true identities until they'd become his disciples, but Miyuki was oblivious at the time because she and her brother had been unaware of their shortcomings.

"I don't know yet."

Yakumo didn't seem to realize the unintentional irony, either. His mind was probably on something else, on another acquaintance who wasn't present.

"I think Kazama would know, though."

"You mean the major is keeping the information to himself?" Tatsuya shot back.

"That's not quite right. He doesn't have any responsibility to leak information to us."

Yakumo was correct and left no room for argument. Tatsuya

felt ashamed of his own poorly chosen remark. He belonged to the JDF as a special-duty officer, but this was a matter of convenience at best. He wasn't yet a soldier in a real sense, and even considering military organizational hierarchy, Kazama outranked him. Superiors weren't required to convey every last detail to their subordinates.

And Tatsuya was a member of the Yotsuba, too. No matter how many of his relatives refused to acknowledge him as part of the family, he was objectively one of their combat personnel. The 101st Battalion was a potential rival organization to the Ten Master Clans, and Kazama was essentially its leader. With the Yotsuba occupying a leading position among the Ten Master Clans, Kazama keeping secrets from one of its *members* was the natural thing to do.

"In any case, if we don't know anything about the tests Kudou is trying to conduct, we can't put together any countermeasures..."

Yakumo made a show of griping. However, a competitive light had entered his eyes. The light of confidence—he'd get to the bottom of what these P-Weapons were in no time flat.

"You'll investigate first, then?"

Setting Yakumo's feelings aside, his comment that they couldn't decide how to respond without knowing exactly what their targets were trying to do left no room for debate.

"Yes, well." Yakumo nodded to his disciple's question, which had mostly just been to keep the conversation going. "I'll probably have to go to Nara."

"To old Lab Nine, right?"

"A place we have a deep connection with."

Tatsuya, too, knew of the discord between ancient magicians with ties to Lab Nine and the Numbers with the character for "nine" in their name. Yakumo's proactive stance made Tatsuya think, in a twisted way, that perhaps *that* was why Yakumo seemed more enthusiastic about this than he usually did...

◇ ◇ ◇

July 5, lunch break, three days after the Nine School Competition's new-rules notification.

Tatsuya was looking through First High student data in the student council room.

Not to say he didn't feel like the emergency was more important, but the *public* preparations for the Nines had become an emergency in and of themselves. Tatsuya had simply decided to leave the *covert* response in Yakumo's hands during the weekdays and devote his own efforts to the public arena.

The documents Tatsuya and Hattori, the club committee chairman, were viewing were a summary of practical exam grades they were using to choose participating athletes. They'd *utilized* them under the assumption that this year's events would be the same as last year, but the documents contained comprehensive practical testing data, so it would be useful in selecting competitors for the new events as well.

While biting into a sandwich, Tatsuya flipped through one piece of data after another, organized in card format. He was using one hand to work his keyboard, making a list of candidates.

Incidentally, his sandwich was one Pixie had made and passed out to everyone. Miyuki and Honoka would stop working on their consoles every once in a while to eat more politely, but Azusa had a half-eaten sandwich in her mouth as she pounded away at the keys, drawing silent shade from Izumi.

Hattori was the first one to speak up. "I think we can just take the Pillar Break, Mirage Bat, and Monolith Code entries and adjust for the multiple events rule. What do you all think?"

"We probably can, but we'll need to split them up into solo and pair entries for the main Pillar event," said Tatsuya.

"For the girls, can't we have Shiba solo and Chiyoda and Kitayama be a pair?" offered Hattori, catching the ball again.

"What will we do about the boys?"

"There's not much difference in ability between the three male entrants. We should probably pair them off and decide based on compatibility."

"I agree."

"For Rower and Gunner, I'd think we can choose from our candidate reps for Speed Shooting and Battle Board, but…"

"For the pair that should work, but the solo spot would need multicasting ability at a high level. I believe we'll need to take that into consideration as well."

"I see. Then which do you think we should treat as more important— shooting skills or boating skills?"

"We can anticipate the boats in Rower and Gunner to be more stable than the boards in Battle Board, so I think we should concentrate on shooting skill while moving."

"In that case, the corresponding clubs would be the SS board club, the biathlon club, the hunting club, and…"

The reselection of competitors was the goal behind gathering during this lunch break, and the conversation continued to progress in this way, mostly between Hattori and Tatsuya.

After school, Tatsuya paid a visit to small gymnasium number two. Not, however, because he was skipping out on his desk work—this was yet another part of competition prep.

The two smaller gymnasiums were both fitted with cleaning mats in the entrance, which would completely scrub the soles of your shoes just by walking on it, so going inside while wearing outside shoes didn't present any particular issue. However, Tatsuya purposely removed his shoes, then stepped up into what they called the arena, where the floor switched to plank boarding.

Despite regular exams being right around the corner, the jaunty sounds of club members wearing defensive gear batting their *shinai* together could be heard. With faces invisible behind their masks,

Tatsuya relied on movement quirks to seek out the student he was looking for.

The one he was after was sitting against the wall. She was removing her helmet, as though she'd just been taking a break. Despite clearly intending to relax, she maintained her posture so well that it was fascinating.

"Erika."

"Is that you, Tatsuya? You almost never come to watch."

As Tatsuya raised his hand to her and walked over along the wall, Erika displayed slight surprise. As she said, this was the first time since Tatsuya took the seat of vice president that he'd come to watch the kendo club practice.

Incidentally, Erika wasn't part of the kendo club—she was in the tennis club. Of course, she was more like a ghost member. The tennis club wasn't very active, so they wouldn't scold her if she took time off from it.

Erika, considering that convenient, would occasionally come to the kendo club like this to help out—not because she necessarily wanted to but because Sayaka was constantly asking her to.

Tatsuya, too, had a rough understanding of those circumstances. But he hadn't known today would be one of those *helping out* days. Tatsuya had gone to the tennis courts before coming to small gym number two. Essentially, he'd wasted time, but it wasn't Erika's responsibility, so he didn't mention it.

"Did you need something?" said Erika in place of a greeting—she didn't know he'd visited specifically to look for her.

"Yeah. I've come to ask you for a great favor."

When Tatsuya sat down formally and made that proper remark to her, Erika unintentionally gave a blank, defenseless look. It was the type others might have called a *dumb face*, if not for her beauty—even that expression looked good when she made it.

"Huh? This is sudden. What's wrong? You never ask me for things…"

There was a hint of caution in her eyes that couldn't be hidden, doubtless because Erika had grasped a part of Tatsuya's true character, however small.

"It's not really me asking—it's the student council."

But this time, she'd been overthinking it.

"What did they want?"

Having understood that, the tension disappeared from her eyes, replaced by a strong sense of doubt. The suspicion she had was simple—what were they going to try to make her do?

Of course, Tatsuya didn't have any reason to keep secrets now, so he gave her the answer straight. "We would like to request for you to serve as a practice partner for the Shields Down event in the upcoming Nines."

"Oh. That event did look interesting. Wait, are you okay with me being a practice partner?"

Erika realized that her own magical capabilities were remarkably skewed. She doubted she could be of much help as a competitor, of course, but that went for being a practice partner, too.

"Yes, I'd very much appreciate it."

But Tatsuya didn't seem to doubt Erika's suitability one bit. Erika unconsciously averted her gaze from his straightforward gaze—she was embarrassed.

"...If you really insist, then I guess I'll do it."

Even when she purposely used a high-handed tone to conceal her embarrassment...

"Thank you."

...Tatsuya never broke from his completely serious attitude. It felt intentional to Erika. *Is he making fun of me?* she grumbled to herself... And she knew quite well that it had been no more than a false accusation.

After changing into her school uniform, Erika did as Tatsuya asked and headed to the small conference room on the first floor of the prep building.

"What the heck are *you* doing here?"

There she saw the unexpected face of a *certain* classmate—and without meaning to, that was the first thing she said. If it had been just the two of them or among their friends, nobody would have thought anything of it. But there were also several upperclassmen she didn't know in the room, and she hadn't even greeted them yet.

Crap... I did that so automatically. Now what do I do?

Looking, it wasn't just Erika—those upperclassmen were wearing bewilderment on their faces as well.

"Oh, shut up. Tatsuya called me here, too."

But the awkward mood about to spread through the room dissipated thanks to the mood-blind Leo's retort. Though one would need to ask him whether he purposely hadn't paid attention to the mood or if he simply couldn't.

"Erika, Leo."

Tatsuya's gently chiding words, however, were clearly mood specific. Once they'd closed their mouths, Tatsuya introduced Erika to their Shields Down representatives.

"Shiba, you want me to pair up with Saijou to practice, right?"

"I'll be going with Chiba when I practice, right?"

The first one who asked was their boys' solo pick, Sawaki. The remark after that came from a senior by the name of Tomoko Chikura, the one chosen as their girls' solo representative.

"That's right."

Shields Down was a competitive event. But they'd only have three boys and three girls, one each solo and the others in pairs, as their representatives. Each of them would be missing one person to practice two-on-two with. That was why Erika and Leo had been selected as practice partners.

"You two will be the solo practice partners as well."

In addition, the plan was to have a three-person rotation with the two of them.

"Mm. Well, these recommendations came straight from Shiba. Saijou, it's a pleasure!"

"...Right."

"Chiba, don't be too rough on me."

"Same to you."

He'd already explained this to the two of them, but Erika aside, Leo—who would be up against Sawaki, whispered to be the finest martially inclined student in First High—had a bit of awkwardness in his polite smile.

It would, perhaps, be disingenuous to call them the conspiracy's epicenter. Going back chronologically, the Kudou family had done nothing more than avail themselves of the military's plan to accelerate the usage of magicians in the military. That said, no matter how severe the plan's substance was, it was none other than the Kudou family who had brought *secret weapons* intended for military use into the Nine School Competition, a mere high school event. Notoriety was something they would have to accept without complaint.

And the Kudou family had no reason to mind such a thing. They—and in particular Retsu Kudou, who had proposed making the Nines the stage for the performance tests—were fully aware that he was doing something deplorable. It was for that very reason, however, that he was under mental pressure to not, under any circumstances, allow the Parasidoll testing to fail.

Retsu had taken command at Lab Nine again today, from sunrise until sundown. If he hadn't already made plans for afterward, he might not have left the institute until well into the night. And even then, his dinner engagement was an invitation he'd answered in order to smooth things over with politicians who were formerly in the military and held powerful influence over the competition.

It was after six o'clock. Retsu had left for a restaurant serving Japanese cuisine in Osaka, and Makoto, left in charge of things, had just settled into a seat in front of the desk when the internal line rang, a message from the security guards that a guest had arrived.

"A guest? We weren't expecting any guests. Who is it?"

"He's calling himself Gongjin Zhou, from Yokohama Chinatown. He requests to speak to the master directly. How should I proceed?"

Gongjin Zhou from Yokohama Chinatown—Makoto had heard the name. It was a name that couldn't be ignored by anyone from a family of "nine" originating in Lab Nine, even if the other twenty-eight families would have never heard of him.

"I'll be there in a moment. Show him to the reception room."

And as he himself said, Makoto immediately got up to go.

Upon seeing the Yokohama Chinese expat rise from the reception room sofa as he entered the room, the first emotion Makoto felt was envy. To his eyes, Gongjin Zhou was young and dashing. His cool, graceful features emitted an energy old men like himself couldn't possess.

"Welcome. I am Makoto Kudou, head of the Kudou family."

Forcing down the dark emotions welling up within him, Makoto offered an outwardly magnanimous smile and held out his hand.

"My name is Gongjin Zhou. Please call me Zhou."

In response, Zhou, with a polite and—at least visibly—humble attitude, accepted his outstretched hand and shook it.

"I'm very much familiar with your name. You're a celebrity, Mr. Zhou—at least, in these parts."

The remark was very deliberately spoken, and Zhou answered with a meaningful smile in lieu of any pointless modesty. Zhou's calculations had included being known. Besides, the negotiations he was attempting to conduct wouldn't succeed unless Makoto knew what he was doing in "these parts." In fact, behind his smile, Zhou was thinking that this saved him time.

"I'm flattered you know of me. I've come today with a request regarding our business, hoping that you might be accommodating."

"When you say *our business*...?"

"Yes, I believe you have the right idea. I would like to discuss the future course for my comrades who have escaped the iron hand of the GAA."

In addition to assisting with GAA anti-Japanese schemes, Zhou also provided those who wished to defect from the GAA with various amenities. His main activities were acting as an intermediary to find ultimate destinations for the defectors arriving in Japan and to provide boat passage there, including covering various expenditures. However, he also gave financial support to their post-defection political activities.

The GAA was actually aware of these defection-broker activities. The information wasn't that widespread and not all governmental officials and high-ranking military officers knew about it, but it was at the very least an open secret among soldiers and those related to government who were connected to anti-Japan outfits.

As for why Zhou was not on any GAA purge lists—the defection dealings were rather convenient for the GAA government as well. Anyone who was willing to defect was another person who was discontented with the government. If they promptly defected, there would be fewer governmentally dissatisfied elements. The GAA had no lack of manpower, and their coffers benefited because those people couldn't bring all their assets with them when defecting.

The troubling things about people engaging in political activities wherever they defected to were it extending to their nation, it producing negative diplomatic effects, or it being used as an excuse for embargoes.

None of those were a problem for the GAA in its current state, though. The GAA government had established hegemony over the eastern mainland after the *internal* strife with Dahan. At present, GAA leadership had full control over everything, down to the smallest units of the military. They understood well that without the backing of the military, anti-government movements wouldn't get very far. And without sympathetic armed forces within the GAA's borders, foreign plots would never become powerful enough to topple their administration. The GAA government still hadn't forgotten its history of local forces going out of control, leading to Dahan's pretended independence—*pretended* being the GAA's own perspective on the matter—and to internal warfare.

Diplomatic criticisms weren't particularly problematic for the current GAA, either. States only needed international backing if they weren't politically independent, usually because they were militarily or economically reliant on one nation or another.

But with the current state of geopolitics, no military alliance could form and pose a serious threat to the GAA. All four of the world's superpowers—the USNA, the New Soviet Federation, Indo-Persia, and the GAA itself—all adopted militarily independent policies. The USNA and Indo-Persia possessed allies, but those relationships were superficial. The tight-knit alliances from before the most recent world war no longer existed. If one of the four great powers attempted to expand its territory, the other three would likely not be silent, but none of them would interfere with another's internal politics.

The GAA was highly self-sufficient economically as well, so embargoes wouldn't harm or even irritate them. Their energy situation was a source of unease, but other countries were in the same boat. Quite frequently those who defected were the wealthy, and as long as there weren't *too* many people defecting, it was actually a net benefit for the government's pockets.

For those reasons, the GAA administration *incentivized* Zhou's defection-broker activities.

Incidentally, Japan currently had a strict limit on the acceptance of defectors (political refugees). This wasn't restricted only to Japan, either—the very framework of the Refugee Treaty had collapsed because of the outbreak of the Twenty Years' Global War. But they only limited the entry of defectors—they didn't prohibit it. And if a person who requested asylum was beneficial to the nation, that was an entirely different story. Talented scientists, for example. Famous artists, for another. And of course—powerful magicians.

"To tell the truth, we are planning on accepting three Taoist immortalists from the mainland next week, but there has been a slight mishap... The destinations where they will settle down have not yet been decided."

"A mishap?"

"Yes, though it shames me to say. It appears our investigation into the enmity between various sects has been insufficient."

"I see. I can understand why practitioners of the ancient arts would be concerned about it."

Makoto was casually intimating that modern magicians didn't worry about sects or the like. Still, Zhou's remark, feigning to be a defense, had drawn this appeal out; Makoto had understood that and purposely leaned into it.

"Still, however, they are a sort it would be somewhat inconvenient to have stay with us," Zhou noted.

"What sort of inconvenience? Ah, excuse me—if you have no objections to telling me, I would like to know."

"No, not at all. It's nothing I'd need you to keep to yourself. The luminaries defecting and coming here possess considerable power, and... There is no doubt the mainland administration will silently allow them to escape. Mainly to preserve their own honor."

Makoto directed a firm stare at Zhou. It made his interest in what Zhou was saying quite clear; in fact, it displayed an intent to become involved in Zhou's business dealings. On top of that, Makoto wanted Zhou to be the one to broach the main topic himself.

"I would not be able to shelter them alone. That's what I'd like to request of you, Lord Kudou."

Zhou, too, had a wealth of tact in this area.

"Would you welcome these Taoist priests as your honored houseguests?"

And as Makoto had ordered, Zhou continued, always the one bowing his head. Makoto's lips loosened for a moment in satisfaction, but he soon replaced it with a dubious expression.

"Would it be wise to do this, considering your relationship with the Traditionalists?"

That was the heart of the reason why the name Gongjin Zhou was something the Numbers of Nine couldn't ignore. The Traditionalists was the name of a magic society formed across religious lines by local ancient magicians centered in Kyoto. Dignity or perhaps arrogance could be glimpsed in the fact that they simply named themselves Traditionalists, without hoisting a location or methodology.

The Traditionalists' goal was to protect the individuality of ancient magic against modern magic. One might otherwise state it as an adherence to identity. Needless to say, that meant they were aligned against Lab Nine. The Traditionalists were a federation of ancient magicians of various styles bound together by their anger and enmity toward Lab Nine, an organization that had *betrayed* them. The natural course of events led to that hostility being directed at all current Numbers with the character *nine* in their surnames and especially their leader.

And common custom was for the mainland's ancient magicians Zhou guided in their defections to temporarily reside with various families in the Traditionalists. After all, Zhou was known to each of the Nine families as someone who bolstered this latent hostile force.

"My role is purely to provide my comrades who have escaped oppression with a place to live peacefully. I do certainly have a responsibility to those in the Traditionalists for cooperating with me so much. That, however, is not something to weigh against my main objective."

"You say a place to live peacefully, but without very unique circumstances, governments do not allow defectors to naturalize."

"It can be a temporary respite. For someone who has suffered under despotism, being able to live in peace even for a short time has immeasurable value."

Zhou appeared to be ever earnest, only concerned about his comrades' well-being. It wasn't 100 percent believable, of course, but Makoto didn't care if it was an act. At the very least, he decided he could believe that Zhou wasn't solidly allied with the Traditionalists and trying his best to bring down the Kudou family. It was enough for him just to confirm this wasn't all a Traditionalist conspiracy.

"All right. One of the Ten Master Clans' principles is to produce humane living situations for magicians. You might say it is a natural obligation of the Ten Master Clans to extend aid to magicians who seek freedom so badly that they would abandon their homeland. However, this is also not a proposal I can accept irresponsibly, so please understand that I can't give an answer right this moment."

He couldn't immediately agree to everything. As the Kudou family patriarch, being treated lightly by someone he had just met was something he needed to avoid, even if he was overthinking it.

"Oh yes, of course." Zhou showed no offense at Makoto withholding an immediate answer. Probably because he'd realized his conversation partner's heart had stirred after hearing his proposition. He took a small envelope out of his inside pocket and held it out.

"I've prepared profiles on the Taoist priests here. I will await a favorable reply."

"I will make inquiries, but I'm optimistic about them. You can likely expect an answer by the end of the week," said Makoto to Zhou as he took the envelope, which had a data card in it.

"I'm much obliged. Would it be permissible if I intruded again on Monday?"

Makoto removed a notebook terminal from his pocket and

lowered his eyes to it, then looked up a moment later. "If it's at four PM, then yes."

"I'll come at that time. Thank you very much for seeing me today." Zhou gave a bow that was as elegant as the rest of his appearance.

After scanning the data Zhou had given him, Makoto called up the main security guard in the institute and ordered him to keep silent about Gongjin Zhou's visit.

"My predecessor must not be informed of this, either. Understand?"

Makoto was particularly thorough about including Retsu Kudou among those who had to be kept in the dark about this meeting. After watching the head security guard leave with a dubious look on his face, Makoto summoned an informant he personally used. His agent arrived in a little under an hour, and Makoto requested he do background checks related to Gongjin Zhou's request.

After completing these arrangements, Makoto leaned back into his chair and breathed a heavy sigh.

"Yellow Turban Strongman..."

He was muttering to himself about a profile description that went over the immortalists' fields of expertise. According to the document, the three about to defect to Japan were researching Yellow Turban Strongman, a lost art of divine immortalism.

"It's too convenient."

A sales pitch from an expert, who had brought it to him as though perfectly timing it with their parasite doll development: that was how Makoto interpreted Zhou's request despite the Parasidoll development being a top-secret project. Zhou must have obtained intelligence on it.

"If I assume there is an information leak, that would be a worrying state of affairs. However..."

But when it came to techniques to control lifeless dolls from afar—such as puppet magic, soldier-creation arts, or golem magic—ancient magic was one or two steps ahead of modern magic. The technology the Parasidolls required was not magic to manipulate inanimate puppets but a technique to control an evil spirit residing within a mechanical doll. Still, the parallels with ancient magic, which turned spiritual beings into agents to control puppets, were numerous.

Putting it all together, the magicians researching the secret lost art from the mainland, Yellow Turban Strongman, were desirable indeed for the Kudou's continuing development of the Parasidolls.

"No matter. If they become pests, then I need only crush them in my fingers," said Makoto, ending his monologue, adding to himself: *whether those pests are snakes in the grass or the three worms.*

[3]

Once the weekend came, First High was finally shaking itself free from the competition's "operations shock." Having reconsidered their representative selections after the notice that came on July 2, event practice resumed on Saturday the seventh. Regular exams would be starting on Tuesday, but the new reps were supposed to get at least one practice in together before that. In particular, for the new events Rower and Gunner and Shields Down, mock battles had been planned so the competitors could get a feel for the event. The Cross-Country Steeplechase's setup was too involved, however, and hadn't yet been prepared.

For Rower and Gunner practice, they used the Battle Board waterway as it was, procuring targets from the biathlon club and the hunting club. For Shields Down, they created a makeshift ring on the athletic field for each gender, and mock battles for that had started right after school ended.

Right now, in the girls' ring—though the standard of twenty meters long and wide and one meter high was the same for the girls and the boys—the girls' solo rep, Tomoko Chikura, was facing off against Erika.

Apart from the difference in size, Shields Down enclosures looked like a boxing ring with no ropes or posts. However, the floor was made of material that made it harder to slip on and kept vertical vibration to a minimum. On that canvas perfect for running around on, Erika was, in fact, running around as she pleased.

"Ugh, she's fast…!"

For a while, Tomoko had been trying to push Erika out of the ring using Deviation Release. The spell's original use was compressing air on one side, then rapidly expelling it on the other side where the target was located.

Unfortunately, the spell hadn't been able to keep up with Erika, who was using self-acceleration magic. Erika's body stepped in zig-zagging patterns, and the moment Tomoko lost sight of her, her shield was blasted by a fierce impact.

Erika had applied Landslide to bash her shield into Tomoko's. The technique could be called a shield-bash version of Landslide. At the moment of contact, she'd maximized her own shield's inertia. As a result, her attack had launched Tomoko and her shield clear out of the ring.

After Tomoko Chikura fell onto her back atop the cushions laid outside the field, Erika jumped down from the ring, offered a hand, and pulled her up. Hattori, watching from beside Tatsuya, sighed. Noticing Tatsuya was glancing at him, he turned to look at the boys' ring, where Sawaki and Leo were crossing swords—or more accurately, crossing *shields*—with the chosen pair team consisting of Kirihara and Tomitsuka.

The shields used in Shields Down were made of wood; the boys' were over 0.5 square meters and the girls' over 0.3. Their forms were defined to allow a handle and no more than two curved surfaces. In other words, as long as the shield didn't have an undulating surface, edges that folded in on it, or anything of that sort, it could be circular, rectangular, or even star-shaped.

As a result of attack pattern simulations on its athletes, First

High had adopted spindle-shaped shields. Kirihara pointed the tapering point on his at Leo and thrust.

Leo, having dropped his weight in the center of the ring, caught Kirihara's attack. It was amazing that he didn't even budge, but Kirihara, who didn't lose his balance even with the recoil of being completely blocked, was just as skilled.

They both stopped. Aiming for that opening, Tomitsuka launched an attack on Leo.

Avoiding Sawaki, whom he'd been staring down, Tomitsuka quickly wheeled around to Kirihara's right side. In contrast with Kirihara's shield, which was one-handed and fixed to his right arm, Tomitsuka's had two handles running along its length and was designed to be held with both hands. Readying the shield to his front right, he tried to aim a skewering thrust on Leo.

"Ahh?!"

But a moment before he could land his move, a sudden gust of wind hit him. Just as he'd gone around Kirihara's right, Sawaki had come around to Leo's left. Sawaki, with his one-handed shield fixed to his left arm, sent his right fist flying toward Tomitsuka.

A pneumatic-pressure wave caused by the speed of his fist—this was Sawaki's specialty. The spell worked by layering his hand with a thick covering of air, accruing no extra weight but widening its surface area, then using his magically accelerated fist to blast an opponent with a mass of air. The Shields Down rule forbidding direct attacks on parts other than the shield only applied to physical attacks involving solids or liquids—there were no restrictions for gas-based strikes.

Tomitsuka's short body tumbled onto the canvas. He barely managed to avoid getting knocked out of the ring, but without any means of fighting at long distance, he was effectively neutralized for the moment. Kirihara, shield locked against Leo's, saw this and moved his empty left hand to the CAD wrapped around his right arm.

There was a trick to get out of this two-versus-one situation. The spell he planned to use to destroy Leo's shield was a High-Frequency Blade using his shield as a medium. He applied both a high-speed vibration spell and a self-destruction prevention spell to his shield.

The vibrations transferred to Leo's shield through the contacting edge, and—

"Guh?!"

——Kirihara's shield half shattered. He'd given a groan of surprise without meaning to, but no one could blame him. If his shield had broken from the vibration reaction, that meant Leo's hardening spell had beaten his self-destruction prevention spell with brute force.

Kirihara now stood stock-still, and this time Leo rammed his shield edge into his. The magically hardened shield split Kirihara's clean in half.

Another sigh escaped Hattori's lips when he saw the practice match's outcome. He shook his head a few times, then reluctantly spoke to Tatsuya.

"Shiba... Was it really the right choice not to have Chiba and Saijou be our reps?"

They'd actually had this conversation during the competitor selection process, but the one who had most firmly opposed it had been Tatsuya.

"If not for the restriction on attack areas, they would be powerful competitors in their own right."

"You mean they can't win with the current Shields Down rules? You said that during the selection, too, but now that we've seen them in a match..."

"Chikura and Kirihara just aren't used to how to fight in Shields Down yet. Minami?"

After mildly rejecting Hattori's concerns, Tatsuya spoke up to

Minami, who was watching the practice from just outside the girls' ring.

"Yes, Big Brother Tatsuya?"

Minami was about to run over to him, but Tatsuya stopped her with a hand, then walked over to the girls' ring himself. Next to Minami was the freshman girl who would be the other half of the pair team in the rookie Shields Down event, her face taut with tension.

"Erika?"

"What?"

As Tatsuya walked, this time he beckoned to Erika. She had been keenly watching Leo's fight but immediately came over.

"Erika, could you be Minami's practice partner?"

"For a solo match?"

"Yeah."

"Hmm... All right."

After giving Minami a comprehensive sizing-up stare, from the tips of her toes to the crown of her head, Erika nodded, seeming convinced for the moment, and got into the ring.

"Minami?"

Calling after Minami to stop her from getting right up into the ring after her, even though she was confused by this unexpected development, Tatsuya whispered something into her ear.

When Erika saw that, the corners of her lips turned up in a smirk.

"I'm sorry for making you wait, Chiba. I am ready when you are."

After Minami stepped up into the ring and gave a polite introduction...

"Can't wait to see what strategy he left you with."

...Erika responded with a dangerous-looking smile.

"Both of you, on your marks."

The Nine School Competition didn't have judges in the field, and Shields Down was no exception, with no staff on the canvas. Instead of a beep to signal the match's start, Tatsuya blew a whistle.

Erika immediately charged Minami. She didn't feint but it wasn't because she was underestimating Minami. She couldn't restrain her curiosity over what kind of plan Tatsuya could have given her.

As Erika rushed toward her, Minami quickly and calmly used her CAD.

Erika's body stopped dead for a moment. The motion was made possible only because the inertia applied to her body was neutralized, but the fact that she had stopped was not because of something Erika had intentionally done.

Minami had deployed an anti-object barrier and hit Erika's shield with it. Erika didn't feel any recoil because the target inertia had been minimized. But the same went for Minami, too. Without receiving any impact whatsoever, she moved to her next spell.

Erika's body floated up into the air. She hadn't jumped. She'd been stranded on the barrier Minami had made diagonally. Gravity still worked even though inertia had been neutralized, which meant she could still plant her feet. But now that she'd been cut off from solid footing, she had no way to resist.

"Hey…!"

Erika frantically tried to knock out the neutralization spell, but unfortunately with her skills, she couldn't change a spell's ending condition on the spot. And if she maximized her inertia now, it would only cause her uniform motion to continue. As a result, the advancing Minami's barrier carried Erika out of the ring like a feather.

"Was that…Juumonji's Phalanx?" murmured Hattori, shock in his voice.

"No. That spell was just continuously moving a single-layered anti-object barrier." Tatsuya denied Hattori's speculation out of hand. "The principle is the same as simple movement magic. Movement spells continuously change a target object's position. All she did was switch the target of that change from an object to the barrier's deployment coordinates."

"Is it really that easy…?"

Hattori's shock wasn't allayed—in fact, it had intensified. If such a thing was so easy, anyone would be able to recreate the Phalanx's offensive capabilities.

"The spell Minami used and Phalanx have different difficulty levels," answered Tatsuya. "The offensive type of Phalanx sacrifices the anti-object barrier's duration to push its strength and speed to their limits, continuously creating more layers. Minami's spell emphasizes durability; you can't expect it to have enough pressure to crush a target."

Tatsuya left Hattori's side and walked over toward where Tomoko Chikura was. Erika, who had fallen from the ring, and Minami, looking embarrassed after emerging from the ring, had also assembled there.

"Man, you sure got me. Never thought someone would knock me out that easily."

"If you charge in so obviously, of course she'll hit you with a counter. That trick of yours requires enough speed that your opponent can't perceive it happening."

"…I'm impressed you knew."

Tatsuya shifted his gaze from Erika, who was disappointed at her *secret technique*'s flaw being mercilessly pointed out, to Tomoko.

"I believe you now understand how to cope with opponents who rush in for close combat."

"…I can't use barriers like that, you know."

"But vector-inversion spells are your specialty, right?"

Apparently thinking Tatsuya wasn't aware of her magical forte, Tomoko's eyes widened slightly.

"…Well, yes, but…"

"All you have to do is reverse the appropriate vectors right before your opponent's shield makes contact, raise them into the air, then throw them out of the ring with a movement spell."

It was more unexpected from Tatsuya's perspective that she'd thought he *wouldn't* know about her specialty. He was both an engineer and a chief of operations for this year's competition. For both roles, not knowing the competitors' strengths and weaknesses would've been ridiculous. Perhaps that was why his remark came off as a little brusque—although it was more likely that was simply his true character.

Whatever Tomoko thought about his attitude, though, she seemed convinced for the moment of his advice. Erika looked like she wanted to say something in her place, but Tatsuya's attention had turned to the vibrating information terminal in his inside pocket.

He took out the terminal and read the message. Then he turned around and spoke to Hattori, who was standing behind him.

"It looks like Pillar Break is all set up. I'll be heading there, so could I trouble you to take over here?"

"Yeah, thanks for your work. You can leave it to me."

This had been planned from the start so Hattori agreed at once.

Just to be sure, Tatsuya looked toward the boys' ring. Next to a senior engineer, who had taken Sawaki's CAD to perform minor adjustments on it, Chiaki Hirakawa was intently listening to something Tomitsuka was saying. She was probably asking him what he thought of the competition CAD. Deciding she wouldn't cause an issue, Tatsuya bowed to Hattori and Chikura before calling Erika and Minami and heading toward the Pillar Break practice area in the training woods.

Every year, the fifty-meter outdoor pool in the back of the training woods was used for Pillar Break practice. It wasn't a pool for swimming, but for fluid control practice. It was normally empty and covered up, but when the time came, students would fill it, create ice pillars, then use magic to stand them up. Only after going through that process would the Pillar Break practice finally be able to start.

The prep work had traditionally taken quite a lot of time, but this year, they finished it in a quarter of the time.

"Oh, Brother. The preparations are complete."

This was all thanks to Miyuki, who had refrained from doing so last year because she was a freshman, taking on a major part of the work this year. Tatsuya, too, had estimated it would take about half as much time as last year, but Miyuki's skills had gone above and beyond his expectations. ——It had taken almost the same amount of time filling the pool as it did to finalize preparations for Pillar Break practice.

"Good work. That was pretty fast."

"I couldn't possibly make you wait, Brother."

Miyuki's remark was, suitably for her features, very in line with the ideal that Japanese women traditionally aspired to, but the gaze she fixed on Tatsuya betrayed her voice and face. Her eyes spoke volumes. Her true intentions had been to *take back* Tatsuya as soon as she could and it was obvious to anyone who bothered to look. Kanon, for example, was making a clearly fed-up expression in the background.

"Who in the world could've known she'd make twenty-four water pillars simultaneously, then freeze them all into the right shape all at once," muttered Kanon sardonically.

On the other hand, Shizuku seemed interested in the spell Miyuki had used. "Did you put that fluid-control spell together, Tatsuya?"

"It was my idea to apply similar-figure duplication theory, but Miyuki is the one who brought it to a usable state."

"Oh, but it was you, Brother, who built an activation sequence based on the magic that I use intuitively."

The older brother and younger sister each yielded the achievement to the other. Not only Kanon, but even Shizuku, turned aside as if to say *Yeah, whatever.*

"...Anyway, if we're done setting up, let's get started."

At Tatsuya's words, Miyuki immediately assumed her position.

Kanon and Shizuku had been somewhat slow to react, and that couldn't have been purely their fault.

* * *

As previously noted, the fifty-meter-long, twenty-meter-wide, five-meter-deep pool was not meant for swimming. Therefore, sanitation management was not very strict. Judging by the pool's walls and bottom, the foundation was simply highly water-repellent clay that had been pressed into place. All that made this the perfect place for Pillar Break practice.

The bottom of the pool was divided by white lines the same size as a Pillar Break field, and a slender pole stuck up out of each of the four corners. Scaffolding was laid across the ground ten meters from each of the pool's lengthwise ends, and the competitors faced off from atop them.

On one stood Miyuki.

On the other stood Kanon and Shizuku.

It was a two-on-one handicapped match, but that didn't mean Kanon and Shizuku definitely held an advantage.

Save for special exceptions, magic could not be compounded. If Kanon and Shizuku both flung spells at the same time and didn't work well as a team, only one of their spells would activate. In the worst-case scenario, sometimes neither spell would have any effect. This problem was present in the other pair events as well, but they predicted it would be particularly arduous for Pillar Break.

"Shizuku, do your best!"

Honoka cheered Shizuku on. Setup for Mirage Bat was taking a while, so she'd come to watch Pillar Break practice—that was the "official" reason, but she mostly wanted to be near Tatsuya.

"Miyuki, you can do it!"

As if competing with Honoka, Izumi rooted for Miyuki, though she was slightly embarrassed about doing so. She was a Pillar Break rookie rep, and despite harboring somewhat biased thoughts, she was actually there to observe.

"Then let's begin."

Following Tatsuya's remark, the simple signal they'd set up glowed red, then changed to yellow. As it shifted into green, magic sprang forth in the pool.

Kanon, sitting on a folding chair, was looking away from everything, her expression aggravated. Miyuki and Shizuku, both standing, exchanged troubled looks, wondering what to do.

This was the fifth practice match in a row, and despite Miyuki doing almost all the Ice Pillars setup, she'd won all five. This wasn't a reaction unique to Kanon—anyone would be unhappy with results like that.

"Chiyoda on offense and Shizuku on defense—I think your tactics are generally correct."

And without paying attention to Kanon's attempted appeal to her own displeasure, Tatsuya spoke to her unreservedly while adjusting her CAD.

"Are you saying I didn't lose in magic? Then what's the problem?"

"There isn't a problem, per se—you just don't have enough practice as a team. That's natural, of course, since you only started today."

"...What went wrong?"

"Chiyoda's magic activation area and Shizuku's Information Boost area were slightly overlapping."

Upon hearing Tatsuya's explanation, Shizuku stepped in front of Kanon and bowed her head.

"I'm sorry, Kanon, it was my mistake."

"Right. You probably spread the boost effect to our entire playing field to oppose Miyuki's area-of-effect magic, but Information Boost is meant to be used on single objects, not on areas. And you don't lose until literally every pillar is gone, so you'll want to think about narrowing your Boost target down."

"Okay, I will."

"Brother, don't you have any advice for me?"

While Shizuku continued looking up at Tatsuya with a face like a puppy waiting to be petted, Miyuki moved in front of her with a *smile*.

"If you lose, I'll give you advice. But if you go easy on them, I'll scold you instead."

"Scold me...? I—I would never purposely lose. It would be rude to Chiyoda and Shizuku."

Miyuki replied with a tone that seemed blustering, but the edges of her averted eyes had slightly reddened.

Kanon watched them with a dumbfounded look. In truth, she wasn't satisfied with Tatsuya being the engineer in charge of their *practice* instead of Isori. She had wanted to nitpick the job Tatsuya was doing somehow, but seeing Miyuki and Shizuku practically hanging from him made her think to herself that she'd endure until the real thing while she laughed bitterly on the inside.

July 7, Saturday night. During this season marked by long days, you could still call it early evening, but the Saegusa family's principal residence was deathly quiet.

The current family head Kouichi's eldest son had already married and now lived in an apartment with his wife in the heart of the city. His second son was always sleeping at the magical institute the Saegusa family had established separate from old Lab Seven, and that had essentially become his living quarters. The two older children were sons of his late first wife, and there was a chance that they were avoiding their younger sisters, who were born to his second wife. They certainly weren't on bad terms, but reservations likely lurked somewhere in their hearts.

As for his daughters, his eldest, Mayumi, was at yet *another* party and still hadn't come back. Tonight's wasn't a social gathering connected to the Numbers at a salon but a Tanabata party held by the university. Still, *as always*, she'd probably be back close to midnight.

Kasumi and Izumi had quickly taken baths and shut themselves up in their rooms. They'd given him the rapid-fire "I'm tired today," so they might have already been asleep by now.

Kouichi, however—though he was exhausted like his youngest daughters—couldn't rest. While he was working in his study, the subordinate he'd been waiting for arrived.

"Enter," he responded to his knocking, urging entry.

The person was Nakura, his *current* confidant.

"What did Gongjin Zhou say?"

Blocking Nakura, who was about to offer the usual niceties, Kouichi asked for a simple report. Nakura, actually appearing to be glad to have cut the pleasantries, answered impassively.

"He requested the current Kudou leader accept defectors from the GAA."

"Hmm... What was his true reason for contacting the Kudou?"

"To interfere with the performance testing of the Parasidolls, combat gynoids possessed by parasites, during the Nine School Competition and to make the gynoids go berserk and harm the competitors. Our source said he will not go so far as to kill them. I believe this point is trustworthy."

"How will he do it?"

"By using a madness-inducing spell made for the parasites."

"...Exotyped magic to interfere with spiritual beings." Kouichi said that to himself, appearing very interested. But then, wiping that interest from his face, he turned to his desk. "Excellent work."

The words implied that he wanted Nakura to leave. But Nakura didn't silently obey.

"Would it be wise to leave this be?"

"It doesn't matter," answered Kouichi, his back still facing the man. "The Parasidoll performance tests will be conducted during the Cross-Country Steeplechase event. Freshmen won't be entering it."

"Then it doesn't matter as long as your relatives don't come to harm?"

Nakura's voice held no criticizing tone, but Kouichi, as if he'd noticed something he couldn't overlook, swiveled his chair around to face Nakura.

"Why should I have to bend over backward for the children of other families?"

At Kouichi's question, Nakura admitted his own mistake and lowered his head. The simple fact that they were connected to Zhou meant that caring about other families would be hypocrisy.

"And the hard-liners in the JDF were the ones who meddled first this time. The Parasidoll test itself is how the Old Master is taking advantage of this series of events to try and create an opportunity to replace magicians with machines. It'll make no difference at this point even if another conspiracy or two is layered on top of it."

The mastermind was in a group close to him, so Kouichi knew all about how the large-scale changes to the Nines had been made.

The ones who had started the whole thing had been a group of anti-GAA conservatives in the JDF. They were the faction that had opposed the peace treaty they had signed with the GAA last November.

They'd insisted that they should take advantage of the GAA losing one-third of its total fleet to deal even greater military blows, removing the threat of the GAA over a long period of time. In other words, they wanted open war. Before the Yokohama Incident, almost nobody in the JDF agreed with that opinion, but afterward, their group had certainly gained some supporters.

But in the end, they hadn't gone any further than threatening military action. The circumstances had strengthened the hard-liners' bonds, and they'd grown into a faction that JDF command couldn't afford to ignore.

Accepting pressure on the magic society as tolerable was, in large part, to soothe the hard-liner dissatisfaction. As a result, the Nines had chosen events with strong military overtones.

Anything beyond that was Kouichi's own speculation, but Retsu

Kudou was probably trying to bend the current state of affairs for his own benefit rather than cut it off entirely. He had drawn the hard-liners' interest with the pretense of magic weapon experiments, and he wanted to show the Parasidolls taking down normal magicians to convince them it would be more effective to strengthen their military by advancing Parasidolls research, since they were made to be weapons from their inception rather than being magicians turned into weapons.

Kouichi didn't have any proof of this. It was nothing more than a hunch deduced from what he knew of the situation. But however he thought about it, that method, rather than sacrificing young magician boys and girls to develop weapons, was more like the Retsu Kudou he knew.

"Nakura, there's no need to worry. Even if Lord Makoto is caught in the trap, things will be wrapped up as necessary."

Kouichi trusted his former master that much.

Sunday, July 8: Tatsuya was visiting FLT's R & D Section 3. "Despite it being the weekend" would not have been an appropriate way of putting it. It would perhaps actually be more suitable to say it was *because* he didn't have school that day.

Unusually, Tatsuya was alone. Regular exams would be starting Tuesday, so Miyuki was at home studying. Tatsuya could always cram if he had to.

As always, the lab was filled with researchers who had forgotten the concept of weekdays and weekends. Everyone seemed to be working like busy bees, since Section 3 was just coming to the end of a new product's development.

A CAD controlled entirely by the mind—a product that would cause a technological breakthrough in machine-based magic-casting assistance. Six months ago, Rosen Magicraft had released a fully thought-controlled model, said to be the first in the world, and FLT's new product would be an extension of it, intended to seriously compete in the market.

Still, Rosen and FLT were approaching the product concept from two different directions. Rosen's CAD was a specialized one, fitted with a mechanism that allowed the user to control the buttons with psionic waves; for a portable object, it fell into a fairly broad category of devices.

In contrast, the fully thought-controlled CAD that FLT had developed specialized in a single function: outputting an untyped magic activation sequence to control the CAD. All CADs, of course, output an activation sequence corresponding to the target spell. Controlling it with an untyped spell instead of using your fingers, however, was the concept this device had first realized.

Although FLT's fully thought-controlled model required the additional installation of pairing software onto the CAD, one could use it with a device they were already familiar with, which was a great advantage. At least, that was what R & D Section 3 assumed. The pairing software covered 80 percent of CADs sold within the last five years, whether it was a multipurpose type or a specialized type. And users could control them with nothing but psionic waves—this new product would create a large additional market demand that went beyond manufacturer boundaries.

Today was the day of its final testing before being made into a product, and if they didn't find any problems, the plan was to announce its imminent commercialization. By the time Tatsuya showed up in the monitoring room, the tests had already begun.

"Good morning. Am I a little late?"

"Good morning, Prince! No, you're right on time. I'm sorry— We couldn't wait, so we started early."

Ushiyama lowered his head, his face apologetic, but his eyes were sparkling with joy.

It wasn't a smile that made fun of Tatsuya but the kind offered when a craftsman created satisfactory work.

"I see. I suppose I don't mind…"

Moving his eyes to the wall-mounted monitor, Tatsuya wore a smile much like Ushiyama's.

"It looks like it's going smoothly."

The large display showed twelve testers simultaneously going through the trials. They used each of the eight types of magic, one after another, replacing the CAD each time.

"Oh yes, everything thus far has been perfect! We've brought the time lag down below our assumptions as well."

The testers were only using beginner-level magic. It was a common sight to see during testing of newly developed CADs, but two things set this scene apart: One, they weren't touching the CADs' buttons with their hands. And two, a medallion-like device hung from a small chain around each of the testers' necks.

Hidden inside their clothing was a silver matte disk, three centimeters across and six millimeters thick. That was the fully thought-controlled CAD. The monitor, which was set up to make psionic light visible, showed the medallion CADs drawing in the testers' psions and outputting activation sequences. As Tatsuya used his information body-perceiving vision ability to watch one tester through the monitor, he *saw* the activation sequence output from the medallion at his chest change into a psion-controlling magic program within the tester and *saw* the psionic waves converging and being absorbed with pinpoint precision into the button on the bracelet on his left hand.

CAD buttons were both electrical switches and psion signal receptors with a mounted reaction stone antenna. The touchless button already fitted into the CAD beforehand sent psions directly to this antenna, thus serving as a replacement for finger-based controls, but frequently if the user wasn't used to controlling their psions, they would specify the wrong activation sequence, so the CAD's own misrecognition rate was no small value. This time, their fully thought-controlled model had been developed with the concept of allowing even magicians inexperienced with psion control to accurately designate activation sequences and to eliminate CAD misrecognition rate.

The means Tatsuya and the others had adopted for that purpose was the development of an untyped spell that would send the converging psionic waves precisely into the induction stone antenna. Users would output the activation sequence for casting magic by using magic. It was certainly a roundabout method, but the psionic waves required to operate a CAD only needed to have a simple construction, so the added burden on the magician was very close to negligible. Given the merits of being able to accurately specify an activation sequence just by thinking about it made this circuitousness a mere triviality.

"Why don't I test it as well?" Tatsuya asked.

"Yes, please do. Hey! Bring the Prince a prototype!" Ushiyama called.

Accepting the medallion-shaped, fully thought-controlled CAD from a researcher who ran over, Tatsuya headed into the testing room.

In the afternoon that day, the Shiba siblings went to the city subcenter. More accurately, Miyuki brought her brother there.

The new model CAD tests progressed without any issues and ended in the morning. Because of that, the time originally set aside for bug fixes became a moment to rest instead.

Tatsuya had returned home with a souvenir—one of the fully thought-controlled CADs, no longer dubbed a prototype but a finished product—only to find his younger sister waiting for him with a sullen look, stress having spoiled her mood. She didn't take it out on him, of course—she almost never did anything like that—her eyes just seemed unhappy and as if she were struggling against something.

Tatsuya, however, couldn't leave his little sister like that. Ever since enrolling, she'd kept her written exam grades at number two in her class. (Her overall grades were, of course, static at the top.) There was never a topic of study she wouldn't be able to understand, but she also wasn't the type to care about rankings. Exam studying couldn't have been the source of Miyuki's obvious stress.

Is it competition prep...? wondered Tatsuya, before proposing that they go out for a change of pace.

"An outing with you, Brother? I'll go! Yes, please!"

Miyuki's answer was, as expected, fervent enough that Tatsuya winced. Basically, she'd just wanted him to pay attention to her. He felt like she was going a little too far with it, but in the end, it was just a sister fawning over her older brother. Tatsuya realized this belatedly—but he certainly wasn't *averse* to his sister doing that, either.

"Minami, what about you?"

Tatsuya asked mostly to be considerate of a housemate.

"No, I have studying to do as well, and I'd like to get a little bit of cleaning done."

Minami answered with a polite bow and politer refusal. She was conflicted—perhaps she *should* accompany them to carry out her Guardian duties. In the end, though, the feeling that won out was that she had better things to do than keep herself inside their mushy little bubble.

Tatsuya had been the one to suggest going out, but it had been a spur-of-the-moment idea, so he had no actual plan. He decided to leave their destination up to Miyuki; as a result, though, they went shopping in the Shibuya city subcenter.

Miyuki had something of a love of finery. Her interest in makeup was still weak, but Tatsuya believed she liked trying on clothes. Her real feelings were slightly different—she liked showing herself off, all dressed up, to Tatsuya—but in any case, whenever the two of them went out, they tended to visit stores of that nature. Even now, they were going through a fashion mall that had just been built.

The many tenants of this building weren't running their own businesses individually but rather jointly doing sales on each floor; nothing demarcated them. One section would have party dresses on display, while the one right next to it might be an underwear shop, making it an awfully uncomfortable place for a man to accidentally walk into.

At first, Tatsuya had made sure to be careful, but since all he was doing was simply following Miyuki around, he couldn't avoid all of it. And it wasn't as though he was harboring any inappropriate thoughts, so he decided it would be strange to claim he didn't want to pass by underwear shops or swimsuit stores.

Today, however, that backfired.

When Miyuki asked an employee if she could try on a few *very airy* summer outfits in a casual clothing shop, they found that unfortunately, none of the fitting rooms nearby were vacant. Both Miyuki and Tatsuya would have been fine with waiting for the previous patrons to finish, but the employee, whether flustered by Miyuki's beauty or oddly taking a liking to her, forcefully guided Miyuki to an empty fitting room on the same floor.

It was the fitting room in a swimsuit store.

Tatsuya waded through the women's swimsuits crammed into a line in the same manner he always walked, but even he decided it wouldn't be good to stand right in front of her fitting room. As Miyuki disappeared behind the door, he told her that if she needed something, she should call him on his terminal, then began to wander away from the area.

His consideration, however, went unrewarded. As he tried to walk from the farthest of the four fitting rooms, hidden from the floor by a wall, past the other three and out onto the sales floor pathway, he came face-to-face with two girls in front of the front-most fitting room. Girls who were underclassmen he was well acquainted with.

"Shiba?! What are you doing over here?! This is the women's changing room!"

Crying out and approaching him was Kasumi Saegusa, in a boyish outfit with an animal-print T-shirt and jean shorts cuffed at the bottoms.

"This isn't a changing room, Kasumi, it's a fitting room... Wait! You're with Miyuki right now, aren't you?! Where might she be, if it's okay for me to ask?!"

Drawing near to Tatsuya with sudden excitement on display after sighing and correcting her older twin sister's mistake was Izumi Saegusa, in a somewhat revealing sleeveless dress of a feminine, very frilly design, with a wide neckline and a skirt that came up five centimeters above her knees.

And if these two were here, he had a pretty good guess as to who was in the fitting room. Tatsuya, overwhelmed by a sense of crisis, quickly moved to leave—but he was one step too late.

"What are you two shouting ab...out?"

The fitting room being so ridiculously sealed had worked against her. Mayumi could hear her little sisters making a racket outside, but she couldn't tell what they were saying. Meaning to reprimand them, she opened the door.

He could feel her staring at his back. If he were to run away after all that, he'd come under suspicion of *peeping* instead. Staying would be better than being accused of crimes he had no recollection of ever doing, but it would still be awkward for a while. Making those calculations quickly in his head, he steeled himself and casually turned around.

The situation was very close to the worst possible scenario he could have envisioned.

She obviously would never have come out naked, but the worst scenario would have been Mayumi in her underwear.

As she stood there dumbly, eyes wide, in front of Tatsuya, the *cloth* she wore was just barely covering her chest and below her waist and only down to the base of her thighs—a white bikini.

Her ample chest, out of place on her petite body, wasn't entirely hidden by her top, which ended up displaying some very visible cleavage.

Her surprisingly plentiful hips and slender waist produced voluptuous curves.

Her defenseless thighs appeared as smooth as marble and seemed soft wherever Tatsuya looked.

"Wha... Ta... This..."

"Please calm down, Saegusa."

He held both palms out in front of him toward Mayumi, who had begun to tremble, and shook them slightly to try to defuse the situation. In other words, he tried to communicate with body language that exactly matched what he'd just said.

Surprisingly, his persuasion (?) succeeded. Mayumi, still facing him, eventually stepped back, returning into the fitting room, then shut the door with a soft sound.

"Kyaaaaaa!"

What he heard from inside the fitting room was doubtlessly Mayumi shrieking. This time, Tatsuya managed to successfully withdraw.

"I was wondering what on earth could be going on..."

"I'm sorry for the noise..."

After Miyuki gave her simple, honest thoughts, Mayumi made herself small and offered an apology.

"No, it isn't your fault. In fact, I should be the one apologizing."

They were in a café being run in the fashion mall. Around the table were Tatsuya, Miyuki, Mayumi, Kasumi, and Izumi.

"I was the one who dragged Brother into a place like that... I'm terribly sorry to both you and him."

Miyuki had been the one to invite the other four here. She'd said to Mayumi that she wanted to have a proper conversation about the clamor that had just occurred, and the Saegusa twins, going with her, marshaled Tatsuya as well.

"No, you're not at fault here, Miyuki. It wasn't like…he saw me naked or anything. I-it was just a swimsuit, so it was strange of me to get embarrassed. Sorry for screaming like that, Tatsuya. I was just a little surprised, that's all."

Mayumi was trying to play the part of their senior or perhaps of an adult. But at the same time, it was clear to everyone but her that her remark was an effort to admonish herself as well. Considering how her cheeks had gone red and her eyes were wandering unsteadily, it was obvious she was still rattled by what had happened.

Tatsuya didn't say anything at first. If he denied what Miyuki had said, it would come off as him covering for a family member, and apologizing to Mayumi, too, would probably just end up making her more embarrassed.

"No, I can't blame you," was about all the response he could manage.

One girl here, though, wasn't satisfied with that. Kasumi was secretly—though it almost wasn't concealed at all—fuming about him embarrassing her sister.

To put her feelings into words, it would be *You're the one who saw my sister in an embarrassing outfit without permission!* But the fact that it wasn't *You're the one who was peeping!* seemed enough to imply she still had some reason left, but either way, it was unfair anger as far as Tatsuya was concerned.

Fortunately for him, perhaps, was that Izumi didn't sympathize with Kasumi's silent outburst.

"What plans might you have after this, Miyuki?" Izumi asked.

Right now, her attention was on one person—Miyuki.

"I was going to look at some Western clothes for a bit longer, then go home," the female Shiba explained. "Exams are next week, after all."

"In that case, may I possibly come with you?" Izumi asked.

Izumi, her ability to think rationally having gone completely out the window, pleaded to come along with Miyuki. While giving her a look that was a bit too rife with desire to be characterized as "innocent." Izumi was faithful to her nature, and Miyuki struggled to maintain her smile against the request.

"Well, if Brother says he's okay with it."

"Izu, you can't cause trouble for other people's families."

Miyuki's answer was neither a yes nor a no, but Mayumi's response was clearly reproving. Izumi was always quick on the uptake, though—and once her sister had gently reprimanded her, she snapped out of it.

"You're right. Please excuse my rudeness, Miyuki."

If that had been where it ended, the Shiba siblings and Saegusa siblings would have parted ways peacefully. Kasumi, however, was a little more honest with her own feelings than her twin.

"Yeah, Izumi. You can't get in the way of the Shiba-Shiba date."

"Date?!"

The flustered cry came, for some reason, from Mayumi.

"Kasumi, we're not exactly on a date here," explained Tatsuya calmly. In fact, his response could accurately be expressed as impassive—and that ruffled Kasumi's feathers, *as usual*.

"Saying it's not a date when *a boy and girl in high school* go shopping by themselves isn't very convincing, you know."

Mayumi, with much trepidation, took a peek at *Miyuki's* face.

The Shiba sister, for whatever reason, had a look that implied she was trying to keep herself from breaking into a smile.

"When the boy in high school is her older brother and *the girl* in high school is his younger sister, I think it's very convincing."

"Well, siblings going on a date seems very unproductive to me!"

"Kasumi, you're really being rude," interrupted Izumi, her tone of voice purposefully strict. She could very easily tell that Kasumi was being stubborn and unwilling to back down.

Kasumi herself could tell she was stepping into a bottomless swamp, too. But for some reason, whenever she talked to Tatsuya, she ended up being stubborn over trivial things. It was rare for Kasumi, who was essentially openhearted, and even she felt doubt, since this wasn't like her.

Independent of her feelings, though, her mouth moved on its own.

"Talented magicians have a responsibility to the next generation! Or are you saying you'll be with Shiba until—"

"Kasumi."

But Tatsuya stopped her tongue running out of control with a voice that was purposely not too loud.

"If that's the case, then wouldn't spending your day off with your siblings be unproductive, too?"

"!" Kasumi grimaced, and her face went red.

Tatsuya returned her frustrated glare with a cool expression.

Then, a moment later, he looked away, stood up, and bowed his head to Mayumi. "Saegusa, we'll be taking our leave now."

"Oh no, allow me."

Seeing the payment slip in Tatsuya's hand, Mayumi hurriedly got up.

"No, I did something immature in front of an underclassman, so this is my apology."

But Tatsuya didn't take her up on the offer and headed for the register instead.

Miyuki stood up, bowed to Mayumi, and followed after him.

Kasumi, lips drawn back as though she were about to cry, and her two sisters, watching her worriedly, were left behind at the table.

After leaving the store and walking a short distance, Miyuki turned around. The Saegusa sisters weren't following them, of course. With a slightly relieved expression, she spoke to her brother.

"Umm, Brother, I don't think Kasumi meant anything by what she said."

Tatsuya replied with a momentarily confused expression, but then he gave a pained grin and nodded.

"I don't, either."

Miyuki's tension loosened at his answer, and she breathed a sigh.

"I know Kasumi didn't mean to say *that*. I used that logic because I didn't want to let her say anything beyond that, but... Maybe it was a little too mean of me."

Tatsuya was smiling in a self-deprecating way, but Miyuki knew he wasn't really beating himself up over it.

"...I do like how you aren't *too* kind to other girls."

"...You have a wicked streak of your own, don't you?"

"Hmph!" said Miyuki, puffing out her cheeks.

The childish act made Tatsuya smile, this time without any pain in it.

[4]

Monday. At the promised hour, Gongjin Zhou visited Makoto Kudou.

Makoto welcomed him and answered that he would take the defecting immortalists into the institute.

Zhou and Makoto each offered a satisfied smile, shook hands, and parted.

And this meeting, despite a strict gag order, was known to Retsu Kudou after one hour.

"...As you've heard, Lord Makoto has pledged to accept the defecting immortalists. And for it, Gongjin Zhou has requested no special reward or conditions. His objective was likely only to plant these immortalists into our ranks."

"I see."

At the report from the old man who was dressed in a suit with hair shaved off in the style of a monk, Retsu Kudou, himself wearing a three-piece suit with his pure-white hair neatly combed back, nodded unhurriedly.

"Would it be wise to remain a spectator, Sensei?"

This old man who called Retsu "Sensei" was one of the Numbers of Nine, the previous head of the Kuki family, Mamoru Kuki. He was over sixty, but compared to Retsu, who was almost ninety, he was still not quite at retirement age. He had entrusted the family estate to his eldest daughter in order to fully serve at Retsu's beck and call.

The families of Nine had a stronger sense of unity than the other Numbers. They weren't equal to members of the Twenty-Eight—the Ten Master Clans and the Eighteen Support Clans—but more like a main family and branch families or a master and retainers. This relationship had originated from their Lab Nine days, when they had fought against a common enemy, the Traditionalists, with the Kudou family as their center; the reason it wasn't the Kuki or Kuzumi who had become the leader but the Kudou was because of Retsu Kudou's charisma. Recently, Retsu's authority had also greatly waned—at least, to the point where Makoto could place a gag order on members of the institute—but for the generation of the previous leaders of the Kuki and Kuzumi (in other words, Mamoru's generation), Retsu was still their leader.

"It doesn't matter. Though we will need to revise our plans."

"In what way, Sensei?"

"The hard-liners are the masterminds—contriving reasons to use immortalists from the GAA for Parasidoll development, whose performance testing just happens to be on the same day as the Nine School Competition, as well as trying to manipulate public opinion by badly injuring the competition athletes. Which means Gongjin Zhou, instigated by the Traditionalists, is the one who sent the immortalists into our institute in cooperation with the hard-liners."

Retsu's hypothesis was rough, to say the least. Anyone who had common sense would say that everything Retsu claimed was far too convenient.

But Mamoru didn't object to the plan. The important thing wasn't to construct an elaborate scheme but to stay a step ahead of the opponent, to outsmart and ensnare them. Both Makoto and Retsu understood that.

"We will have to make arrangements to prevent sacrifices among the magic high school students…"

When Mamoru referred to sacrifices, he meant deaths. He didn't consider injuries something that needed to be avoided.

"Don't worry. The Parasidolls have always had limiters preventing them from attacking noncombatants. We planned to have them use guerrilla combat mode during these tests, but if we deploy them with normal settings, no students in plainclothes will come under attack."

Even knowing that, Retsu guaranteed there wouldn't even be injuries.

"Won't the immortalist spells affect the limiters?"

Mamoru's concern was a reasonable one, but Retsu's confidence didn't waver.

"To begin with, it's impossible for a Parasidoll to go mad. The parasite and gynoid are linked together with a loyalty spell. The limiters programmed into the spell have the same effects as a *geas*, from ancient Celtic magic. The parasites receive the necessary supply of psions for their activities from the gynoid under the condition that they're bound by the loyalty spell. If one tries to act contrary to the restrictions of its limiter, the parasite will immediately expel all its psions and fall into a hibernating state. In that way, the gynoid's frame becomes a container sealing the parasite within. It's described in the loyalty spell as a penalty to pay should the limits be violated."

"Meaning that if we wished it, we could render Gongjin Zhou's entire plot pointless...?"

"Yes."

Retsu and Mamoru shared a private smile.

"But then the Parasidolls wouldn't have any targets in the first place," pointed out Mamoru in a half-joking tone.

Retsu, however, answered him very seriously. "If there is a soldier not identified as an ally, in other words an armed person, the Parasidoll will mark that person as an attack target. I'm thinking of having them go up against Kazama's subordinates."

Retsu's targets didn't stop at the hard-liners and the Traditionalists.

He was trying to take care of every opposing faction at once. Mamoru, after realizing that, unconsciously straightened up.

"Will Kazama take the bait? And I can't imagine Saeki would stay silent."

"He'll take it. One of his subordinates will, at least."

Whatever idea passed through the back of his mind at that moment, Retsu erased his expression and continued like this.

"If he learns the competition is being targeted, Miya's son will surely act. Even if he knows he will end up playing the fool, he won't have the option of not intervening."

"Lady...Miya, you mean of the Yotsuba? Did Kazama have a subordinate like that?"

Mamoru's question was hushed. Retsu didn't return an answer.

"If he acts, Kazama will have to act as well. At least, he will have no choice but to tacitly permit it." Retsu breathed a quiet sigh. "Neither Kazama nor Saeki can stop *him*, after all."

July crawled into its final third, and Tatsuya eventually got some breathing room. The prospects for dealing with the competition's new rules, which had been piled on during exam season, looked bright as well. The players had gotten well used to the new events Rower and Gunner and Shields Down, and this week's results saw the competitors winning out against their practice partners. The only concern was the Steeplechase, but they couldn't do much other than get used to running through the training woods over rough terrain. They couldn't even guess as to what sort of obstacles would be in store for them, so they just had to do what they could.

And then finally, Tatsuya managed to wring out some free time on the night of July 21, a Saturday. He was now deep into the investigations of Lab Nine that he'd planned with Yakumo.

At the moment, he was relaxing in a private room on a linear train headed for Nara. This wasn't the long-distance transportation mechanism called a trailer with a bus or cabinet loaded onto it, but an old-timey multiperson train. This type of train had survived as a means of transportation that prioritized trip comfort over the convenience of never having to transfer. In old-fashioned terms, one could describe it as an express train with only green cars.

So why was Tatsuya, who was off to play secret agent, indulging in such a luxury? The reason was his traveling companion.

The plan had originally only included Tatsuya and Yakumo.

Currently, four people were in this room. Miyuki had steam-rolled him by asking him to bring her along, and Minami had been right behind her, saying that if *Lady Miyuki* was going on a trip, she would be there to look after her; they were both with him now.

"This is much more comfortable than I expected, Brother. And it feels to me as though it's going quite fast, at that."

Miyuki seemed thrilled about their linear train trip. She was right—the cushioning was good, with the train almost not shaking at all, and it was pushing speeds comparable to short-distance aircraft. But more than anything, it was first and foremost a novel experience. In modern times, with ground-based transportation having shifted toward decentralized methods with lower concentrations of people, even riding a bus was out of the ordinary. It was both Tatsuya's and Miyuki's first time on a train many people rode at once and a high-class one at that, with the interior split into individual compartments. Even Tatsuya was a little out of his element, so he couldn't blame Miyuki for being excited. Looking more closely, Minami seemed a bit buoyant as well.

Yakumo had been the one to arrange this transport for them. Their initial plan had been to take a wagon car driven by one of his disciples and rush there at high speed, but once he learned Miyuki would be coming, he'd changed the schedule. Part of it was that they'd check into the hotel quite late if they used a car, but it was mainly as a safety measure.

The possibility that Lab Nine and the Numbers of Nine knew

of their actions was slim to none. Encountering obstacles, then, was unthinkable, but in the very worst case, the car would have run the risk of causing an accident—like the one on the way to the Nines last year.

With a linear train, as long as they didn't hesitate over the chances of indiscriminate terrorism, it was impossible to make an attack look like an accident. Other passengers were on board as well, so an assassin could have been lurking in their midst, but with this group, assailants would be easier to deal with than a traffic accident.

Still, they also knew the possibility of actually being attacked was equal to zero.

In the end, his true goal was mostly seizing a chance to make Miyuki and Minami happy.

Once Tatsuya's party reached Nara Station, they split into two groups. They'd been informed of this beforehand, but Yakumo wanted to move separately, so he got in a cabinet headed for Kyoto.

After seeing him off at the station, the other three first checked into their hotel. Tatsuya opened up his luggage in the rooms and immediately changed. He swapped his travel clothes for a riding suit with a blouson over it. Material science had become quite advanced, but in the middle of summer, the outfit was still hot. Still, he had no choice if he wanted to conceal the CADs under his arms. It was only a temporary comfort, but once he sprayed some cooling substance under his blouson, he was all set.

As Tatsuya was about to leave the room, he ran into trouble, which was, in a certain way, just as he expected.

"…Then you must leave me here no matter what?"

Miyuki was looking at him with an overly dramatic gaze, as though she were seeing off a hero starting on a journey to a distant world. With her hands clasped in front of her chest and everything. Even Tatsuya, as indulgent as he was with his sister, couldn't go along with it—his answer was a cold, short one.

"It's dangerous. I can't take you along."

"I promise I would never be a burden!"

"Young women shouldn't be going out at this hour anyway. I don't remember you being a poorly behaved lady, Miyuki."

The current time was a little before nine PM. On days she had lessons, it wasn't unusual at all for Miyuki to be out at this hour. Tatsuya had made the offhand remark knowing full well it would be unconvincing, but it yielded a surprising effect.

"...All right. I'll do as you say, Brother."

Miyuki made a face like she was in shock before nodding and hanging her head.

Tatsuya wondered to himself where on earth she'd learned this kind of acting.

"Minami, take care of Miyuki for me."

But he couldn't waste time in this situation. The only time they had to use was tonight. Tatsuya ordered Minami to take care of her, a pretext for keeping an eye on her, and placed his hand on the door.

"Of course."

He could tell without looking that Minami had politely bowed. A hint of joy that she'd be able to carry out her responsibilities made it into her voice. Tatsuya decided to leave before he got a headache.

After leaving the hotel behind on a rental bike he'd arranged in advance in Tokyo, Tatsuya headed for the old Lab Nine—even if he didn't have a reason or pretext to get in by normal methods. On the public road in front of the institute, at exactly the halfway point between two streetlights, where their light was weakest, he parked the motorcycle on the shoulder.

Around old Lab Nine—which currently held the official name Class Nine Magic Development Institute—were only detached homes one couldn't even tell if anyone lived in and no unmanned convenience stores, either. At best, it was a quiet environment.

With how inactive it was, even a quiet voice would easily be picked up on a microphone. The incredibly low amount of traffic meant even one person would stand out. The conditions were tighter than anticipated, and Tatsuya's actions became more cautious to match.

He took an information terminal out of the side bag hooked onto the front of his bike seat. Pretending to open a map app to figure out where he was going, he directed his Elemental Sight at the institute's interior.

Publicly, old Lab Nine's current research theme was perception-type magic development. The reality might have been different, but if they were using it as a pretext, they'd have to at least be conducting token development into perception spells.

It wasn't as though Tatsuya knew every spell in existence. Chaotic battles were one thing, but if he used his Elemental Sight in a situation like this without any extra noise to cover him, there was a very real chance they'd notice his spell through some method unknown to him.

But it's still less risky than sneaking inside.

Reassuring himself with that thought, he used his eyes that gave him a commanding view of the Idea.

First, he placed the entire institute within his vision.

They'd chosen the Nines as a testing ground, so these P-Weapons were probably something that used magical abilities. If they were testing them against magicians, then they were either weapons that used magic or weapons that blocked it.

In Tatsuya's estimation, there were two types of weapon that could use magic. The first was one that utilized a stored magic program, like the Ni no Magatama. Over half a year had passed since he'd begun analyzing the jewel, but he hadn't gotten any results. But maybe old Lab Nine had been able to successfully store a magic program.

The other type was a combat robot, a fusion of a parasite and a humanoid machine. Pixie's existence already proved that concept was practical, so there was a good chance the weapon was similar.

Whichever it was, he would be able to observe dense quantities of psions. If it was a magic program–storing weapon, then the stored magic programs themselves—if it was a combat robot, then the psions stored within the parasite residing inside it.

He decided not to consider the possibility the weapons were the magic-blocking variety. Using antinite was one thing, but if it was some kind of tech that tried to emulate the Cast Jamming that Tatsuya himself possessed, he wouldn't have been able to tell the difference between that and a regular CAD. Searching for something he wouldn't be able to find would be a waste of time.

As he looked very carefully across the institute, sure enough, he saw one spot particularly thick with psions. He narrowed his magic vision's focus down to that section.

And that was how he saw it:

Parasites, residing inside…female-type robots?

At about the same time as Tatsuya discovered the Parasidolls…

"…Yes."

There had been a telephone call from the desk to the room Miyuki and Minami were staying in.

"Yes… Please wait a moment."

Minami, who had picked up the antique-style telephone with the receiver and speaker connected via an arm, covered the speaker up and turned around to Miyuki.

"Big Sister Miyuki?"

Sometimes at home she would accidentally call her Lady Miyuki, but in a place where others could possibly have been listening to them, she made an unconscious judgment to use the decided-upon title.

"You seem to have a visitor who wants to meet with you."

"What? With me? Ask them their name."

"All right."

After a few more exchanges through the receiver with the front desk, Minami turned around, her countenance this time slightly tense.

"It's Lord Mitsugu Kuroba and Lady Ayako. They seem to be in the lobby."

The tension was transmitted from Minami to Miyuki.

"Tell them I'll be right down."

After giving instructions to Minami thusly, Miyuki hurriedly went in front of the mirror.

Once Miyuki, accompanied by her bodyguard Minami, arrived in the lobby, she indeed saw the Kurobas there.

"Oh, hello there, Miyuki. It's been so long."

Keenly spotting Miyuki, Mitsugu addressed her, but Miyuki simply returned a slight bow and walked up to him.

"Uncle, it has been a long time."

Approaching to a properly courteous distance, Miyuki bowed deeply.

"Yes, and I'm so glad to see you well."

Mitsugu answered with a friendly smile. It wasn't only in his expression, but in both his eyes as well. Miyuki's powers of observation, at least, couldn't see through his act.

"And it's been about three months since I've seen you, Ayako. Thank you for helping us with so much during the incident in spring."

Miyuki wasn't confident she was smiling in the same way as Mitsugu.

"You're very welcome. It was only helpful because you and Tatsuya worked so hard."

When she saw a challenging light emanating from Ayako's eyes in her smile, Miyuki felt a little relieved.

"Well, let's not stand around. Why don't we sit down to talk? And you—you're Minami Sakurai, right? Please, you should come as well."

Mitsugu gave Miyuki and Minami an instruction in the form of a proposal. Miyuki had no responsibility to obey him, but she didn't have a reason to spurn him either, so she obediently followed after him.

Mitsugu brought the two of them (three of them, when including his daughter) not to a sofa in the lobby but to a hotel tearoom—and a private lounge for conversation at that.

"This hotel is under the main family's personal patronage. I doubt you would have known that, though."

Hit by a sudden preemptive strike from Mitsugu, who spoke of it in a mischievous tone as though it were a silly confidence, Miyuki struggled to maintain her smiling face.

"Oh, is that so? It was Master Kokonoe who arranged for our stay in this place, so... What a coincidence."

"Ah, Yakumo Kokonoe? We may have to look into whether there's actually some subtle contrivance in place, then."

Mitsugu Kuroba, and the Yotsuba family at large, couldn't help but be cautious at the mention of Yakumo Kokonoe's name.

Miyuki's answer seemed to have received passing marks under Mitsugu's standards, so the corners of his lips softened slightly.

"Come, come—take a seat. You too, Minami. No need to be shy."

Mitsugu, who had sat down first, gestured with a hand to the chairs.

"Thank you very much."

In response, first Miyuki sat down, then Ayako, then Minami, in that order.

"It's getting late, so if you don't mind, I'll get right down to business."

"We're sorry for rushing you. We have a car waiting outside," added Ayako, bowing lightly to Miyuki.

"Please, you don't need to worry about it. If you devoted time on your way back home to come here, it must be something important, right, Uncle?"

Indicating that she fully understood the implication that they wouldn't be staying here tonight, Miyuki returned a nod.

"That's right. We didn't have any plans to stay over tonight." The preface made Mitsugu's intentions obvious before he took up the main subject. "We're here about the experiments certain persons are attempting to carry out during this year's Nine School Competition."

"You're referring to the P-Weapons' performance testing—the ones they planned to use the Cross-Country Steeplechase as a location for?"

"You knew about the P-Weapons?" Mitsugu asked, a note of surprise in his voice.

He didn't seem to have thought Miyuki would know the code name. But he quickly pulled himself back together and rearmed himself with a smile that left his true thoughts hard to read.

"No, only the code name. Brother has actually gone to investigate the details."

"Oh…"

Mitsugu made a point of looking like he wanted to say *drat*.

"Is something the matter, Uncle?"

She knew it was an invitation, but she couldn't tell what kind—beneficial or harmful. Of the two choices, going along with it and not, she picked the former.

"To tell the truth, we've been conducting our own investigations into them."

Confusion rushed through Miyuki's eyes. She said nothing—not because she'd swallowed her words but because she'd had none to begin with. Next to her, Minami's eyes went wide and she put a hand to her mouth.

Not batting an eyelid at Miyuki's response, which was in a sense just what he'd been after, Mitsugu glanced at Ayako. His daughter took out a data card for use with portable terminals from her handbag.

The look on her face as she handed the card to Miyuki was smug.

"Here are our investigation results regarding the P-Weapons, also known as Parasidolls. Please feel free to peruse it, Miyuki."

"Parasidolls? Why, that's…"

"I believe you have the right idea. Parasite dolls are weapons that use parasites."

Miyuki's brows furrowed, while Ayako answered her with a grin.

"Even we struggled this time. Up against another one of the Ten Master Clans and about the development of weapons that involve demons, with information that would doubtlessly become a media target if it leaked. Their security system was incredibly rigid. I doubt even Tatsuya could thoroughly investigate it in one night."

At Ayako's remark, which one could have taken as a boast, Miyuki found one point she couldn't overlook.

"And you got this, Ayako…?"

"No, no, it wasn't only her efforts," Mitsugu said. "Besides, as you know, Ayako's magic is geared toward intelligence work. It's only natural she would work on this, given that her field of specialty is so different from yours, which is combat and suppression."

What Mitsugu said was objectively true. Especially when it came to situations that required neutralizing a group of enemies, Ayako didn't even begin to compare to Miyuki. But at the moment, with this data card in her hands, that thought wasn't in any way comforting to her.

Right now, what Tatsuya needed was the ability to expose the conspiracies of the JDF and the Kudou family.

And right now, the one helping him was not Miyuki but Ayako.

"Sorry for calling you so late. If you'll excuse us, we don't have much time, so we'll be taking our leave now."

"Please give our regards to Tatsuya."

As the two stood from their seats, it was all Miyuki could do right now to mechanically return the gesture.

◇ ◇ ◇

In the spot of old Lab Nine that was particularly dense with psions stood figures of the same variety as Pixie—parasites possessing gynoids. As Tatsuya stared, wondering why they were specifically female shaped, Tatsuya realized that conditional-activation spells had been cast on them.

What are these? They look like mental interference–type spells, but...

A spell similar to Luna Strike had been implanted in all the gynoids. They didn't seem to be part of the machines' assembly. He sensed an instability from the magic programs, like they'd actually been added on after the fact.

Luna Strike uses an illusory impact to paralyze a person's awareness, intentionally loosening their mental inhibitions and causing them to go berserk. Is this...a spell to make the parasites go on a rampage?

Tatsuya was baffled—it was pointless to make a weapon lose control on purpose. Just then, his information terminal alarm went off. He pulled his mind out of the information dimension and back into the physical plane—this world.

It was the sound of an urgent message arriving. He quickly opened it. The sender field was blank. The same as the one delivered to his house. The text read: *Get away from there right now.*

The situation and the message. Someone knew Tatsuya was here, and they had the motive to send him a warning. He was sure of their identity now, and a moment later, his "eyes" saw the signs of a magical attack.

An emission-type magic—an electric attack spell—and a mental interference–type illusion spell were coming. He'd been caught completely unawares. He wouldn't make it if he pulled out his CADs now.

Making that snap decision, he struck his hands, filled with psions, together hard.

With a clapping noise, psions exploded everywhere.

Program Demolition. An anti-magic spell that used psionic pressure to blow away magic programs.

Since he hadn't given it a direction, he'd used a larger quantity than usual, spreading highly dense psions into his surroundings.

He leaped onto his bike, then used the fastest method possible to take off.

The thick psionic mist was like a smoke screen, and it cut off any pursuit from old Lab Nine.

The next morning, in the train car on the way back to Tokyo, Miyuki, in contrast to yesterday, looked glum. She thought she was the same as always, but to Tatsuya's eyes, her smile looked clouded.

It wasn't that their private room on the linear train, same as what they traveled out with, was disappointing. Last night, Tatsuya had returned to the hotel close to midnight. At the time, she'd seemed simply tired. And when he'd seen her again this morning, the only impression he got was that she felt slightly unwell.

But once they were facing each other in the compartment after meeting up with Yakumo—for some reason, Miyuki didn't sit next to Tatsuya like she always did—a shadow quickly began to fall over her smile, and soon enough it had become a forced one.

That wasn't the face of someone not feeling well. They'd reach Tokyo in about fifteen minutes, but the mood wasn't one he could leave alone until they got back home. He was also curious about what Yakumo, who had taken a separate route, had found out. But he felt that right now he had to prioritize his sister.

"Miyuki, did something happen? Or are you worried about something...?"

"Big Brother Tatsuya—"

"It's fine, Minami."

Minami tried to interrupt to cover for her. Miyuki in turn

interrupted her, reaching into her pouch. She held something out—a small data card for use with portable terminals.

"What's this?"

Tatsuya asked while frowning at the card he received.

"Last night, at the hotel, Uncle Kuroba and Ayako gave this to me."

"They visited you at the hotel?"

His brow still furrowed, Tatsuya turned toward Yakumo. How did the Kurobas know what hotel Miyuki was staying at? They hadn't kept it particularly hidden, but even the Yotsuba didn't exactly keep tabs on her constantly. And she wasn't someone they could immediately get hold of if they needed something.

"Ah, right. That hotel belongs to the Yotsuba. Should I have picked another place?"

Tatsuya's gaze was fairly sharp in its own right, but Yakumo, sitting next to him, without appearing ruffled in the slightest, confessed easily. No, the term *confess* would be inappropriate. After all, Yakumo didn't think he'd done anything wrong. And Tatsuya didn't have any reason to criticize him.

"They said it contains data on the P-Weapons—the Parasidolls—and the results of their investigation on the experiment," Miyuki stated in a low voice.

"Parasidolls... Is that what the P-Weapons really are?" Tatsuya repeated, remembering the female robots he'd discovered last night.

Parasidolls—dolls with parasites in them.

It was so plain, he thought, and it didn't show much of a naming sense, but it was easy to understand. The gynoids sleeping in old Lab Nine were exactly that, dolls with parasites residing in them—parasite dolls.

"That was what Ayako said."

Not Mitsugu but Ayako. When he heard that, Tatsuya guessed why Miyuki was so *depressed*. It was obvious to everyone that Ayako had a competitive streak when it came to Miyuki ever since they were little, but Tatsuya knew that Miyuki also secretly treated *her* like a rival. Their fields of expertise were completely different, but Miyuki was still too much of a child to be convinced with logic.

Tatsuya put the data card he'd taken into his pocket, still in the case. He was interested in the data stored within, but they would be arriving in Tokyo momentarily, and there was no telling who could be spying or eavesdropping on them... Or rather, that was the excuse he gave himself. Tatsuya didn't want to compliment Ayako's efforts in front of Miyuki.

——There was no way the information Ayako and Mitsugu had given to Miyuki would ever *not* be worthy of praise.

"Tatsuya, would you mind letting me see what's on there?"

But Yakumo was going to ruin his considerate act.

"Master, we'll be at the station soon."

If he argued too strongly, it would instead cause Miyuki to worry, so Tatsuya was careful about his tone of voice as he made a roundabout refusal.

"We still have ten minutes, don't we?"

"We *only* have ten minutes."

"It's all right, Brother."

Though Tatsuya kept on trying to decline, Miyuki leaned toward him, peered up into his eyes, and shook her head.

With words of objection on the tip of his tongue, Tatsuya wordlessly nodded at Miyuki. He'd ended up worrying her anyway, but he understood that going any further than this would be for himself, not for her.

"Master, did you bring a terminal?"

"Yeah, I've got one right here."

Tatsuya pulled a wired connection cable out of his own terminal. Partly because their trip was only for one night, he'd only brought a portable terminal along. He'd immediately decided cozying up next to Yakumo to look at the tiny screen wouldn't be a very pleasant setup.

After seeing Yakumo connect the cord to his terminal, Tatsuya played back the card he'd received from Miyuki. The contents were only characters and simple diagrams, so he scrolled through it quickly as usual. Yakumo kept up with his pace without an issue.

After scanning a quantity of information that would normally have taken fifteen to twenty minutes to read in three minutes, Yakumo looked strangely satisfied.

"It looks like it was worth the trip."

Perhaps he was acting out of consideration in his own way. If Miyuki had been acting like she always did, he'd have broken out into a mean smirk. Before Tatsuya could ask what he found so interesting, Yakumo sent him data from his terminal.

The information that flowed through the cable to him was a simple career report. Of three people, mugshots included. Their names and features were both Chinese.

"Is this...data on immortalists defecting from the GAA?" Tatsuya asked.

"Yes, they're *fangshu* users from the mainland who illegally entered the country last week."

Adding timely information, Yakumo nodded. Tatsuya immediately realized the reason.

"The timing does seem too convenient."

The report included the magic these immortalists specialized in: Chinese arts meant for controlling marionettes made of wood, stone, or metal. Spells to affect the independent information bodies that gave the puppets temporary sentience. A special note said that they were skilled in techniques for stealing control of independent information bodies from other casters and ones for severing independent information bodies from their casters' control and causing them to go berserk. This special note matched the magic Tatsuya had found in the Pixie look-alikes—the Parasidolls—at old Lab Nine.

"Doubt it's a coincidence. Someone trying to take advantage of the experiment probably invited them here."

"Take advantage of it? You mean it wasn't the Kudou family's intent to invite them—no, wait, I see what's going on."

As he asked the question, he arrived at the answer himself. He'd considered it last night on his own: It was pointless to make your *own* weapons go out of control. *Normally*, the only ones who would benefit from making weapons go berserk were enemies.

"It looks like this incident will be another tricky one to handle. Though it might end up being a simple setup once you figure out how it works."

Yakumo was absolutely right, thought Tatsuya. You prepare for one scheme, and then someone else integrates their own plans, and once you get to execution, it comes to light that all kinds of other ambitions have gotten twisted into it. In the end, they wouldn't know until everything was over what the true nature of this incident truly was...

Just then, a message that they'd be arriving at the station soon appeared on a panel in the compartment. No announcements could be heard.

"Minami, thanks for this. That's enough."

They were out of time, so they'd have to adjourn here. With that sort of intent in mind, Tatsuya addressed Minami.

Minami nodded and suddenly relaxed. An announcement, which abruptly began to play, reached their ears. Minami had removed the psionic shield and the sound-blocking field.

Still sitting, Minami lowered her head once more at Tatsuya's show of appreciation.

[5]

This year's Nine School Competition was scheduled to have its opening banquet on August 3, begin competition on the fifth, and hold closing ceremonies on the tenth. The events schedule alone spanned eleven days, one more than last year.

While much had changed, the event location was the same. First High's competitors, as they did every year, would assemble at school at eight thirty AM on the same day as the party on the eve of the competition, split up into a large bus and a work vehicle for the engineers, then head for the hotel adjacent to the venue.

Their full group numbered twelve boys and girls each for the main competition, nine boys and girls each for the rookie competition, eight technical staff members, and four strategy staff members, for a total of fifty-four people.

There were two more than last year because of the changes to the event rules. But despite the extra people, the large bus still had seats left over. Until last year, the entire technical staff had traveled in the work vehicle, but this year they would have one person per vehicle for a total of four, with the other four riding the bus. Among the bus's passengers were Tatsuya and Isori. They were in essence, part of the strategy staff as well, so with the logic that they should ride the same bus as the other strategy staff members, someone had strongly insisted they be together—and it went without saying who that was.

This year, two freshmen were on the technical staff, one male and one female. Tatsuya was currently giving Kento Sumisu, the boy, a few tips before they got moving. Meanwhile, a female student was directing a cold stare at him.

"Why is that man bringing a maid robot to the Nine School Competition?" muttered Kasumi bitterly while watching Pixie climb through the back door of the work vehicle assigned to Kento.

"Kasumi, calling him *that man* is rude. And it isn't a maid robot. It's a Humanoid Home Helper," corrected Izumi, her voice flustered.

For a time, Kasumi's feelings toward Tatsuya had taken a turn for the better, but ever since the incident right before regular exams, her loathing of him had intensified.

As for the reason she hated him, Izumi kind of understood it herself. More than half of what had happened before exams had been Kasumi self-destructing. Still, Izumi too felt like Tatsuya's counterattack had been a little more caustic than necessary, and people not seeing eye to eye or having poor affinity with one another didn't obey logical rules. Therefore, Izumi had no intention of criticizing Kasumi for the act of speaking poorly of Tatsuya in and of itself.

But she didn't want Miyuki to hear her elder twin saying those things. Miyuki revering Tatsuya was an understatement, and she probably wouldn't brush off any vilification toward her brother as a joke. Basically, Izumi warned Kasumi because of the egotistic motive of not wanting her to do anything that would give the upperclassman she so adored a bad impression of them.

"Maid robot, 3H, same thing. They work the same way."

Fortunately, Kasumi hadn't caught on to her sister's maliciousness. Not because she was dull or pure and naive but because her mind was focused on disparaging Tatsuya.

"It's an interface for a HAR, right? They didn't *need* to design them as cute girls, did they?"

"A 3H's basic appearance is of a twenty-five-year-old woman. I don't know if you can call that a girl…"

"Th-that's not the problem! I'm saying they didn't need to make them pretty! HARs mainly get used by women, so they *should* have made them average-looking older ladies. Would have been perfect."

Izumi didn't necessarily agree with all of her sister's opinions, but she had a point, so she didn't say anything this time… Besides, if she did, it wouldn't get through the heat haze in her head anyway.

"When you think about it, they probably made 3Hs pretty women and girls because *men* are perverts and wanted to have pretty girls take care of all their needs! I can't believe he'd bring something like that to the Nines…"

"Kasumi?"

Kasumi, who'd been beside herself with her impassioned speech, didn't notice that an upperclassman had approached her from behind until she said something to her. Her spine straightened up, and she turned around slowly.

"What are you so surprised about?"

Shizuku was standing there with a mystified look. "N-nothing."

"Oh? Well, we're leaving soon."

Kasumi was relieved—she didn't seem to have heard their conversation. But that only lasted a moment, too. When she looked left and right, her classmates and upperclassmen were already on the bus.

"I'm sorry, Kitayama!"

"…We're sorry for the trouble."

Shizuku seemed to have come to collect Kasumi, a friend from the disciplinary committee, and Izumi while she was at it.

With apologetic expressions, the twins followed Shizuku and quietly boarded the bus.

This year, without any accidents on the way and without any disturbances sweeping through the bus, First High's competitors arrived safely at the hotel. Everything went just as planned, without even minor trouble occurring, and now the evening party was about to get underway.

Tatsuya had already entered the venue as well—in his own school uniform, no less. Seeing the eight-toothed gear emblem embroidered on his shoulder, Miyuki, who waited next to him, smiled happily.

"Miyuki, what are you smiling about?"

Tatsuya could tell the difference between insincere smiles and sincere ones, though only when it came to Miyuki. Casually curious as to why she suddenly had such a happy-looking grin, Tatsuya asked her directly.

"I was simply overcome with happiness that your magic engineering uniform looks so right on you."

"What's going on? You've been seeing it for four months now."

Tatsuya looked slightly taken aback. ——Minami, waiting behind Miyuki, watched with cold eyes as though she wanted to say *What's going on with you?* But in this situation, she was in the minority—or rather, completely isolated.

"I think so, too, Tatsuya!"

"Me too."

Enthusiastically (or in competition with?) Honoka agreed with what Miyuki had said, and Shizuku also chimed in.

"Yeah. Maybe because it was borrowed before," Subaru remarked. "Last year, it felt like it didn't quite fit."

"Yeah!" agreed Eimi, nodding several times. The competitors chosen from the junior girls seemed like they all stood with Miyuki.

Entrants in the main competition were chosen not only from the juniors but from among the seniors as well. Despite the now-juniors who had delivered incredible results in last year's rookie competition, only five of those twelve reps had been chosen this time.

For Pillar Break, Miyuki would be the solo entrant, while Shizuku and Kanon would enter the pair event. Honoka and Subaru would appear in Mirage Bat, while Amy would be in the Rower and Gunner pair. Five of these people, plus the freshman Minami, were flocking around Tatsuya. Seen from the outside, though Tatsuya would have resented it being described that way, it looked like a harem situation. In addition, Tomitsuka and Morisaki, also juniors, and Mikihiko, chosen as a Monolith Code entrant, had been caught by Sawaki, their senior in both club and disciplinary committee, and were now buried behind the other seniors.

It wasn't that Tatsuya was particularly bad with women. In fact, he didn't have any problems with them. But in a situation with one man and six women, and all the women being cute girls, even he couldn't quite stay calm. During last year's eve party, Subaru and Amy had given him a wide berth. Things had changed this year. Of course, considering Subaru's previous remark, they seemed to have checked up on him back then, too.

Not in a position to stare at the girls too much, Tatsuya took in the venue. Then he spotted an *acquaintance*, surrounded by girls like he was.

He seemed to have noticed Tatsuya, too. Maybe he'd sensed the foreign gaze. Bringing along a throng of female students, also in Third High uniforms, Masaki Ichijou walked over to Tatsuya.

Tatsuya, too, began to walk toward him. Honoka and Amy naturally parted to let him through, allowing Tatsuya and Masaki to face each other, female students waiting at their backs. ——Masaki, though, wasn't the only boy. Next to him was Shinkurou Kichijouji.

"...It's been a while, Shiba."

But the first words out of Masaki's mouth were for Miyuki.

"Yes, it certainly has been, Ichijou."

Excluding Masaki, with his tense, drawn-back smile, and Miyuki, responding in contrast with a wonderfully insincere one, the entire party looked on as though someone had thrown a wet blanket over them. Kichijouji was the one to play support, wanting to stop the awkwardness from settling in before it happened.

"We haven't seen you since Yokohama. I'm happy to see you're the same as always, Tatsuya Shiba."

"Glad to see you're in good health as well, Kichijouji."

His wording was rather gruff, but Tatsuya responded with what was a friendly expression in its own right, then looked to the side.

"And you too, Ichijou. You played a big part in Yokohama. The Crimson Prince lived up to his name."

"...Could you give it a rest, please?"

When Tatsuya mentioned his alias in a serious voice, Masaki frowned slightly.

"You don't like it? I wasn't trying to make fun of you, honest."

"It just sounds pompous, and I don't like it. Can't you just call me Ichijou?"

"Sure."

Tatsuya nodded without argument—or perhaps, without interest. Masaki responded with a look of light surprise. But he didn't mention what exactly he found surprising about it.

"By the way, Shiba—er, is it okay to call you that?"

"Of course."

The First High girls and the Third High girls had begun talking among themselves, leaving them on the sidelines. The Third High girls seemed somewhat reserved (the reason they felt that way was obvious), but they were still having good, lively conversations. With the female students' voices ringing out in the background, Masaki lowered his tone and spoke to Tatsuya.

"Something's going on with this year's competition, isn't there?"

It was a very abrupt topic change, but Masaki's face was all too serious. Kichijouji, too, wore a similar expression.

"Is it that strange? I only know about last year's competition, so I don't really get what you mean."

What Tatsuya replied with was half to conceal his own position.

In reality, he had a guess as to what Masaki was worried about. But there was no guarantee it was correct. Tatsuya wanted to hear it come more clearly from Masaki's mouth.

"A change in events? Sure, that I can accept."

"After all, the way the competition is managed assumes that there could be event changes," added Kichijouji, not satisfied with just a greeting.

"It does seem a little biased toward combat, but considering current events, I think it's actually quite appropriate," Masaki added.

"But the last event, Cross-Country Steeplechase, is the exception."

"That's right. They're going too far with that—it's in a completely different league."

"It's originally a type of training the army undergoes for forest warfare. It's a mystery why they're even calling it an *event* in the first place. They've barely given any official information about it, so we only have rough information, but… Even units in active service barely ever do similar exercises for four kilometers. It's like the training regimen for a large-scale military exercise."

"This may be a competition for magicians, but we're high school students. And they're holding it on the last day, once everyone is tired, too. The risks are too high."

"Plus, any junior or senior can participate. It's not mandatory, but if everyone can get points for running the whole thing in under an hour, I doubt anyone will stay out of it."

"Other things about it are weird, too. I could put it more nicely, but the Nine School Competition is basically a show. You can't deny that part of this is magicians appealing to general society."

"And yet, we have no idea what the Steeplechase will be like. Even Monolith Code's forest stage lets you see the battles in front of the monoliths, at least. This Cross-Country Steeplechase event won't even offer that much."

"The only thing I can think of is that they have another reason besides showing off to spectators and cable news."

"The Nines is for high school students to compete in magical ability. The fact that an event like that was permitted and put into practice makes me feel like someone has other ideas, and they're eroding the very competition itself."

As he listened to Masaki and Kichijouji's conversation, Tatsuya was honestly quite impressed. He'd only begun looking into what was going on behind the scenes of the competition after receiving that anonymous message. But these two were probably on the trail of those intervening intentions backstage having used only their own powers of insight.

"Is that a result of something the Ichijou family investigated?"

"Hmm? No, we didn't go that far... Do you think we should?"

"It's better to investigate things you're worried about if you have the means. Though if you don't have the resources to devote to this, that would be a different story."

That was how Tatsuya answered Masaki's question. He didn't mean to provoke him, but with the way he said it, Masaki couldn't help interpreting it that way.

"We always have that much power in reserve! What I was trying to ask was whether the situation warrants going that far."

"Some say ignorance is bliss, but that's a lie. Sometimes you get into trouble because you don't know enough, but I've never encountered a case where more knowledge was a burden. Do you have experience like that, Ichijou?"

"I don't, but that's not the issue—"

"The Steeplechase is on the last day of the competition, in twelve days. It's hardly enough time, but it's not so short you'd have to give up, thinking you can't do anything."

"Masaki, I think maybe Shiba's right."

As Masaki's mouth bent into a frown, Kichijouji spoke up from beside him, trying to soothe him.

"It's too much for us, but maybe Mr. Gouki can figure something out."

Mr. Gouki referred to the head of the Ichijou family, in other words Masaki's father. Kichijouji's words were ones that supported Tatsuya's opinion.

"...All right. I'll ask the folks back home to look into it."

Masaki said that not to Kichijouji but to Tatsuya.

Guessing that Tatsuya, Masaki, and Kichijouji were speaking of serious matters unbecoming of the party venue, both the First High and Third High girls continued enjoying their own conversations among themselves, without trying to talk to them. That was when a Fourth High male student's voice came up.

"Shizuku."

"Harumi?"

After this exchange, Honoka, who was nearby, seemed to know the boy as well, and they also exchanged greetings.

When she heard Shizuku call out to him, Miyuki recalled that Shizuku's older cousin was enrolled at Fourth High. By remembering that, she succeeded in averting her attention from the Fourth High freshman behind him, pretending she didn't know who he was.

Shizuku, leaving the group and exchanging words with her cousin, nodded several times before returning to Miyuki's side.

"Miyuki, can I ask you something?"

Her face as she said that contained a trace amount of apology.

"What is it?"

"My cousin says he wants to introduce Tatsuya to his underclassmen."

"Really?"

Looking dubious, Miyuki thought, *Here we go.*

"Yep. He goes to Fourth High, but the freshmen heard rumors about Tatsuya and wanted to meet him."

Each of the magic high schools had its own coloration. First and Second High conducted education in accordance with national evaluation standards. Third High held up martial spirit as school tradition, emphasizing magic as a means of fighting. In contrast, Fourth High leaned toward magical techniques that might be used in laboratories and magic engineering. For a Fourth High freshman to look up to Tatsuya, who had displayed such advanced skill as a CAD technician at last year's competition, wasn't strange at all.

"I'll ask him, but I doubt he'll say no."

After answering, Miyuki trotted over to her brother. It was good timing, as he'd gotten to a pausing point in his conversation with Masaki and Kichijouji.

"Brother, might you have a moment? A freshman from Fourth High wishes to say hello."

"To me? Yeah, sure."

The reason Tatsuya was comfortable with this and why Masaki and Kichijouji looked convinced were different. That was how well the phrases *Fourth High* and *Tatsuya's accomplishments* worked together.

"Ichijou, Kichijouji, might I borrow my brother for a moment?"

"Y-yes. That's fine with me. We were actually just finished talking."

Giving a cool smile and a bow to Masaki, who had tensed up again when she'd spoken to him, Miyuki led Tatsuya to where Shizuku was waiting.

"See you, Ichijou."

No response came to Tatsuya's voice. Masaki's mind was glued to Miyuki's smile.

"My name is Fumiya Kuroba. Pleased to meet you, Shiba."

"And I'm Ayako Kuroba. I'm Fumiya's older twin sister. It's a pleasure to make the acquaintance of an upperclassman."

Introduced by Shizuku's cousin, Fumiya and Ayako gave *first-time* greetings to Tatsuya. Their greetings didn't feel unnatural at all.

"I'm Tatsuya Shiba—it's nice to meet you."

That applied to Tatsuya's words, too.

"I'm from First High, though, so I'm not your upperclassman…"

"We go to different schools, but you're still our senior as a magician."

"We may attend Fourth High, but technical fields aren't quite our specialty. Still, if at all possible, would you be willing to give us a little coaching? Both my little brother and I were moved by your capabilities."

This, of course, was simply an act to make it easier for Fumiya and Ayako to interact with Tatsuya in the future. Therefore, Miyuki didn't mention anything that would waste their efforts, either, and since she wasn't confident enough to treat them like total strangers, she didn't speak up.

"It may be difficult during the competition, but if we have another opportunity, I'd be glad to."

"Really?!"

"Thank you very much. We greatly look forward to it."

It was unnatural that the two of them, especially Fumiya, who was a boy, didn't want to talk to a beautiful girl like Miyuki, but it wasn't strange enough to give away that this wasn't their first time meeting. Successfully leaving an impression of being strangers to Tatsuya, Fumiya and Ayako returned to the group of Fourth High students.

The eve party was a buffet-style one without assigned tables, but the same as every year, each school generally had its own spot. When Masaki returned to Third High's table, the female students from his school followed him.

It was also almost time for the guest speech. Tatsuya, too, returned to First High's table, with a female classmate who hadn't had anyone to talk to.

"Tatsuya, those Fourth High students before..."

No sooner had he gotten back than someone had sidled up to him and spoke—it was Mikihiko.

"You mean those two freshmen?"

Though he may have intended to be sneaky, Tatsuya had of course noticed him. Therefore, he didn't do anything like panic at being suddenly addressed and, naturally, didn't blow his cover.

"Yeah... I think they said their last name was Kuroba."

"Wait, were you reading their lips?"

Disapproval was thick in Tatsuya's voice. He'd done it on purpose, of course.

"Sorry. I know it seems like I was eavesdropping."

On the other hand, Mikihiko's guilt-ridden voice was unaffected. For someone with such a serious personality, he probably couldn't avoid feeling guilty whether he'd actually done it or not.

"It's fine. We weren't talking about anything private anyway."

After being absolved by Tatsuya, Mikihiko looked a little relieved.

But a moment later, he gave a darker expression.

"Did you find something wrong with them?"

Now that the ball was in his court, Mikihiko hesitantly opened his mouth.

"It's just a rumor that started this spring... If it's right, there's a branch family called the Kuroba under one of the Ten Master Clans, the Yotsuba. Apparently, they're a very powerful one among the Yotsuba families, too."

"This spring? That wasn't long ago... Do you think they could be related to the Yotsuba?"

"Well, I don't have any proof."

"Kuroba is definitely an uncommon last name, but it's not like it's one of a kind, you know."

"True, but *Yotsuba* isn't all that unique, either."

Tatsuya's makeshift, leading response met with Mikihiko using the same logic for his argument, which ruined it.

It would be counterproductive if Mikihiko thought he was getting irritated about it, Tatsuya thought, changing course.

"I see. Then did you want to warn me not to go near the siblings?"

"Not exactly... Well, maybe. At least, maybe you shouldn't be the one to approach them."

"Then it's okay if they come to me?"

"Trouble does always seem to find its way to you."

That's an awful way of putting it, thought Tatsuya. He considered giving a sarcastic quip in response, but unfortunately, he ran out of time. The illumination in the floor-sized room switched, and the guest speech began.

The event began first with short greetings from the commander of the base providing the Nine School Competition venue—which almost felt like a briefing—then the director of the Magic Association, then the acting president of the National Magic University, each taking turns stepping onto the stage. On a regular year, after the prominent faces, whom these high school students probably would never have had a chance to see otherwise, the schedule had Retsu Kudou wrapping things up with a final guest address.

This year, however, the guest addresses ended without any words from the Old Master.

A murmur rippled through the room at this unexpected development. Not only through the students but among the other guests as well.

First High's students were no exception. But one among them was aware of the exceptional, shall we say, *circumstances.*

"I heard the Old Master has fallen ill."

As a visibly confused Honoka was repeating the process of *look right, look left,* Shizuku, who had disappeared without them knowing, spoke up from behind her.

"Really, Shizuku?" asked back Honoka, turning around with a surprised look.

Shizuku nodded. "I heard it from over there."

She looked toward the Magic Association's head of office staff, who was conversing with a guest Diet member. Miyuki, listening from the side, wondered which one exactly she'd heard that from... though it could have probably been from either.

◇ ◇ ◇

Of the First High female competitors, the juniors numbered five and the seniors seven. Their hotel rooms were twin bedrooms, so one junior and one senior would inevitably be paired up. (Speaking of which, there were an odd number of same-sex freshmen, nine, which left one out, but this year, for learning purposes, they'd chosen one boy and one girl for the freshman technical staff, so with ten freshmen of each gender, they fortunately avoided having to share a room with an upperclassman.)

The junior girls' rooming assignments saw Honoka and Shizuku in one room and Amy and Subaru in the other. Miyuki, left over, would be sharing a room with the extra senior, Kanon, *on paper*.

Incidentally, the engineering staff had three senior boys and one senior girl, one junior boy and one junior girl, and one freshman boy and one freshman girl. Each of the gendered pairs had a senior and a junior together. As a result, Tatsuya would be sharing a room with Isori, *on paper*.

What sort of thing might happen as a result?

There would be no night roll calls or anything of the sort during their stay at the Nines. As a military facility, the night duty soldiers would be patrolling, but they wouldn't enter any of the rooms. Miyuki and Kanon were in a room together. Tatsuya and Isori were likewise.

In the end, it was not a very difficult question. At least, most of the First High reps save for the freshmen had accurately guessed what would happen. In front of Tatsuya, who had left the party, was not Isori but Miyuki.

"His Excellency Kudou was absent, wasn't he?"

Miyuki sat politely on the edge of a bed and spoke to her brother, who was currently changing. At her feet lay her own suitcase. If she'd just come to talk or hang out, she wouldn't have needed that.

"From what Shizuku heard, he's apparently fallen ill…"

"It's a lie. Well, maybe something *has* befallen him physically or mentally, but he wasn't at the party for a different reason."

A liberal translation of what he meant might be that Retsu Kudou had gone mad. Miyuki had to sigh at Tatsuya for being so certain. The siblings were the only two in the room at the moment, but the remark was a bit candid considering he was talking about the revered elder of Japan's magic world.

Speaking of having to sigh, however, Tatsuya felt the urge far more strongly and fiercely when it came to Miyuki. He wondered what this whole thing was about—maybe Kanon had asked her to and maybe Kanon and Isori were engaged, but why had she actively *helped* a young not-yet-wed couple spend the night together?

He felt no reluctance at sleeping in the same room as his sister. There wasn't even any resistance. If he was worried about anything, it was only how her reputation might be harmed if word of this got out. On the other hand, he knew it would be more convenient for what would happen in the future if he was rooming with Miyuki instead of Isori. That was the reason he hadn't chased her out.

"…Still, if sickness was his chosen reason, he would be cooped up at home. He wouldn't come here, at least. I don't know what he's plotting, but him not being nearby is good for us."

Retsu Kudou was of very advanced age, close to ninety. Neither his magic output or stamina would be what it was in the past, but the magical abilities of someone once called the world's greatest trickster were still a threat. They'd caught a glimpse of his skills a year ago—his vision, which allowed him to immediately *discern* the mental interference spell applied to the entire eve party venue or the Electron Goldworm lurking within a competition CAD, informed Tatsuya that the nickname of the world's *greatest trickster* was not yet a thing of the past. Should he have come face-to-face with him as an enemy, what he'd need to be particularly cautious of was not an open and direct clash but a more roundabout battle. No—even if he was being perfectly cautious, the man was skilled enough that Tatsuya might have found himself on the back foot regardless. Not to make light of

Kudou family magicians, but it was more comfortable for Tatsuya that Retsu wasn't there.

"Miyuki, I'm going out."

Having changed into an entirely black outfit, Tatsuya spoke. He'd really wanted a stealth suit or a modified MOVAL suit with better stealth capabilities, but he knew that was asking for too much.

"Please be careful, Brother," Miyuki replied, standing up from the bed.

She didn't offer to come with him because she knew her aptitude and was being patient. Her eyes spoke the fact that she wanted to, but Tatsuya pretended not to notice it.

"You be careful nobody finds out you're in this room, too. If that happens, be honest and say Chiyoda forced you to, and how you couldn't go against her."

Tatsuya's comment was neither a lie nor a shirking of responsibility—it was the truth. But he was essentially telling her to lay the blame entirely at an upperclassman's feet, and she giggled, finding herself belatedly amused at Tatsuya's lack of reservation.

Tatsuya's target of investigation was the cross-country course. He didn't think the P-Weapons, the Parasidolls, had been placed there yet. Still, if he could learn the lay of the land, he figured, he could predict where they'd lay traps and have troops waiting in ambush.

But Tatsuya couldn't get into the course.

If their security is this tight, how did they let No-Head Dragon invade last year?

He tsked, looking around at the security systems laid out so densely not even an ant could crawl through them. And immediately he realized his misunderstanding.

Actually, I guess it's because of last year...

In olden times, a regular military base allowing a mere criminal organization to get inside would have been grounds for seppuku.

The base's officers had probably burned with enough humiliation to possibly die from it. This strict, even paranoid security layout was doubtlessly grounded in last year's incident.

He carefully broadened his *field of vision* so as not to allow the JDF magicians to detect him. His *visual power* wasn't the sort of thing a psionic radar would pick up, but they might have someone with ESP on watch—one who would detect his abnormal ability. Stealthily, so he'd be able to cut off access at any moment, he began letting his mind permeate the world.

In his wider field of vision, he struck on a *presence* he was familiar with. What he was seeing wasn't an image but information. In his unconscious region, information regarding physical structure was converted into signals easier for his mind to understand. Its coordinates in the physical dimension were not that far off. The fact that the physical distance was small and yet the *information distance* was large spoke volumes of *her* abilities to conceal herself. Praising her in his mind, without speaking it, he headed for where the *two people* were. After walking about five minutes, he spoke at the shadows hidden in darkness.

"Ayako, Fumiya."

There was a sense of surprise at suddenly being spoken to. A moment later, the shadows solidified, taking shape. Tatsuya, adept at seeing in the dark, recognized them as Ayako with her eyes wide and Fumiya seeming happy.

"Tatsuya... Please do not scare us like that."

"I didn't intend to."

"Then I would object to how you said our names in a scary voice."

A fair amount of Ayako's objection was serious. Her short exhalation of breath seemed like a sigh of relief, and the corners of her eyes had teared up slightly, probably out of reflex.

Tatsuya didn't argue with Ayako's critical words. They weren't quite in the middle of combat, but right now his mind was in a similar state. He realized his own words were not coming through as gentle.

"Did you two come to check the course, too?"

Even so, he didn't bother apologizing.

"...Yes. Security is tight, though, and..."

"We couldn't get inside."

Fumiya answered for the part Ayako stumbled over.

"Even your magic couldn't get inside, Ayako?" Tatsuya asked, taken by surprise. "Ah, I mean, sorry. I wasn't trying to criticize you."

And seeing Ayako's eyes turn downward, he apologized right away this time. He understood without having to think about it that she was more frustrated than he was surprised.

The singular magic Ayako specialized in was called Supreme Diffusion. The spell equalized the distribution of any gaseous, liquid, or physical energy within a specified area and made it impossible to identify.

Supreme Diffusion was classified as a convergence-type spell. One could also program it into an activation sequence, and in that sense, it was a normal spell. Mastering it to a point where it had actual, practical meaning, however, could be said to be nearly impossible. Normal magicians could, at most, use a lesser version of Supreme Diffusion called Diffuse. The only Supreme Diffusion user Tatsuya knew of was her.

If one equalized sound, for example, voices and music alike would all become flat noise, its contained meanings impossible to pick out. But one couldn't hide the fact that there was noise, that sound itself had occurred. This was still on Diffuse's level.

To expand the equalized zone until the sound's strength went below audible range: only in doing so did the Diffuse spell become Supreme. Ayako's magic activation speed and event influence were both weaker than Miyuki's, but she surpassed her in the breadth of an area she could alter events in, boasting the greatest of that talent in the Yotsuba.

Outdoors at night, where light was scarce, was Ayako's territory, where she could best bring out her abilities. She could blend into the darkness by instantly and selectively equalizing the diffusion of electromagnetic waves either she or her team reflected or produced. She evaded auditory and olfactory detection by equalizing the distribution of sound waves and shifts in air currents. In doing so, she became one with the night air. Her code name, Yoru, used one of the characters in her first name, but at the same time, it represented the traits of her Supreme Diffusion spell.

And even she couldn't break into a man-made forest under cover of night. Tatsuya's surprise was inevitable, and Ayako biting her lip in frustration was natural as well.

"Did you come to investigate, too, Tatsuya?"

Fumiya didn't ask Tatsuya that to steer the conversation away from Ayako. He earnestly thought that maybe Tatsuya could do what they couldn't.

Tatsuya's Dismantle and Ayako's Supreme Diffusion were similar in their event alteration direction. Dismantling matter into its component parts was, from a different angle, breaking down the matter's structure and scattering the distribution of its component parts into an unstructured state. You could also look at dismantling magic as being Supreme Diffusion with added depth and reduced scope.

And in fact, the reason Ayako could use Supreme Diffusion was because she'd received training from Tatsuya at the Yotsuba main house. He'd still been in elementary school at the time, but he'd already mastered the use of dismantling magic and *self*-regeneration magic and was accustomed to combat training with adults. It wasn't unusual for Kuroba magicians to be chosen for that, either. And though he was worrying about not understanding his own special qualities, he had shown Dismantle to Ayako, who had been practicing magic with one of her father's subordinates, in an *easy-to-understand way*.

Tatsuya understood from Elemental Sight that she had the same magical qualities as him. When he was still young, meaning to make *comrades* for himself, he'd shown Ayako how to use Supreme Diffusion with Dismantle as a base.

Ayako's Supreme Diffusion was essentially taught to her by Tatsuya. It wouldn't be an overstatement to say that because of him, she had established her own identity as Ayako *Kuroba*, a magician of the Yotsuba.

Therefore, Ayako never looked down on him as a *mere Guardian*. This was one of the reasons Fumiya looked up to Tatsuya so much, too. At the same time, though, it was one of the reasons the Kuroba siblings *overestimated* him.

"Yeah. But I was just wondering what to do myself. I can't get in."

Tatsuya's fields of specialty were combat and assassination. His skills at sneaking into enemy territory were close to first-rate, too, but that was because of Yakumo's teachings. In terms of natural aptitude, Ayako was far and away his better. Tatsuya would have no way of remaining undetected if even Ayako couldn't get inside.

"I see..." murmured Fumiya, not hiding his disappointment. "Should we try again? If we all put our strength together, maybe..."

But he immediately put forth a constructive plan—though it wasn't very specific.

"No, pushing it and making noise would be the worst thing we could do. We should probably leave quietly for tonight."

"*I agree.*"

The one who responded to Tatsuya's remark was neither Fumiya nor Ayako.

"Who's there?!"

At Ayako's sharp demand for an identity, a slender figure appeared from the trees.

"Master, could you please make your entrances more normal?"

His identity was, as Tatsuya mentioned with a sigh, Yakumo.

"Tatsuya is right. We should pull out for tonight."

Without responding to his pupil's grievance, Yakumo continued what he'd been saying.

"...Tatsuya, is this person...?" Yakumo's identity perhaps coming to mind, Ayako loosened her guard.

"I think whatever you have in mind is right, Ayako."

"Then he is *the* Yakumo Kokonoe?"

This time, Fumiya nodded, deeply moved. As the two entrusted with the next generation of the Kuroba, the Yotsuba's intelligence division, the name Yakumo appeared to hold great meaning.

"Anyway, Master, did you learn anything?" asked Tatsuya.

Yakumo shook his head. "Nope. They hadn't put anything in the course yet."

"You got into the course?!"

Ayako unintentionally raised her voice, then quickly covered her mouth with a hand. Warmed by the slip, Tatsuya gave a slight smile. But he immediately erased it and turned back to Yakumo.

"We'd already given up on the security system. You are really something else," he said, glancing at Ayako. She still had on a frustrated look, but he didn't get the impression that she was blaming herself.

"No, no. Not at all."

Yakumo, on the other hand, appeared triumphant, without a shred of circumspection.

Act your age, thought Tatsuya. But he changed his mind—maybe he'd done it to purposely get Ayako's mind off herself and on something else, on him.

"What was it like on the inside? You said there was nothing?"

Ayako's magic could disable any kind of passive sensor, so it was active sensors that were at issue. How had Yakumo gotten past them? Tatsuya would be lying if he said he wasn't curious. But he clearly wouldn't tell him if he asked. Yakumo didn't have a reason to reveal his tricks so easily. More importantly, thought Tatsuya, they needed to prioritize their original goal.

"I meant what I said. Right now, it's *just* an artificial training forest, with only the planned *normal obstacles* set up."

"Can you predict where the Parasidolls will be?"

"Nope. It wouldn't make much of a difference no matter where they put them. That's how they made this place."

"Would that mean the Parasidolls can at least operate regardless of the terrain?"

"If they were, then that would make them built for combat."

In the end, sneaking out of the hotel tonight had been a waste of effort. Tatsuya thanked Yakumo, said farewell to Fumiya and Ayako, and they all returned to the hotel separately.

It had been a pointless visit for Tatsuya and the others, but the situation was proceeding without stopping. Maybe incidents always happened at the scene. But at the same time, by default, incidents were always planned *away* from the scene.

For Major General Saeki, leader of the JGDF's 101st Brigade, mornings started early and nights ended late. She laughed about it, saying her superior officers pushed all the unreasonable work on her because she'd lived as part of the staff for so long, but for her subordinates, it was no laughing matter. The brigade's staff officer reported almost habitually that part of a commander's job in an uneventful time was to go home early, but Saeki showed no signs of cooperating, saying that the current situation was in fact an emergency for a general. She was up late again tonight, looking over the organization reports for the team she'd be sending to the Nine School Competition.

Her preference for paper documents was a result of her attaching great importance to secrecy, and she read low-confidentiality reports on screens as most did these days. Seeing the incoming call sign light up on the videophone in the corner of the display, she frowned.

The 101st Brigade wasn't assigned to a particular area. A call coming in from General HQ on the brigade commander's direct line was unthinkable unless there was a *real* emergency, like coming under surprise attack or something. All the more if it was a business call from the Ministry of Defense. Wondering who on earth was contacting her, she accepted the call.

"General Saeki, I apologize for contacting you so late at night."

A senior gentleman, older than her, appeared on the screen. Saeki knew the man's name.

"Mr. Hayama of the Yotsuba, was it? It has been a long time."

"Oh! I am honored the one renowned as the most resourceful general in the JGDF would remember the name of someone rank-and-file like myself."

Without changing her expression, Saeki thought, *What about* you *is "rank-and-file"?* She knew who Hayama was, obviously through the Independent Magic Battalion having taken Tatsuya in. When they'd pulled Tatsuya out of *there*, she had gone to negotiate directly as the highest responsible party, attended by Kazama. At the time, the opposite negotiating party had, in essence, been Hayama. Saeki had met Maya in person, but other than introductions, they hadn't ever exchanged words. It was this old man, however, who had taken charge of the Yotsuba's end of the negotiations with the 101st Brigade.

"The reason for my rude call at this hour is because I wished to speak of something I am rather hesitant to let others hear. Should this time be inconvenient for you, however, I will call another day."

While Saeki's attention was on her memories, Hayama once again referred to her conveniences. She was about to turn him down without thinking much about it, but then frantically hit the brakes on her tongue.

"…I'll hear it."

"I very much appreciate it. In that case, I will hand you over to the mistress."

Saeki sucked in her breath before she understood what those words meant.

With a respectful bow, Hayama's visage disappeared from the screen.

"We haven't talked in a long time, General Saeki."

The one who appeared on the switched-over camera was a beautiful woman wearing a dress of deep, almost black crimson. Her gorgeous features hadn't faded at all compared to three years and ten months ago.

"Yes, it has been a while, hasn't it, Ms. Yotsuba?"

An unintentional nervousness ran through her spine. The current head of the Yotsuba family—Maya Yotsuba. Saeki knew of the woman's own strength, of course, but also the Yotsuba's strength, from her long career as an intelligence officer.

"I know you're quite busy, General, so allow me to keep the matter short."

Maya's tone was more than polite—it was friendly. She didn't give off any dire impression from her gentle smile, either, which made her look far younger than her age.

Saeki, however, wrestled down the information coming in through her eyes and ears with the data in her memories. No direct correlation existed between a spell's range and physical distance. A spell reaching someone or not wasn't determined by physical distance but by informational distance. In fact, she'd been told the head of the Yotsuba two generations prior, Genzou Yotsuba, Maya's father, had once placed an opponent under a spell by showing himself through a TV screen. Maya Yotsuba might be able to kill her just by connecting to her through a video line like this. Saeki had come this far without knowing flattery or reverence, even with her superiors or other high-ranking officers. But when it came to someone who might quite literally be holding her death in her hand, she couldn't afford not to be prudent.

"What would you like to talk about?"

"It's regarding a plot to ensnare your brigade, General."

The only reason Saeki got away with keeping a straight face was her steely grit. However, if she hadn't braced herself beforehand, she might not have been able to conceal her confusion.

"A terrorist attack, written and performed by one and the same, is planned to take place during the National Magic High School Goodwill Magic Competition Tournament, specifically staged in the Cross-Country Steeplechase."

"…Would you happen to know who's behind it?"

The question *Is that certain?* didn't come out of Saeki's mouth. It didn't have to be Maya—nobody would have said something like this as a joke.

"A group centered around Colonel Sakai from JGDF General HQ, in other words the faction of anti-GAA hard-liners, are being treated as the masterminds."

Saying that, Maya let out a quiet laugh. It was nothing else but an implication that the true mastermind was someone else, but Saeki didn't ask after that. It was clear she wouldn't get an answer if she did.

"And the role assigned to your brigade, General, is to be the unit that carries it out."

"I've no plans to take part in such a farce."

It would be a lie to say Saeki hadn't prickled at that. She was sure she wasn't foolish enough to fall into such a blatant trap, and she knew her subordinates weren't that idiotic, either.

"I believe you. That was why I asked for some of your time like this."

Maya, for now, seemed to be complimenting her. But Saeki didn't feel like being happy over it. Maya may have been one of the world's strongest magicians, but she was still over ten years Saeki's junior. In fact, conspiracies of this sort were Saeki's expertise, not hers. She was grateful for Maya providing the information, but she'd grown tired of her condescension.

Of course, she didn't let out a peep of any of that. She wasn't that green.

"Then what did you want to tell me?"

"They plan to involve my relatives in this."

"…Are you referring to Specialist Ooguro?"

"A clear insight—I'm impressed. Though with his *traits*, it's really unavoidable."

The sigh she gave on the screen seemed real to Saeki, not an act. Saeki had a very similar opinion as her, too.

"Still, I have no intention of acting out a role assigned to me."

"Should I stop him?"

"No. They've so politely set the table for us—I thought we could make the hard-liners the *real* masterminds."

Saeki stared hard at Maya's face through the screen. However, even her insight couldn't see through to Maya's true intent.

Still, it wasn't as though she understood nothing. Clearly, Maya wanted to destroy Colonel Sakai's group for some reason.

Saeki, too, had found the hard-liners shameful for some time now. True, if they opened hostilities now, the GAA would win. But the world wasn't made up of just Japan and the GAA. It was the same reason she'd given her support to Kazama back then. The anti-GAA opportunists during the Dai Viet conflict and the current anti-GAA hard-liners being two sides of the same coin would be far too simple. Any military action required thought from the perspective of a single factor in a multinational diplomatic situation.

Saeki didn't believe the idea that soldiers shouldn't give input on internal affairs or diplomacy. They had to follow orders, of course, but she didn't think they had to be so prudent in things they hadn't been ordered to do. But even still, Colonel Sakai's faction seemed to her to be deviating from their restraint as soldiers.

That, however, only applied to within the JDF. The Yotsuba shouldn't get any merit from purging Sakai's group—Saeki knew well that they didn't have a desire for more authority. She was one of the few high-ranking officers with a direct line to the Yotsuba; they wielded their might based on their own interests for the sake of self-defense and retaliation. Still, Saeki wasn't confident enough about this situation to say that for sure.

Was a faction desiring elimination of the hard-liners lurking behind the Yotsuba?

Unfortunately, that question was not one she could ask right now. Because before she could, Maya came forth with her request:

"In that regard, I'd like to know if you could provide support, General."

"You want me...to use my troops?"

"No, I'd like you to deal with the aftermath. I cannot appear in public, after all."

That was a shameless remark to say the least. She wanted to mess up the JDF and have a JDF major general wipe her ass.

But Saeki didn't get emotional. She inquired as toward her own material gain. "What sort of benefit would this bring me?"

Maya gave a bewitching smile. "I can weaken the Ten Master Clans' interference with the JDF."

She understood without explanation that when Maya said the Ten Master Clans, she didn't mean all of them together but specifically Retsu Kudou.

She closed her eyes to escape Maya's smile, then thought for a while before nodding.

"Was that wise, madam?"

Once Maya had finished her negotiations with Saeki, Hayama came forward with a question.

"Was what wise?"

Maya's response was a return question, even though she knew why he had asked it.

Anyone but Hayama would have held his tongue then. Such makeshift lip sealings, however, didn't work on this old butler.

"Lord Kudou's involvement is still in the realm of speculation."

"That was why I didn't say his name. And..."

After giving a bald-faced explanation, Maya floated a mean smile.

"In that case, we don't have any proof of the hard-liners' self-written terrorist attempt, do we?"

Without batting an eyelid, Hayama simply nodded. "It would in fact be a false accusation. But I believe perhaps saying so doesn't matter. It was *their* wish that we purge the hard-liners, after all."

Maya nodded back, the same smile on as before. "Indeed. We cannot go against the wishes of our sponsors. If not for this incident, we may have had to choose more violent methods ourselves."

An air drifted between them: not a master-servant one but a more conspiratorial one.

"In that sense, this Gongjin Zhou's secret maneuvers were convenient for us as well. Considering Mr. Tatsuya's support, however, is enough to make one's head hurt."

"We can't have any gaudy displays like last year... I'd prefer it if he kept to himself, *at least for another half a year, until New Year's next year.*" After speaking, Maya heaved a dramatic sigh. "Still, if the embers leap to Miyuki, I can't tell him not to do anything."

"Madam, do you believe General Saeki will give her support to Mr. Tatsuya?"

"Oh, she will. She can't stop us, so ultimately, she'll have to help us. Would the JDF have the nerve to neglect the most brutal magical weapon there is?"

Hayama felt like he heard a silent remark: *Even I don't have that.*

It was past noon the day after the banquet. Tatsuya had been invited by Honoka and Shizuku to have lunch in the hotel room—not in his but in theirs. After returning to the hotel in a group of four, including Miyuki, he spotted a student in the lobby who had come to cheer them on and would be staying over to do so. It was a friend of his, and she was looking confused.

"Heya!"

The situation was worthy of déjà vu, but she was wearing something quite a bit more docile compared to last year. A sleeveless overshirt and three-quarter-length pants, specifically, were what Erika was wearing as she waved to them.

"Did you come to root for us?"

"Of course. Oh, and the other two are here, too," Erika said, and just as she did, Leo walked up from behind her.

"You know, you should really be carrying your own luggage... Oh. Hey, Tatsuya." Two bags hung from his hands; the one with the bright coloring must have been Erika's.

"Erika, your key— Oh, hello, everyone." Then, from behind Leo, Mizuki appeared, drawing along a wheeled travel bag.

"Have you had lunch?" Tatsuya asked.

"Nope," Erika answered simply.

"Guess I'll call Mikihiko, too."

A twin bedroom would be cramped with this many people. The group headed for a café permitted for use by Nine School Competition entrants.

Peak hours were already over, so the eight secured seats without a wait. Just as they were sitting down, Mikihiko came out with a sudden question.

"You guys were later than planned. Did something happen?"

The one Mikihiko was asking was Mizuki. But the one who responded to his words first was Erika.

"Hmm..."

"Wh-what?"

As Erika gave him a smile—one with a bit of sadistic nature coming through—Mikihiko withdrew.

But his reaction was a mistake and also too late.

"You were asking Mizuki about our plans."

"I got an e-mail from her, that's all," retorted Mikihiko with a slightly frantic look. It had the opposite effect, though, since the franticness had made it into his expression.

"Really? Miki, you traded e-mail addresses with Mizuki?"

"Yeah, well, friends usually do that, you know."

After Mikihiko gruffly brushed it off, Erika's gaze shifted from him to Leo, who was sitting next to him.

"Do *you* have Mizuki's e-mail address?"

"Nope. Don't really need it."

With group chats via videophone being widespread these days, if someone wanted to communicate in text format, most would use a message board that only a group member could access. Electronic mail was superior when it came to sending summarized information and how people often conducted secret communications with narrowly defined recipients. ——In passing, Tatsuya knew both Erika's and Mizuki's e-mail addresses, but he didn't share that with Mikihiko. Feeling guilty, or *having been convinced* he should feel guilty for the fact that he knew a girl's e-mail address, Mikihiko's face had gone completely red.

And Erika was already grinning from ear to ear. Next to Mikihiko, Mizuki was looking away, her face as red as his. (Notably, to prevent misunderstandings, the group had pulled two round tables together and were sitting around them, with the order being Erika, Mizuki, Mikihiko, Leo, Shizuku, Honoka, Tatsuya, then Miyuki.)

Unable to endure the situation anymore, Mikihiko finally blew.

"Look, you've got it all wrong! I'm not the only one who got Shibata's e-mail. Miyuki and Mitsui and Kitayama all have it, too!"

But getting angry about it only pulled him deeper into the swamp.

"What about you, Tatsuya?"

"Nope."

Mikihiko looked at Tatsuya as though he were a traitor, but Tatsuya wasn't one to be ruffled by false charges.

"By the way, Erika..." But then, seeing that not Mikihiko but Mizuki was about to hit her own limit, Tatsuya decided to change the topic. "Were you really late?"

Erika frowned. "Yeah, kinda."

With modern ground transit systems having eliminated traffic by way of structure, if their arrival was late in such a way that it went beyond the acceptable range, it meant they'd hit trouble on the road. The trouble had probably been unpleasant enough that they couldn't ignore it. Erika's attention veered away from Mikihiko.

"The bus with all the people who came to cheer ran into demonstrators at the base entrance," put in Mizuki immediately, perhaps seeing this as a chance to wrest herself free.

"Demonstrators?" asked Honoka. This hotel and the base entrance were pretty far away, so they wouldn't have known what had happened even if there had been major noise.

"Yes, well… The humanists."

Everyone present—not only Tatsuya and those who hadn't been there but Erika and Leo, too, who had been at the scene—all responded with tired looks.

"It was the same stuff as always." The distaste was plain in Erika's voice. "It's wrong for the majority of magic high school students to go into the army—wake up—the military is only using you. That stuff. Who asked them anyway?"

Perhaps getting riled up again while she was speaking, Erika was growing more and more excited. In contrast, Leo said nothing, as though he didn't even want to think about it.

"What do they mean, *majority*? What's the point of adding post–high school advancement rates to post-university employment rates? They're different populations. I wish they could figure out that you can't add those or subtract them or multiply them or divide them."

Erika must have been pretty upset, because she was acting more *rational* than usual. For all the emotions she kept out of this, she'd probably keep on going. Without a choice, Tatsuya set about putting out the fire.

"Demonstrations and propaganda speeches don't need to be accurate, they need to be impactful. They know it's sophistry at best. And it is true that 45 percent of Magic University graduates are employed in the JDF or somewhere related to them, which is a pretty high number by itself. I don't think arguing over the math is going to help."

"Come on. Are you taking their side, Tatsuya?"

"Me? Really?"

The bitter smile Tatsuya gave meant *You mean the one already in the army?*

"Right. Sorry…"

Erika understood that, of course. Vaguely, she'd also guessed that he didn't have a choice not to do that.

"Anyway, Miki—"

"My *name* is Mikihiko."

Mikihiko purposely revived his usual retort because he realized Erika was trying to shift the mood.

"You're still calling her Shibata? You call Miyuki by her first name, so you should just call Mizuki by hers, too."

"That's not what we're talking about!"

But the consideration he showed was repaid with the opposite.

[6]

On August 5, the 2096 Nine School Competition OPENED at last.

Both the events and the way they were held had been changed. To begin with, Pillar Break and Shields Down would have qualifying leagues, each with nine entrants (or teams) split into three entrants/ teams each, then the finals league, with the three first-place entrants (teams) from those three groups. In Rower and Gunner, each individual entrant or pair would run the course alone, competing with others for time adjusted for accuracy rate.

Though the rules of Mirage Bat had changed the least, they had still been altered so that its number of qualifying entrants was twenty-seven—three from each school—with the groupings changed from four entrants per group to three groups of four and three groups of five. Entry into one over the other was determined via blind draw. In addition, the maximum continuous duration of flight spells had been limited to sixty seconds. In other words, they'd created a rule saying the players had to land back on the ground in under a minute.

Monolith Code had been changed from an irregular qualifier/ league-finals tournament format to a two-day-long round-robin league. Using all five stages to the fullest, they would have ten rounds, each with anywhere from four to eight matches. This meant the Monolith Code players would be in eight matches during days nine and ten of the competition, and on top of that, they'd enter into the Cross-Country Steeplechase on the eleventh and final day. It was predicted that this would place considerable physical and mental burdens on them.

The competition's first day would consist of the Pillar Break paired qualifiers for men and women as well as the Rower and Gunner pairs.

"I would have had to trouble you greatly if our event times had overlapped, Isori."

"But it looks like we don't need to worry about that anymore."

Accessing the tournament HQ's competitor information page from the First High tent first thing in the morning, Tatsuya made a comment in relief, and Isori answered it with a smile. They were looking at the schedule for today's matches.

The Pillar Break qualifiers would consist of nine matches each for men and women. This was half what it was before this year. One pair would also only be playing in two matches in one day. For this event, at least, the competitors' burdens had been greatly reduced.

But because of that, though they'd had two courts for each gender until last year, they'd only have one for each this year, meaning the overall schedule was no less dense. However, it did create some leeway in each school's schedule.

The reason Tatsuya had sighed in relief: because he'd learned Eimi's race and Shizuku and Kanon's matches wouldn't overlap.

Tatsuya was in charge of Shizuku's CAD for Pillar Break and Eimi's CAD for Rower and Gunner. This was due to strong requests from each of them, but if Eimi's race and one of the Kanon-Shizuku pair's matches had overlapped, he would have had to ask Isori to support both Kanon and Shizuku for that match.

Normally, whether it was Pillar Break or RG (the competitors' shortened nickname for Rower and Gunner), the technical staff wouldn't have much to do during the match itself. They could only do minor CAD adjustments and coaching during matches in Shields

Down, which had a two-round format, and Mirage Bat, played over the course of three periods. Even for pair events, one staff member for each wasn't a problem, but Tatsuya would have still felt bad for leaving someone he was assigned to completely in someone else's hands. If that possibility had become reality, he himself would have felt it to be something reprehensible.

The actual match schedule had Eimi's race first that morning, with Shizuku playing in matches four and seven. Their match times wouldn't overlap.

"I'll be off to the RG course, then."

"Do your best out there. Even though I don't need to worry about you, Shiba."

With a smile that seemed almost a waste to use on a guy, Isori saw Tatsuya off.

Of the three waiting rooms for players and staff built next to the starting line, Tatsuya opened the door for the first team. Nobody was inside. Even so, it was still over thirty minutes until race time. The technical staff would have to start getting set up now, but the players had time left.

"Good morning!"

Just as he said that, Azusa entered with an enthusiastic greeting.

"Morning, Shiba!"

Before Tatsuya could return it, Eimi appeared from behind her. Tatsuya felt a little like she'd spoiled his start, but he decided to respond one by one.

"Good morning, President, Amy. You came together today?"

By *together*, he was referring to the senior in Eimi's pair, who had come inside with her. Of course, she had a quiet personality and had only given Tatsuya a light nod. Tatsuya returned the gesture in kind.

"Yep, we ate breakfast together. You weren't waiting for very long, were you?" asked Eimi, not appearing particularly worried about it.

Tatsuya would be troubled if she had been, so he shook his head normally. "No, I pretty much just got here."

"Oh, good!" She put her hands together and smiled sweetly. It may have seemed like a quite sly gesture depending on the viewer, but it suited Eimi well.

"Let's get started on tuning your CAD right away, then," Tatsuya said.

"We'll start from there, too," Azusa suggested to her own assigned player.

The first day's results were in: Eimi and her partner had placed first in the pairs, and the male Rower and Gunner pair had placed third. The Kanon-Shizuku pair won a spot in the finals league, and the male Pillar Break pair also made it out of the qualifiers.

"Eimi, that was a nice race. You almost didn't miss any of them."

"Thanks, Subaru. I was surprised myself!"

Cheerful voices flew back and forth among dinner table seats, but they clearly hadn't been easy victories.

"We didn't expect Seventh High to do as spectacularly as they did."

The mood in the staff's seating area, where Azusa, Hattori, Isori, Kanon, Tatsuya, and Miyuki were, wasn't quite like a vigil, but their expressions were serious as they began their first-day retrospection meeting.

"We placed third in the men's and first in the women's, but Seventh High placed first in the men's and second in the women's," said Hattori in response to Azusa's comment, reviewing their results for the day. Only the first event had ended, but they were second in the rankings. And tomorrow's solo entrant Rower and Gunner was the event they'd predicted they'd have the most trouble with.

"People don't put *Seventh High* and *water* together for nothing, huh? I don't think we were very far behind when it came to spell accuracy, but their level of skill was amazing."

After Isori's honest remark, Hattori spoke again, in a circumspect tone. "It might be more beneficial in terms of wins and losses later if Seventh High takes first place in both the solo runs tomorrow."

"Because it won't open too much of a score difference with Third High?"

"Yeah, and I know it's a pessimistic idea."

Third High had placed second in the men's and third in the women's, giving them 60 points. Today's point rankings had First High with 20 more than them. It was the result of only one event, but the idea of not being able to put a bigger point difference between them when they were leading was certainly a negative way of thinking. That was just how little confidence they had in the solo event tomorrow.

"...Shouldn't we have, you know, had Shiba assigned to the RG solo event? Anyone he's assigned to would probably win."

It was Kanon who had suddenly come out with that wild idea. Still, it was logically correct—but actually saying it was reckless, to put it lightly.

Sure enough, the staff seats felt a freezing pressure hit them. Kanon had flinched out of reflex, but Tatsuya had restrained Miyuki, and Isori, Kanon, thus preventing an off-court melee.

"...It wouldn't be possible to switch engineer assignments now. And just because I'm assigned to someone doesn't necessarily mean the results will turn out better."

The first half of his comment was something everyone—even Kanon—had to agree made sense, but after hearing the second half, their convinced faces turned into suspicious ones. It was clear that the winning women's pair in today's event owed much of their victory to the incredible accuracy and efficiency of their shooting magic.

"From what we've seen today, the first practice run seems to greatly affect the end result. I don't think it would make sense to even have pair entrants give solo entrants advice about that, do you?"

This, too, was a sound argument, but Tatsuya was obviously steering the conversation away. This time, though, nobody could lecture him, apply any brute force, or do anything even more basic than that.

Though Miyuki staying in Tatsuya's room was partly an open secret, being witnessed at the scene would be bad for a few reasons. Thus, they couldn't use his room as a meeting place like last year.

Still, that didn't mean they could stay up all night chatting in the lobby or the café. The hotel was already full—they'd restricted the cheering members who could stay at the hotel to twenty from each school. The present situation was that anyone else in these groups would stay at dispersed places outside the base. If they sat in the lobby or the café for a long period of time, they were sure to have cold eyes directed at them.

Instead, Tatsuya's group had made their small-talk gathering place the spot next to the work vehicle they used for CAD tuning.

"…It's kind of like we're camping out," Honoka noted.

"Camping out on hotel property?" Shizuku quipped.

"But that's why it feels strange, doesn't it?"

"Quite right, quite right."

The exchange became a turnabout victory for Honoka.

The girls were sitting on folding camping chairs. In front of them was a fold-up camping table. Above their heads was an awning tent stretching from the roof of the *camping car*.

In point of fact, the work vehicle First High's technical staff used for tune-ups was an appropriation of a camping car of a type called a cab conversion. It was a marked enhancement considering the simple, small van they used last year, seeming almost extravagant. Students from other schools would actually boggle when they saw it.

The ringleader behind this *outrage* was, though easily imaginable, Miyuki. She had harbored dissatisfaction and anger at how her beloved brother had been forced to move around in a *cramped* work vehicle last year. Even after a year, those feelings hadn't faded, and she'd forced through an improvement to the livability for the technical staff. ——Additionally, the funds for it had been covered by a donation from the Kitayama family. Miyuki, for her part, had planned to make FLT (in other words, her father) pay for it, but she couldn't bring herself to refuse Shizuku's father's goodwill.

Of course, while she'd done all that, she'd also made Tatsuya ride on the bus; when it came to her brother, Miyuki would have her way no matter what. Well, in the end, it had resulted in an improvement in comfort for the rest of the technical staff and not for Tatsuya's, so perhaps she had actually acted impartially.

——All of which, too, was no more than reasoning based on hindsight.

"Here's your coffee."

"Right, thanks."

This conversation wasn't between Miyuki and Tatsuya. Against her will, it had been Pixie who made the coffee for him. And not only for him—she passed out coffee to everyone else, too.

"…Thanks."

"…"

Miyuki and Minami couldn't completely hide their displeasure. But from a system standpoint, Pixie had full control over the camping car's kitchen. Neither of them had any way to stop her.

"Oh, thank you."

The one who looked at Pixie in the most natural way, like any other human, was Kento. He had been nominated as a candidate for Tatsuya's aide for this Nine School Competition, and he had won the position splendidly.

"Mizuki, it's not that Erika isn't feeling well, right?"

Perhaps to distract herself from her unamused mood, Miyuki asked Mizuki something she'd heard earlier.

Eight people were here: Tatsuya, Miyuki, Honoka, Shizuku, Mikihiko, Mizuki, Minami, and Kento. And Pixie, who couldn't be counted as one person, was waiting on them.

"Yes… She said she had minor business to take care of."

At this hour, with night having fallen long ago, few students were outside. Still, First High's technical staff weren't the only ones who had parked a work vehicle in the parking lot to adjust their CADs. For a while now, engineers from other schools had been passing by, casually stealing glances at the out-of-place tea party. First High's competitors would probably learn about this by tomorrow as well. If that happened, the following nights were sure to have an increased number of participants.

On the other hand, the only ones here were those Tatsuya and Miyuki had directly or indirectly told about it. And the siblings had obviously invited Erika and Leo as well. They were nowhere to be found, though.

"Leo said he was going to come, but…"

Mikihiko was the one to explain that, his tone sounding somehow like he was making an excuse. He'd only invited Leo over a voice call; it wasn't like they were rooming together. One couldn't blame him for not knowing what Leo was doing, but Mikihiko feeling like he had to defend him somehow spoke to the kindness of his personality.

"Umm, I actually saw Saijou on my way here earlier."

And then an unexpected person provided information. The commenter was a smiling Kento, sitting directly across from Tatsuya (who always had Miyuki and Honoka on either side, so he would have at least been in front of him). He'd been working here ever since dinner, so as they were about to have their teatime, he'd gone back to his room and showered before coming back.

"The president of Rosen's Japanese branch stopped him in the lobby."

"Rosen?" repeated Tatsuya dubiously, as he had advance knowledge from what Mikihiko had told him.

He looked over at Mikihiko, who was staring right back with the same question in his own eyes.

"Yes. I'm sure that man had to be Ernst Rosen."

Tatsuya and Mikihiko only made eye contact for a moment before Tatsuya quickly returned his gaze to Kento. Without noticing, Kento replied to Tatsuya's question with a smile, like a dog running up to its owner, its tail wagging.

"Saijou seemed like he was a little put off by it, though."

A moment after Kento added that—

"What about me?"

—Leo showed up, as though he'd been waiting for the perfect timing.

Kento hadn't exactly been talking behind his back, but it also didn't seem like he avoided the awkwardness of having brought up his upperclassman in conversation.

"About how he saw you and Ernst Rosen in the lobby."

Before it could come to that, Tatsuya took up the mantle of talking to Leo.

"W-well, yeah… Anyway, that's why I'm late. Sorry about that."

"We don't mind. Not like there's any assigned seating or anything."

As Kento had sensed, Leo didn't seem to have particularly enjoyed his conversation with Rosen. Without bothering him any more by asking about it, Tatsuya gestured for Leo to take a seat.

Teatime wrapped up after ten PM. Mikihiko and Leo, as well as Kento just because he was a guy, too, walked Shizuku, Honoka, and Mizuki back, while Miyuki and Minami stayed behind under the pretext of helping to clean up.

It was a well-known secret that Miyuki was staying in the same room as Tatsuya. Nevertheless, Miyuki didn't have the nerve to go back to Tatsuya's room while Honoka and the others were watching. She wasn't *that* defiant toward her—at least, not yet. Honoka didn't want to see the two of them disappearing behind a door together, either. Miyuki had remained here out of a fortunate crossing of their respective feelings… Though for Minami, her sense of duty as a maid was mostly what had kept her here, wanting to at least clean up afterward.

And Minami had her fill of that desire. As for why, it was because

Pixie, ordered by Tatsuya, was currently handling other jobs and wasn't helping clean up the table.

At the moment, Pixie was sitting in a camping chair as Tatsuya looked down at her, her eyelids closed and her hands covering her ears. The bodies of 3H models didn't hear sounds only through their ears, and they could perceive their surroundings with optical sensors even if their eyes were closed. In fact, if she'd wanted to cut off external input, she could have just turned off her sensors, but such an act, *from a mechanical standpoint*, would have been meaningless. Pixie was adopting such a human posture because her nonmechanical feelings were currently at work.

"How about it? Could you detect them?"

"I did not detect signals from any comrades."

After Tatsuya, standing in front of her, asked the question, Pixie answered using active telepathy. Since the moment their little get-together had ended, she'd been ordered to search for the locations of any parasites—what was *inside* the Parasidolls—which had been made to possess and fuse with the feminine robots.

According to the information from the Kuroba family, the Parasidolls and Pixie were essentially the same. Retsu Kudou had probably made the Parasidolls after he found out about Pixie in an attempt to copy her. That was Tatsuya's read on it. Their bodies wouldn't have been made from housework-supporting robots, of course—doubtless they'd been built for use in combat. But he felt strongly that, considering his usage of gynoids rather than androids, he'd had Pixie in mind first and foremost.

Parasites could sense other parasites. Not only could individuals possessing humans sense one another, ones residing in humans and ones residing in machines could also sense their kin. The incident in February had proven it. In that case, they should have been able to mutually detect individuals both residing in machines.

Tatsuya decided the reason Pixie couldn't sense the parasite dolls' location was because those Parasidolls were currently in a state in which they couldn't be detected. It couldn't be that parasites in machines couldn't detect one another. At the same time, he found it hard to believe that the Kudou family still hadn't brought the Parasidolls here.

Have they put them in a sleep state? They're being very careful...

Pixie had told him before that it was difficult to detect low-activity individuals. Did the Kudou's engineers know that as well? In any case, all he'd learned today was that the only time he'd be able to figure out where the parasite dolls were being stored like this would, at the very least, be right before they took action.

Minami went next to Tatsuya and told him they were done cleaning up. He wouldn't get any more by persisting any further in this. Tatsuya ordered Pixie to move into suspend mode after going back in the vehicle and locking the entrance, then returned to the hotel with Miyuki and Minami in tow.

August 6, before dawn on the second day of the competition.

Though the sun rose extremely early in the summer, the sky was still dark, blue just beginning to creep into the black. It was that odd twilight time, neither night nor morning, as Miyuki sat at the bedside in the dark. She sat patiently, gazing at her beloved brother's face as he slept.

Many would have surely found it surprising to know, but Tatsuya was a heavy sleeper. Miyuki had left the room dark, but it would take more than turning on the lights for him to come to. Even making annoying noises in the same room wouldn't wake him up.

Still, while many would nod and agree with this, Tatsuya was, despite how deeply he slept, a morning person. First off, he would wake up every morning when he wanted to. He didn't need an alarm clock. His biological clock alone was enough. In addition, he was sensitive to malice and ill intent. Even if you snuck in quieter than a pin falling, if anyone who would harm him or Miyuki got close, he'd wake up immediately. And even if you approached within a certain distance without any malice, his mind would rise from its slumber and his eyes would open.

That distance, that boundary, had no regularity and depended on the time and situation. Sometimes he wouldn't open his eyes even if someone got close enough to breathe on him, and other times he'd wake up the moment anyone entered the room. Miyuki assumed that before he went to sleep, he probably decided how near he'd allow someone to come. Her guess was that when he let others get incredibly close to him, it was a result of falling asleep before setting up a chosen distance.

In a situation like this, with them sleeping in the same room, he would have made sure that she could get up and move around normally without crossing the boundary. In fact, even when she brought a chair next to his bed and sat down, he showed no signs of waking up.

But she wasn't sure about anything more than this. Another ten centimeters closer, and her brother could wake up. Or he might not, even if she climbed into the same bed and slept next to him.

Miyuki wanted to know.

How close would her brother allow her to get? At what distance was she *allowed* to be at?

How close will Brother allow me...?

Suddenly, Miyuki felt cold. Her heart hadn't chilled at the idea or anything. It was midsummer but also before dawn, when the temperature was low, and all she wore were thin summery pajamas. If she would wear them the whole time, it was only natural she'd feel cold after a while.

And then Miyuki's mind began to drift in a stranger direction.

Isn't he cold?

This was the first time Miyuki had actually spent an entire night in the same room as Tatsuya. Last night—or more accurately, two nights ago—she'd been so excited it was like she'd tripped her own breaker, falling asleep before she realized it. She'd been knocked out until morning. From last night to this morning, though, she'd been thinking about Tatsuya sleeping in the bed next to her and had woken up several times. Eventually, despite day being yet to break, she'd taken up the mantle of stalker at his pillow side. Her lack of sleep was starting to wear away at her self-restraint.

She reached her hand out for his forehead as though he were a patient with a fever. Her mind seemed clear, but it was actually in the clouds, and in it lay not her apprehension from a moment ago—that he might wake up.

Fortunately, he didn't open his eyes. His forehead felt icy to her palm.

He's cold...

In addition to Tatsuya's body temperature falling during sleep— his body didn't perform *unnecessary* metabolization, so it was normally colder than most people already—Miyuki's perception was affected because in her exhausted, sleep-deprived state, her own body temperature had risen. Her thoughts, however...

How terrible... I have to warm him up.

...had short-circuited.

Umm, I think...in situations like this, body warmth is best.

That was something she'd learned for if she was stranded or otherwise met with an accident. If her brain had been functioning properly, it definitely would have overheated with embarrassment at the idea, but now that she'd, *at some point*, gotten her hands on a pretext—nursing him—she thought it was the natural thing to do.

...I can't take off my clothes, but...

Even so, she seemed to have at least the bare minimum of shame. Forgetting her hesitation at how Tatsuya could wake up, she softly nestled in next to him.

Brother, Miyuki will warm you up...

Miyuki, already half asleep, set forth on a journey to a dream world for real this time, holding Tatsuya close.

* * *

After confirming that his sister was now breathing regularly, Tatsuya opened his closed eyes.

She finally went to sleep...

Gently removing Miyuki's arm from his chest, Tatsuya slowly got out of bed. He'd actually woken up by the time Miyuki had reached out for his forehead. But she'd been acting strangely (he could sense it without having to look), so he'd pretended to be asleep to make sure she was all right.

Even sleeping with a one-of-a-kind beauty like this, *fortunately*, wouldn't set his libido to work. That wasn't to say he had no sexual urges at all, though, and it made him far too uncomfortable thinking about embracing his sister in the same futon. The soft sensation of her skin had felt good, which only multiplied the embarrassment. He obviously couldn't have fallen back asleep like that.

Nevertheless, with a match waiting in the wings tomorrow for his sister, he couldn't wake her back up at this hour. He didn't know how long she'd been up for, but there was at least time for her to get some more sleep.

Careful not to make any noise, he changed into casual clothes. After stroking Miyuki's hair and hoping to himself that she slept well, he quietly exited the room to take in some of the morning air.

"Good morning."

"Oh, good...morning...?"

As Azusa answered Tatsuya and Miyuki after they entered their headquarters tent bringing breakfast sandwiches with them, she tilted her head, confused. That was why her greeting came out so stilted.

Miyuki, who was trailing behind Tatsuya, seemed oddly—or rather, *very* embarrassed about something. As far as Azusa could see, the distance between them was a little wider, about thirty centimeters to be exact. And the corners of Miyuki's eyes were slightly reddened and her gaze was a bit downcast.

The Pillar Break solo event was today, which Miyuki would be participating in. First High's strategy aimed for an overall victory, and it predicted first place in the women's Pillar Break. They'd calculated it to be the event where they could most surely acquire points, and even the ever-timid Azusa wanted to avoid the worst-case scenario of a loss in qualifiers. She couldn't imagine Miyuki, others aside, losing at this event, but her current state still made her feel a tinge of unease.

"...What happened?"

Azusa asked the question because she wanted to rid herself of it, put it down to a vague sense of anxiety.

"What do you mean?"

But when Tatsuya asked her a question back, in a tone that neither confirmed nor denied her own, she found herself unable to ask anything else.

Ultimately, Miyuki fought through the qualifiers without letting her opponents come anywhere close. Their male competitor had been in a bit of a pinch at one point, but he safely made it out of the qualifiers as well. And just like the head minds of First High had been concerned about, both their solo competitors for Rower and Gunner took fourth place, ending with the miserable result of zero points gained.

As for the other schools' results, Seventh High had won both the male and female event to get 100 points each for a total of 200, keeping them at the top of the leaderboard since yesterday. Both Third High's competitors had won second to get 60 points each for a total of 120, overtaking First High and leaping out into second place. Considering the events after tomorrow, Third High would believe they could immediately overtake Seventh High. It was a great start for Third High—or it should have been.

The mood during Third High's dinner, however, was not dominated by jubilance. A heavy air hung over the area where the juniors were sitting. The source of these dark clouds was Kichijouji, who hadn't been able to win the Rower and Gunner solo event.

"Kichijouji, second place is still great. Don't let it get to you."

"That's right. I got second, too, but I don't mind it that much."

As they were cleaning up their trays after they'd finished eating, some seniors passed by to encourage him but to little effect.

"I never thought Seventh High would come out with something like *that*..."

Kichijouji, who had been silently working his chopsticks, albeit slowly, suddenly murmured in frustration. If there hadn't been dishes in front of him, he might have put his face down on the table.

He wasn't shocked purely because he'd lost. The problem was *how* he'd lost. He prided himself on his ingenuity, so it always dealt a bigger blow to him when he lost strategically, rather than in terms of ability. And he felt like it wasn't the strength of his opponent today that had done him in but their game plan.

"Look, you couldn't help it."

It was easier to comfort someone when they were complaining or whining rather than when they were in a silent depression. The juniors around him took the chance to give him a few words.

"He's right. Abandoning shooting with this rule set is absurd!"

Seventh High's tactic had been simple and unexpected. If they could hit the targets with indiscriminate, mechanical shots, all the better—the player could devote his remaining magic power to controlling his boat, shortening the time little by little. Rower and Gunner's rules calculated the time taken to hit a single target by dividing the fastest team's time by the most accurate team's number of targets hit. They then multiplied that time by the number of targets the current teams hit, then subtracted those from their race times. Whoever had the shortest remaining time would be the winner. In other words, if there was a small time difference, whichever team hit more targets would have the advantage—and conversely, as long as there wasn't a big gap in successful hits, whichever team had a shorter time would be in a good spot.

The one who happened to have the most targets hit in the men's solo event was actually Third High's Kichijouji. That would mean the time difference was larger than the one between his pinpoint shooting and their indiscriminate blasting. The result of winning through brute force rather than pursuing precision didn't sit well with him.

"Yeah, all the pair teams focused on hitting the targets."

"And that *was* actually how the First High girls beat Seventh High."

"They just got lucky with random hits. Sometimes that happens in sports. You think so too, right, Masaki?"

The male second-year students turned to Masaki, looking for agreement. And then all the people who had been comforting Kichijouji realized something odd.

When they thought back on it, Masaki hadn't offered a single word of comfort to Kichijouji. In fact, he hadn't said anything since dinner started today. His hands were bringing the food to his mouth, but his heart seemed like it was wrapped up with something else.

"Masaki?"

"Hmm? Right. Like they say, victory depends on of the whims of fortune. Fortune just happened to work against us this time. We lost out to Seventh High, but we turned things around against First High. As a whole, it's not bad—in fact, I think we've done pretty well for ourselves."

He seemed to have been listening to their conversation, but they couldn't help but feel like his remark was somewhat forced. The classmates surrounding Kichijouji, boy and girl alike, exchanged glances.

"I guess… Yeah, we *did* turn the tide against First High."

"Our ultimate goal is to win the whole thing, after all. We've got plenty to do for the rest of the competition, too."

"In other words, dragging this behind me is the worst thing I could do, right? I get it, Masaki."

But Masaki's words seemed to have helped Kichijouji get over it. When their dinner hour ended, nobody came forth to interrogate Masaki about his unnatural attitude.

They'd planned another tea party for tonight, but it would only be starting once everyone's work, beginning with CAD tuning, was done. Tomorrow would be the men's pair Shields Down in the morning and the women's pair finals league for Pillar Break. Tatsuya was already assigned to Shizuku since the qualifiers for the latter, and he was also assigned to Kirihara, one half of the Kirihara-Tomitsuka Shields Down pair. The day after, he'd be with Miyuki, their solo women's Pillar Break entrant, in the morning and then Sawaki during the men's solo Shields Down event in the afternoon. For *Tatsuya*, in the *competition* at least, those two days were estimated to be the busiest.

"Shiba, I finished doing the voltage checks on Kirihara's CAD."

"Could you go through the auto debugger next?"

"Okay."

Using Kento as his assistant, he was tuning Shizuku's and Kirihara's CADs. The work was less *tuning* and more *inspection*, and the reason he had Kento helping him was for educational purposes—to instruct him in the *proper* way to tune CADs. But Kento was very deft and had an abundance of knowledge, so he was a good enough assistant even for Tatsuya.

The surprise was that, as the end of their work was coming into sight, someone came to visit Tatsuya.

"Ichijou? What's wrong?"

The one who had stopped by their work vehicle was Masaki.

"Sorry for coming so late. Do you have a moment?"

"It's not that late for us, so I can spare a little time. Kento, let's take a break."

"All right," he replied.

Tatsuya and Masaki moved to a place where the work vehicle's lights didn't reach.

"You're letting a freshman be an engineer?" Masaki asked as he walked beside him, sounding a little surprised.

"Well, I was a freshman last year, too."

But the somewhat sarcastic response from Tatsuya made him give a pained grin—maybe he'd overstepped his bounds.

"Anyway, what is it? The only reason I can think of for you to visit me is about the Steeplechase stuff." Without matching the relatively friendly attitude Masaki had adopted, Tatsuya tried to head off the next thing he said.

Masaki made a sour face for a moment but then thought better of it—now wasn't the time for idle chatter. "Yeah, that's right. Things are looking a lot fishier than we thought."

"Did you find something out?" Tatsuya stopped walking and turned to him.

Masaki met his question head-on. "We haven't exactly figured it out yet, but it seems like the hard-liner faction in the JDF has something to do with this."

"The hard-liner faction?" repeated Tatsuya dubiously.

Masaki, too, immediately realized he wouldn't know what that meant by itself. "Right, sorry. It's a group of anti-GAA hard-liners in the JDF."

"You're saying they're pulling strings behind the competition?"

Considered on its own, the scheme was easily convincing. A faction that desired victory through war would choose magicians with high military aptitude in order to swiftly expand their combat power. High school students wouldn't serve that purpose immediately, but the hard-liners probably didn't want an outbreak of hostilities in the next few days. And looking at the results of this Nine School Competition, anyone could easily imagine them expanding this methodology to magic sports consisting mainly of university students.

However, the Kudou family—well, Retsu Kudou—and the hard-liners joining forces was a difficult union to imagine. Tatsuya had heard before that Retsu Kudou hated the act of using magicians as weapons. It was secondhand information, to be sure, but highly trustworthy. If he'd only heard it from Fujibayashi, he could consider it to be family bias, but even Kazama, who was against the Ten Master Clans system, had said the same thing.

What Retsu loathed was using magicians as weapons—he did not reject using them as soldiers. Paradoxical, yes, but that was exactly why the old man wouldn't ever make magic high school students into guinea pigs in a way that seemed so underhanded. Soldiers weren't expendable, after all. They were a valuable resource.

"Colonel Sakai seems to want magic high schoolers like us to volunteer for the JDF directly without going to the Academy of Defense first."

Masaki's continued explanation perplexed Tatsuya even more. He understood—if the hard-liners' goal was to secure volunteer soldiers as immediate combat power, they wouldn't stand opposed to Retsu Kudou. If that was also their goal for introducing heavily combat-oriented events here, then that made their intentions pretty clear. They probably wanted to give magic high school students a taste of the thrill of releasing their combat instincts and destructive impulses. By doing so, they'd doubtlessly try to increase the number of young people aspiring to be military magicians.

In spite of being one of those young men—or not even, as he was still a boy—Tatsuya thought about all this as though it wasn't his problem. Stimulating combat instincts and destructive impulses was a trick even the Yotsuba used in their training.

But that alone wouldn't explain the spell to make the Parasidolls go berserk. How much did the hard-liners know, and how deeply were they involved? Were they hand in hand with the mastermind, or were they just playing a supporting role?

And then a little question floated to the surface of Tatsuya's mind.

"...I'm impressed you actually learned about Colonel Sakai by name."

The Ichijou family must have had their own lines into the JDF. But it certainly wouldn't have been easy, ascertaining even the ringleader's name in this short period of time. It wasn't a popular political party or anything, so he knew they wouldn't have created registers for each faction and passed them out.

Masaki gave a pained look at Tatsuya's question, which also sounded like him talking to himself. "Colonel Sakai is an old acquaintance of my dad's..."

This *confession* surprised even Tatsuya. "Ichijou, I know I'm probably wrong here, but—"

"You *are* wrong! Don't misunderstand me, Shiba!"

When he waxed theatrical and tried to draw him out, Masaki rejected it, consternation plain on his face. It was a relief for Tatsuya, too, to hear him reject it. More enemies were manageable—but if the situation got any more complicated, it would be more trouble than it was worth. He was ready to flip over the game board by force if it came to that.

Actually... I might as well just wreck the Steeplechase course. Then it won't matter what *traps they have in place.*

"They were only acquaintances a long time ago!"

Masaki, utterly ignorant of the all too ominous things Tatsuya was considering, was in a rush for a different reason.

"Colonel Sakai was the commanding officer on-site during the Sado Incursion four years ago."

The Kudou family's goals and the JDF's ambitions never had anything to do with me anyway.

"You probably know this, but my father was the centerpiece of the volunteer army that retook Sado. When he did, he asked Colonel Sakai if he could bring a regiment-sized force toward Niigata and the Hokuriku region. The government and the JDF were both paying attention to Okinawa at the time, and since the volunteer army had retaken Sado for the moment, the JDF was planning to settle things with a single battalion."

It's not imperative that First High wins the overall competition, either. Steeplechase is on the last day anyway—Miyuki's victory and Honoka's and Shizuku's and the rest will have clinched first place by then. If the competition ends midway through, right on the heels of the Thesis Competition, the Magic Association will lose all credibility—but what do I care?

"Colonel Sakai answered Dad's request. He's still thankful for it. They did actually field a large force back then, and Dad says that's why they didn't attack after that. And I think so, too."

If I fire a Material Burst at a spot just beneath the surface, they probably won't be able to tell it apart from a conventional weapon explosion. Even with my self-made Third Eye, I can aim at microscopic amounts of matter up to close distances of a few kilometers, and if it's right under the surface of the earth, it shouldn't stress the volcanic chain. In the middle of the night, it wouldn't harm any students from any school. The issue would be convincing Miyuki and making it look like someone else did it...

"But after the battle in Okinawa wrapped up, the colonel tried to launch a reverse invasion against the New Soviet Union! No matter how much my father advised him not to, the colonel never changed his mind. Of course, General HQ wouldn't have ever permitted something that risky. Ultimately, the reverse invasion never came to pass, but apparently the colonel and my dad were in a pretty heated debate until the regiment returned to its regular stations. It was like a falling out, and he hasn't talked to the colonel since."

If only some criminal syndicate guys were hanging around like last year—I could have placed responsibility on them. I wonder if there's anyone who would cause a potential uprising lurking in the JDF.

"When I was talking about this with him last night, he was worried he might do something stupid like cause an uprising, but then he shook his head—saying there would be nothing he could do about that, since they're strangers at this point."

"An uprising?"

Until then, Tatsuya had been thinking about things entirely unrelated to Masaki's *excuses*. But when a term that matched one in his thoughts reached his ears, he naturally shifted his attention to what Masaki was saying.

Masaki, for his part, was surprised at Tatsuya suddenly reacting when he'd been (or so he'd thought) silently listening to his defense and then felt a newfound sense of panic, thinking the term *uprising* was too extreme.

"No, that's not to say he suspects Colonel Sakai's group to be plotting an uprising. Obviously, I don't know the details myself—there's just some rumors saying they might do it soon."

"So there's no evidence?"

"Well, no."

"But it's still a rumor?"

"Seems like it… Anyway!"

Masaki must have felt like this was headed in a bad direction for him. Raising his voice, he veered the conversation back on course.

"Colonel Sakai and the Ichijou family don't have any connection now. They knew each other in the past, which just means they had a lot of common acquaintances. That's where he got information on this stuff from. The colonel's group can't possibly be plotting rebellion, either. If they are plotting something, they probably just want to get a lot of young magicians in one place and get them into their faction so they can attack the GAA."

"That by itself is plenty terrifying in its own right… But thank you. This really helped."

"I-it wasn't like I was investigating this for you, so you don't need to thank me. Anyway, that's how it is, so they probably won't interfere with any of the events while they're happening. They'll most likely act after the competition is over. Either at the closing ceremony party or they'll contact people individually… If I learn more, I'll contact you."

"Thanks."

Tatsuya saw off Masaki, who was leaving more restlessly than he needed to, with a short word of gratitude. He knew Masaki's deduction was wrong, but he didn't intend to get him involved in the parasite doll business.

The hard-liners...

Now that he had a concrete candidate to serve as a stand-in, Tatsuya had actually regained his calm. He clearly didn't have enough time for any covert sabotage. They'd gotten to the point where only ten days were left until the Cross-Country Steeplechase, the appointed time for the experiment to be conducted. Completing any schemes in such a short interval would be difficult even *with* Yakumo's help. The Yotsuba would have made it possible, perhaps. Unfortunately, Maya would never help him bomb part of the Mount Fuji maneuvering ground.

This isn't like me. I seem to be getting too indecisive over this stuff...

By using that phrasing, Tatsuya admitted that he was tired. For tonight, he ordered himself to push the parasite dolls from his mind and relax at the tea party with his sister and friends.

The competition's third day would have the men's Shields Down pair qualifiers and finals in the morning, with the men's Pillar Break pair finals league.

And currently, they were right in the middle of the third match of the men's Shields Down pair finals league. First High and Third High had each won one match in the finals league. Whoever won this match would be the men's Shields Down pair champions.

Tomitsuka held up his shield and charged. Third High's players, who knew from previous matches that both First High's competitors were close combat types, had been constantly fighting Kirihara and Tomitsuka from a distance. However, their long-range spells were directly hitting a narrow but high-density Area Interference deployed by Tomitsuka, or so the Third High players thought. In actuality, they were being blocked without exception by his contact-type Program Demolition. The Third High players, under the wrong impression, fired masses of compressed air at them, but…

"Yahhhh!"

A shock wave fired from Tomitsuka's shield, throwing the compressed air into chaos, reduced them to a mere stiff wind.

It was a compound technique, involving a derivative of the acceleration spell Explosion and the movement spell Stasis. Rather than applying radial acceleration to a population, its event alteration gave an acceleration vector to the gas in contact with the shield, perpendicular to the shield's surface. (Stasis was to prevent the recoil from this.)

Tomitsuka hadn't been able to learn an attack spell using air—a popular technique for modern magicians. For that type of spell, you needed to maintain the air's compressed state until it got close to the enemy or contacted them. Tomitsuka, who couldn't control magic any farther than his hands or feet could reach, naturally felt like he was bad at it.

But the reason he hadn't been able to learn this type of spell *at all* was indeed an issue of the *mind*. As long as you stood on the earth, air was all around you. And that included *within reach of your hands*. Simply accelerating air that was close at hand didn't require a long-distance control spell. For example, all Sawaki's Mach Punch technique did was use air fixed around his fist to push on the air he came in contact with. It was just hard to immediately follow up a spell that accelerated your flesh—even if it was only a single part of it—to the speed of sound with one that moved a fixed air mass at the speed of sound. *Tricks* that fired pressure waves never had any remote control involved.

Tatsuya, also one of the operations staff, had been the one to contrive that theoretical outline. But it had been Chiaki Hirakawa who had successfully modified an activation sequence and optimized his CAD so that he could learn and master Blast.

Chiaki had always been better with hardware, like the CADs themselves, than software such as activation sequences, and while she was fine at adjusting the programs, she wasn't great at arranging them. But when she'd heard Tomitsuka's idea for a zero-range Blast, she'd visited their instructor Jennifer Smith every day, tackled the activation program arranging she found so difficult, and had finally assembled an activation sequence for Blast that Tomitsuka could easily use. One could say it was thanks to Chiaki that Tomitsuka could use Blast now, albeit at zero range.

Spotting the right timing to destroy Third High's attack, Kirihara stepped out in front. In terms of ring positioning, Tomitsuka was in the center, the Third High pair was on the edge, and Kirihara was between them.

Kirihara squatted, went down to a knee and, as though falling down, slammed his shield into the ring.

A beat later, the ring shook. He'd used magic to send an oscillatory wave, its cycle nudged to align with the vibrations leaping off the ring from the strike, into them.

The shaking was greatest in the center. However, the psychological effects were heavier on the Third High pair, who stood at the edge. After all, if they fell from the ring, they'd be disqualified.

The other two didn't let the opening out of their grasp. Tomitsuka dashed in with a self-acceleration spell, overtaking Kirihara and hitting a Third High player with his shield. This time, with a spell he excelled in, one that targeted a fixed object—Explosion.

The other Third High player didn't have time to worry about his partner falling out of the ring. Kirihara thrust the edge of his shield out at him.

A modified High-Frequency Blade. Rather than cleaving the Third High competitor's shield, it shattered it. Without having to wait for round two, First High clinched victory in the men's pair event.

Kirihara grabbed Tomitsuka's hand and lifted it in the air. In the staff seating built right next to the ring, Chiaki clapped her hands in joy. She'd had a sullen look this whole time, probably because she was sitting next to Tatsuya, but in the moment, she seemed to have forgotten even that detail.

◇ ◇ ◇

Day three ended with First High taking third in the men's Pillar Break pair event and first in the women's pair event. In Shields Down, their men's pair had taken first, and their women's pair had lost in the qualifiers. The women's Shields Down pair's results had been a miscalculation, but it was because they'd been in the same group as Third High's pair, which had won first place. If they'd beaten Third High in the qualifiers, the First High pair probably would have won. That was how heated that match had been.

But results were results. In every event today, Third High had taken at least second place. Third High had had 400 points at the end of day two, and so they'd opened their lead on First by 100 points.

Thanks to that, First High's dinnertime wasn't an excited one, filled with celebration for the victorious pairs. Instead—well, not exactly *instead*, but...

"Shizuku, congratulations on winning!"

"Well, you *are* strong, so it's only natural."

"Yep! Congrats, Shizuku!"

...words congratulating Shizuku on her victory were flying back and forth at the nighttime tea party they were holding at Tatsuya's work vehicle.

"Thanks, everyone."

Even Shizuku must have been happy with all the praise. With a subtle smile, she bowed her head slightly.

"Tomorrow it'll be Miyuki's turn."

And then a little embarrassed but certainly not trying to hide it, Shizuku gave Miyuki some encouragement.

"Yes. I must do my best as well," answered Miyuki seriously, a simple smile on her face.

"Actually, maybe you shouldn't think about doing your *very* best. If you tense up, you could get stuck in a pitfall you didn't see coming."

"Miyuki couldn't possibly lose just by getting stuck in her head, would she? The only thing she needs to worry about is getting disqualified from flying too long."

"That would be the greatest pitfall of them all."

"I swear... Subaru, Erika, do you both think of me as that clumsy?"

Perhaps Subaru and Erika had made banter disguised as urges for caution because they couldn't endure the purity of the air coming off Shizuku and Miyuki. Not exactly as though to prove it, when Miyuki came back with a light humor in her tone, the entire group palpably relaxed.

"No, not exactly," replied Subaru with a pained grin, and Miyuki didn't pursue things any more than that, either.

The girls' flowery chitchat rode the breeze up and melted into the night air. As expected, the nighttime tea party held at Tatsuya's work vehicle had more people and was livelier for it.

Erika, too, who said she had something to do and couldn't make it the first day, had been casually participating since last night. Subaru Satomi and Eimi Akechi had joined their ranks today. Soon, their camping table wouldn't be enough. If any more people came, they'd have to get more chairs and tables. ——These were all the second-year girls, at least the athletes, so maybe they didn't have to think about what they'd do if they had more people, though.

Incidentally, their little tea party had already spread to all the First High students by the following morning. And the reason Eimi and Subaru had joined them only tonight was *not* because they'd run out of modesty after one night had passed.

"Anyway, I'm glad you're feeling better today, Amy. I wasn't sure what I'd do if you'd kept pouting like that all night."

"I—I was not! I wasn't pouting!"

It wasn't the most important thing she had to remind her of…but Subaru soothed the angrily arguing Eimi with an "Okay, okay." It was unclear whether or not she was *seriously* trying to soothe her, but that only went to show how bad Eimi's mental state was. At least, that's what Subaru thought anyway.

Subaru and Eimi were in the same room. They weren't as close to Tatsuya and the others as Honoka and Shizuku, and since coming to the venue, they'd stuck together, except for matches, of course. If Eimi was in an awful mood, that made Subaru uncomfortable, and more than that, Subaru wanted to do something for her as a friend.

"What happened?"

The one Miyuki asked was not Eimi herself but Subaru.

"It's nothing, okay?!" cried Eimi from the side, her face red as she tried to interrupt them.

But that wasn't enough to keep Subaru's mouth closed. "Well, that Tomitsuka guy…," she answered, closing one eye, shrugging with a sigh.

Her answer caused not only Miyuki but Honoka and Shizuku as well to suddenly look like things made sense.

"What about Tomitsuka?" asked Mizuki to Shizuku, who was sitting next to her.

But the one who answered the question was Erika. "He was probably flirting with that woman or something."

"That…woman?"

"Hirakawa! Chiaki Hirakawa."

And then, Mizuki too finally seemed to understand what Erika wanted to say. But she still seemed unconvinced as she leveled an inquisitive stare at Eimi.

"Amy, it is Tomitsuka we're talking about. I think he was probably just expressing gratitude." Honoka, who had seen Tomitsuka and Chiaki talking familiarly (well, not quite, considering Chiaki looked downcast for a lot of it) at dinner, offered words of comfort.

"I told you, it's nothing."

Eimi enthusiastically denied it, but Honoka wasn't the only one who'd seen Tomitsuka frequently talking to Chiaki. Miyuki and Shizuku had seen the same. Even aside from that, if you compared Eimi's face to Subaru's, it would be crystal clear which one was trustworthy.

"Amy, that won't work."

"What won't?!"

In fact, given how easily readable her reaction was, it was dubious even whether she wanted to hide it. Of course, the way Shizuku had put that, in her abbreviated way, had at least *sounded* challenging.

"Unlike Tatsuya, Tomitsuka is *actually* dense, so you have to tell him straight."

With the abbreviated part now spoken after the fact, Eimi gave off a queer look. It was the face of someone who didn't feel like defending herself and knew she couldn't even if she did.

Speaking of odd expressions, Tatsuya seemed troubled by the choice of what kind *he* should make, now that he'd been mentioned. But *fortunately*, his confusion didn't last long.

"Master."

Suddenly, Pixie called to him telepathically, and Tatsuya stood up, his face casual despite the inherent stress of the situation.

After all, he'd ordered Pixie not to use telepathy except in specific cases. One of those conditions must have been met.

"Brother?"

"Tatsuya?"

"The machine doesn't seem to be working right. I'll go check on it."

Leaving Miyuki and Honoka with an excuse they could interpret in any number of ways, Tatsuya headed inside the work vehicle.

When he entered, Pixie had called up a map on the data panel in the driver's seat. The cursor was in the middle of it, on a military-use road on the other side of the cross-country course from here.

"I've detected responses from comrades at this point."

"Are the responses continuing?" asked Tatsuya, staring hard at the map.

"Yes. They seem to have recognized me as well."

"Can you tell how many?"

"Sixteen individuals identified."

That matched the number of gynoids Tatsuya had seen in old Lab Nine.

"Oh..." said Pixie with her mind's voice. Lately, this sort of reflexive action had made her much more humanlike.

"What is it?"

"My comrades' responses have disappeared all at once. They seem to have entered sleep."

"Any signs of them moving?"

"Not while I was still receiving responses."

At this stage, the Parasidolls' handlers couldn't publicly do maintenance at a JDF installation. Tatsuya didn't know how many people knew about it, but this performance test was supposed to be a secret project. Tatsuya had figured they'd done something reasonable, like obtaining a mobile lab and transporting them inside the base like that.

He wasn't sure how far their range to effectively monitor the Parasidolls extended. But if they were doing performance testing, they wouldn't want to be very far away so they could monitor them during the tests. The very back of the course matched this condition. The only problem was...

Just as we detected the Parasidolls, they must have learned Pixie was here...

That point was a source of unease. In the same way Pixie could identify the Parasidolls, the Parasidolls could identify Pixie. Which also meant that the Kudou family's experiment team would know their presence had been detected.

If Tatsuya was in their shoes, he'd move right now. Perhaps leave entirely until the day of the test. However, it was highly possible they wouldn't be that cautious, given their safe positions under the patron-age of Retsu Kudou.

Didn't I decide just yesterday that there's no point hesitating? So what if it's a pointless trip? I should just attack them now...

After wavering, he made up his mind.

When he put on gear he'd hidden in the work vehicle and exited it, the tea party had already wrapped up.

"See you tomorrow, Tatsuya."

"See you, too, Miyuki."

"Tatsuya, thanks for the drinks."

"Shiba, Miyuki, thanks for letting us come!"

"See you, Tatsuya."

"Good night, Shiba."

Their friends (plus one underclassman) began returning to the hotel as a lively bunch. After seeing them off, Miyuki looked up at Tatsuya and smiled.

"Brother, you'll be leaving now, won't you?"

"Yeah."

Tatsuya nodded without even thinking of trying to fool her—she always hit the nail right on the head.

"I had everyone return because I thought you would be."

She seemed to have seen through him to an almost scary degree, but figuring it was a little late to be surprised at that, Tatsuya's confusion dissipated in his mind before materializing. But even he couldn't hold it down after the next words that came out of her mouth.

"Brother, please don't go."

"Miyuki...you're, what?"

"No. Brother, I will not let you go."

He couldn't see any agitation in her face. Her eyes glittered with a cold, firm resolve.

"Brother, is it necessary to go to the enemy right now? It does not seem that way to me."

"Pixie's located the enemy. I finally have a lead."

"The problem comes before that. What I want to ask is whether you must act to *preemptively* stop the Kudou family's experiment."

For once, Tatsuya didn't know what to say. Ever since he'd received the anonymous warning message, he'd considered it natural to stop it. But was that something *he* needed to do?

"Perhaps I am being selfish. Perhaps I think of such shameless things because I can't help you in any way this time, Brother."

Miyuki was resolute in her words. She had firmly accepted that shame to stand against her brother.

"I will gladly accept your scolding. However, Brother, before that—please hear me out."

Tatsuya couldn't move his eyes away from Miyuki's gaze. Having decided to head for the enemy, he couldn't move out from in front of her.

"You haven't a single reason to shoulder the responsibility for the Kudou family's experiment. Nor do you have any responsibility regarding the Parasidolls' performance tests."

Tatsuya knew that as well and had mentally said as much to himself.

"You have equally little reason to shoulder the responsibility for every single athlete entered into the Cross-Country Steeplechase."

"..."

He felt like he'd been struck with a Zen stick while in the middle of meditating. Faintly, he began to understand what Miyuki was trying to say—and that she was right and he was wrong.

"Brother, I am about to say something selfish. Something very shallow."

Miyuki's voice contained no self-deprecation or pretense of evil. She was not wavering even slightly...

"As long as you protect me, that is enough. I am the only one you need shoulder responsibility for."

...except for her voice, which trembled as though she was about to break into tears at any second.

"You don't need to concern yourself with anyone other than me—not the students of First High, much less those of other schools!"

Miyuki clenched her teeth. Her bangs hung in front of her downcast face, hiding how her eyes were holding back tears.

"You can leave the Parasidolls for that day. As long as they don't decide to release the parasites' main bodies, those things would never present a threat to you. You can destroy them all on that day. Once the main bodies have been released and the event has ended, I will put an end to every one of them."

Glaring, challenging, Miyuki locked her gaze with Tatsuya's. Her eyes had shed no tears.

"And if you will still go, then I don't mean to be rude, but I will stop you by force."

This time, Tatsuya was actually dismayed.

He sensed the forbidden power rising within Miyuki.

"Miyuki, stop! Are you seriously going to seal my eyes?! If you do that, you wouldn't be able to use magic anymore, either!"

"Yes, and I shall likely have to forfeit tomorrow's event. I may even have to drop out of First High. But all that is better than letting you continue to act unreasonably!"

For the first time, Miyuki let her agitation show. Her tearful voice laid her true feelings bare.

"Brother—Brother, do you realize how hard you're pushing yourself?! From morning to night, you adjust our players' CADs; after every match, you listen to the other technical staff members and give them advice; and you stay up late at night preparing for the next day while instructing an underclassman. Meanwhile, you want to take on the Kudou family and the JDF... Even you won't hold up under all that! You'll ruin yourself!"

Heavy tears fell from her eyes.

At last, Tatsuya realized that he'd been so exhausted that he hadn't realized his fatigue was putting a huge amount of pressure on his sister.

The doubts haunting his mind vanished, and he physically felt his heart growing lighter. "You don't need to do that."

Miyuki looked up at him, her face struck by surprise. The fretfulness had left Tatsuya's voice and peaceful geniality brimmed in its place. "I'll go back to the room now for today."

"Brother...?"

"Miyuki, what you're saying is right. I was wrong."

She hadn't thought her persuasion would succeed. She knew that *truthfully, as a human*, her brother was correct. She couldn't so suddenly believe her brother's change of heart.

"You're right about it. You're the only one I need to protect. As long as I protect you, nothing else matters. If you're here, that's enough for me."

The words Miyuki always hoped for filled her heart and caused her chest to tighten. She stared wordlessly at Tatsuya, as though her earlier eloquence had been a lie. With a gaze that, like before, was straightforward—but unlike before, looked like she was in a dream.

"Let's get back to the room."

Her shoulder gently pushed, Miyuki began walking toward the hotel like a marionette.

——And behind them, Minami, who had been in the background for the entire scene right up until the end, continued to look down, hiding an expression that implied she'd been enduring the whole thing feeling uneasy.

Competition day four, morning. In the women's Pillar Break solo event, Miyuki ended both her finals league matches in under one minute and won the championship.

Her victory was so overwhelming it would make one worry about her opponents being traumatized, but Miyuki showed no signs of concern about that. The audience couldn't even pay any attention to the losers. When she offered a gratified smile, the spectators forgot to applaud, simply watching her. It was as though they'd been entranced.

After lunch would be the men's Pillar Break solo event and the men's Shields Down solo event. Tatsuya would be assigned to Shields Down. As he was heading ringside, he met up with Sawaki.

"Shiba, you seem like you're on your game today."

Although he'd been concerned wholly with Pillar Break (read: Miyuki) that morning, he'd run into Sawaki in the tent during breakfast.

"Is it that obvious?" Tatsuya asked back, feeling like it was both belated of him and abrupt.

"Yeah. Day one, day two, day three, you kind of looked like you weren't totally focused. We were getting the results we wanted, so I wasn't going to say anything, but I figured you were worrying yourself over something."

Tatsuya was inwardly amazed. It hadn't been worries but doubts, but he didn't think he'd shown any of it. In fact, his friends—Honoka, Shizuku, Mikihiko—and others closer to him than Sawaki, like Isori and Azusa, didn't seem to have noticed he'd been in bad form. Maybe something could be said about not constantly being with someone cluing you in to even small changes, but even so, it was incredibly sharp.

"You look pretty refreshed today. I can feel the fighting spirit coming off you."

"I may have been letting the exhaustion accumulate without realizing it. Last night I got a really good night's sleep for the first time in a while, so that probably helped get me back into things."

It wasn't an unnatural excuse, but it also wasn't a good one. Even as he answered Sawaki, he thought that in his shoes, he wouldn't believe it.

"Cool. Then let's keep that energy going, Shiba!"

But if Sawaki had any suspicions, he wasn't letting on. He was pointed only forward. Without thinking about anything unnecessary, his eyes were set only on the approaching match in front of him.

As if in concert with Tatsuya's regaining his form, First High's come from behind began.

On day four, First High's results were third in the men's solo Pillar Break and first in the women's solo. First place in the Shields Down men's solo and first place in the women's solo. They'd reduced the gap between them and Third High from yesterday's 100 points to just 60 today.

First High's drive continued into the rookie competition, too. On its first day, they achieved first place in both the Rower and Gunner men's and women's solo events. Working alongside Kento as the boys' engineers, Tatsuya had guided his underclassman pair to defeat Seventh High and emerge victorious. As for the girls, Kasumi had given a proud look of *it was nothing* from the center of the victory stand.

On the second day of the rookie competition, they reached the finals in both Shields Down and Pillar Break. For Shields Down, the boys ended at third place, but the girls won a spectacular victory. Tatsuya was Minami's assigned engineer, but in that respect, he had almost nothing to do.

Pillar Break went the same, with the boys taking third and the girls winning. Izumi had stolen the show during the women's Pillar Break event. When she'd returned to First High's tent, she'd had on a huge smile—one that smelled faintly of desire—and she'd gone up to Miyuki and hugged her, but for once, Miyuki let her treat her as a (standing) hug pillow for as long as she wanted.

And then on the third day of the rookie competition…

"…Not much we can do about this."

"Yes, it will be difficult to compete against Ayako properly in Mirage Bat… Even I likely wouldn't be able to give her a good match."

Tatsuya, who was off today and tomorrow in preparation for the main Mirage Bat event coming up in two days, watched the Mirage Bat finals from the stands. The First High entrant had won her way into the finals.

Actually, during the entrant selection stage, they had considered choosing either Kasumi or Izumi for the star girls' event. Many had been in support of the plan, but Tatsuya had debated it stubbornly, and eventually Kasumi ended up in Rower and Gunner and Izumi in Pillar Break.

The pretext he'd given for opposing their entrance into Mirage Bat was that Kasumi was more well suited for Rower and Gunner, and Izumi had a better affinity for Pillar Break. Those weren't lies. A lack of weaknesses was a trait distinguishing Saegusa magicians, meaning also that they were suited to all magic and had an affinity with all of it. Cases like Mayumi, who so clearly specialized in one form of magic, were actually the exception.

His true reason, however, was that they wouldn't be able to beat Ayako in Mirage Bat.

The magic Ayako most excelled in was the convergence-type spell Supreme Diffusion, which dispersed and equalized gases or energy until they became indiscernible. The spell had no direct relationship with Mirage Bat. But Ayako had another spell she was almost as comfortable with as Supreme Diffusion.

And that was Pseudo-Teleportation. It could wrap herself or an allied partner in a cocoon of air, neutralize inertia, then move them instantly through a vacuum tube.

A vacuum tube would be seen as interfering with other players, so she couldn't use the spell during Mirage Bat unchanged. But if she downgraded it, the spell still allowed her to leap blindingly fast while creating gusts of wind.

Her speed was unmatchable, even using flight magic. Pseudo-Teleportation was significantly superior to flight magic when it came to movement distance. That wouldn't become a problem in Mirage

Bat, though. If there was any way to beat Ayako in this event, it could only be to eliminate the orbs of light before she spotted them.

As both Tatsuya and Miyuki predicted, Ayako was racking up the points for herself during the rookie Mirage Bat event. Their First High underclassman was faring well, too. If things continued at this pace, she could probably get second.

But that was it. Even now, the points difference was only increasing.

The match-ending buzzer sounded.

In the rookie Mirage Bat, victory went to Ayako Kuroba of Fourth High. First High took second, Third High took third, and Fifth High rounded the results out in fourth place.

Monolith Code on the rookie competition's final day. Even here, First High was struggling but putting up a good fight. Starting this year, the event would be played as a full round-robin. Both the rookie event and the main one would use six arenas over a two-day period, split up into ten rounds where each team would play eight matches total. (In other words, each team had two rounds without a match.)

Day two, round nine. First High's team, led by Takuma Shippou, had won all six of their matches before this. Two matches ago, they'd won a hard-fought victory over Third High, seen as their greatest rival before the competition began, and a triumphant mood had been drifting among the rookie team. But after seeing Third High lose to Fourth High in the previous match, they felt tense, as though someone had dumped ice water on their heads.

"That's crazy. What was his name again?" asked Leo to Tatsuya—they weren't watching the match from the VIP seating but from the general cheering seats.

"Kuroba. Fumiya Kuroba."

"Kuroba—you mean…"

Mikihiko, also spectating from the cheering seats, clammed up as though he didn't want others to hear.

First High versus Fourth High would indeed be a match to end all matches. And unfortunately, things looked grim for the former.

The craggy stage, speckled with big boulders, was modeled after a karst. On the edge of it stood First High's monolith, and protecting it was Takuma Shippou. Surprisingly, he'd volunteered to be the defender, and so far, he'd taken down every single enemy who had made it that far. One could say a big reason for their victory over Third High was that Takuma had annihilated their offense.

And now, Fumiya was pushing Takuma back. Fumiya was jumping from boulder to boulder just like Ushiwakamaru, not letting Takuma get a straight shot. And in midair, the handgun-shaped CAD in Fumiya's hand took aim at Takuma, attacking him with formless impacts.

The untyped magic, Phantom Blow.

Tatsuya had used the spell himself in last year's rookie competition, but the power behind Fumiya's was entirely different. Which made sense—Fumiya wasn't using only Phantom Blow. Behind that, he'd slipped in a spell he specialized in, one only he could use, called Direct Pain, which caused a person's mind to feel physical pain.

He was lowering the force of it in such a way that even the magic researchers in the stands couldn't see, much less the spectators, so no single attack led to knocking Takuma out. As a result, Fumiya's spell was recognized as a strong Phantom Blow rather than Direct Pain.

Still, misunderstanding it wouldn't change its power and the effects it delivered. The pain accumulating in Takuma's mind was draining him of his ability to concentrate.

Declining concentration directly linked to a reduction in spells' power and its success rate. To stop Fumiya from moving, Takuma tried to use Stone Shower, a spell that would use colony control on small rocks, focus them, and stream them toward the enemy.

The rocks danced up from around him.

But instead of coming down upon Fumiya, they hit the boulder he'd been standing on a moment ago.

Direct Pain fired from Fumiya's hand, hidden behind Phantom Blow.

And with that, Fumiya had dealt a KO to all three members of First High's team, clinching Fourth High's victory.

The rookie Monolith Code event closed with Fourth High taking the championship. But First High secured second place, earning them an overall victory in the rookie competition.

As a result, at the time of the rookie competition's end, the difference between first-place Third High and second-place First High became five points. Through the freshmen's successes, the battle for first was right back where it started.

Day nine of the Nine School Competition. The battle moved from the rookie competition to the main competition once more. And under this starry sky, the finals of Mirage Bat, also called Fairy Dance, was about to begin.

First High would be fielding Honoka and Subaru in the final match. Honoka's engineer was Tatsuya, and Subaru's was Azusa. Both were juniors, but the plan was to pull far ahead of Third High at once. With Third High's finalists being limited to one person, the plan had already halfway succeeded. Bringing in the other half was something both Tatsuya and Azusa had worked hard to set the stage for. Now it was all up to the athletes.

Honoka, having changed into a fitted uniform of mainly light lime, stood in front of Tatsuya a little awkwardly. She knew the clothes were for the event, but they were still embarrassing for eyes of the opposite sex to be seeing this close.

"No problems at all. Anything feel out of place to you?"

It was inevitable that, after checking her CAD's tuning, Tatsuya would give her a thorough look. Because for him alone, it was more reliable for him to check her with his "eyes" rather than measure her with a machine.

"No... Nothing does. I'm okay," answered Honoka finally, her voice soft and timid. She had a reason to be embarrassed that went beyond simply a member of the opposite sex seeing her like this. Tatsuya understood that as well, but that was exactly why he had to make sure his expression was casual.

Maybe I'll give her a little time to herself, like before the qualifier, so she can focus on the match…, thought Tatsuya. But just as he was about to say something to her…

"Shiba, I'm coming in."

…in came Subaru, who had been doing final adjustments in the next booth over with Azusa.

"Did you need something?"

His words were quite unfriendly, but his tone wasn't that inhospitable. He'd simply asked a question. She was an entrant from the same school, but Mirage Bat was an individual competition. You couldn't exactly call it nonsensical that she'd visit a player she was about to compete against right before they were supposed to go out on the field, but it wasn't normal, either.

"I just thought I'd come say hi to you before going."

"Say hi? To me?"

"Yes—to you."

Subaru nodded in an affected way. Of course, that was par for the course for her. A year ago, it might have bothered him but not now.

"I'll be winning this match, thank you. Sorry, but I'm putting a stop to your undefeated epic today."

Still, that haughty remark wasn't like Subaru at all.

The "undefeated epic" referred to how every athlete Tatsuya had ever been assigned to, since last year, had been essentially undefeated, only losing among themselves. In this year's Nines, too, Eimi in Rower and Gunner, Shizuku in the Pillar Break pair and Miyuki in the solo, Kirihara in the Shields Down pair and Sawaki in the solo, the boys in the rookie Rower and Gunner, and the girls in the rookie Shields Down had all taken home victory in every event.

"It's not like *I'm* out there winning."

But Tatsuya didn't misunderstand those things as his own accomplishments. Eimi, Shizuku, Miyuki, Kirihara, Sawaki, Minami. Every one of them an athlete who could have won first prize without his help. He felt as though *he* was the lucky one. Even if a pained grin was mixed in with his response, that didn't mean his personality was twisted.

"Even so. Nobody you're assigned to loses, Shiba. And I'm about to end that legend."

Objectively speaking, however, there was no doubt that these achievements had been putting pressure on their competition rivals. Subaru must not have been any exception to the pressure, displaying such an uncharacteristically strong-willed attitude.

To be honest, the attitude made him uncomfortable. But even so, to Tatsuya, Subaru was an athlete from the same school. It would be a bad idea to pile on the pressure with an inept reaction.

"I see."

Other than that short response, he had no way to answer her.

After seeing Subaru off and returning his eyes to Honoka, she was for some reason impassioned.

"Tatsuya!"

No shame was left in her look. In its place burned the flames of fighting spirit.

"I'll do my best. And I'll win! I'll protect your undefeated record, Tatsuya!"

She was so eager he worried about her self-destructing. But in Honoka's case, throwing cold water over her would have the opposite effect. He'd learned about her personality in the year they'd known each other.

"All right. I'm counting on you."

In fact, at times like this, it was better to fan the flames even further.

"Okay!"

Honoka nodded, seeming happy, her smile full of energy.

The Mirage Bat finals match.

Its results: Honoka won first and Subaru second. Third High's entrant clawed into third place, but First High won 80 points total and Third High only 20.

First High, at last, stood at the top of the overall rankings.

"For a while I wasn't sure how it would turn out, but it looks like things will work out again this year."

At the dinner seats where First High's students had gathered, the mood was actually more relieved than overjoyed.

On day ten of the Nine School Competition, First High had won first place in Monolith Code as well, widening their point lead over Third High to 95 points. For now, having opened up a nearly 100-point lead meant they'd completely turned the tables.

"Yoshida wins the medal today. You really did well."

The one who commended Mikihiko was a senior who had been in his Monolith Code team—a British-Indian boy with uniquely blond hair and dark skin named Kerry Minakami.

"No… This belongs to more than just me. You both really supported me."

He glanced toward Tatsuya, who was a short distance away, eating while surrounded by girls.

"Tatsuya helped out a lot, too, so…"

"Yeah. Shiba did a real bang-up job again this year as engineer. Hey, Shiba!"

As Tatsuya looked up and turned to them, Kerry beckoned him over with his hand. Tatsuya rose, holding his tray with half-eaten food on it. Seeing him leave the group of beautiful girls—his sister Miyuki first and foremost among them—and come over to their boys-only table…Mikihiko may or may not have found himself thinking a most uncharitable *I won't let you get all the good stuff to yourself…*

"Come on, sit down."

These words came from Sawaki, leading member of said boys-only group. Without committing the folly of purposely disobeying—he'd come with his tray in his hands, so he probably hadn't been meaning to anyway—he said, "All right," and sat in the seat he'd been directed to.

"Man, you did work today."

"Actually, I couldn't do enough yesterday, so I was thinking I'd like to recover from that a little."

Tatsuya's assignment to Mikihiko hadn't been something decided on the spot. He'd been taking care of Mikihiko's CAD from the beginning. Of course, speaking of *from the beginning*, they'd always predicted the possibility that Mirage Bat would overlap with Mono-lith Code matches. In full recognition of that unreasonable thought, Tatsuya had been chosen as both Honoka and Mikihiko's assigned engineers.

"You can't help what happened yesterday. We knew it going in."

That was something everyone present understood, but Hattori was the one who actually said it, pointing to the conscientious and obstinate nature of his personality.

"That's right. And even yesterday you did so much that a little slipup wouldn't be any problem at all. There's no doubt about it—you contributed to our victory today."

"Now we're sure to grab the overall win. Which means I'll be able to face my upperclassmen with pride."

Following Sawaki, Kerry looked relieved as he made his comment. He'd been chosen as a representative for the first time as a senior, so the tradition must have been weighing even heavier on his shoulders.

If anyone asked Tatsuya, he thought it was a rather premature thought. A turnabout was still possible depending on how tomorrow's Cross-Country Steeplechase went.

But he didn't point that out. Frankly speaking, he didn't care about their placement or the points or the overall championship.

He would make sure tomorrow's event ended safely.

No—he would crush all *obstacles* to tomorrow's event ending, on the surface, safely.

Those were his feelings underneath the inoffensive reply he made.

Tatsuya had come to the hotel's observation deck after dinner. The moon hadn't yet ascended, but the skies were clear. Mount Fuji was dimly showing its outline in the starlight. In front of it was an abyss of darkness. He was looking down from the balcony at tomorrow's Steeplechase, and the man-made forest for maneuvers put together behind it, which would be the stage for violence.

"How is it?" he asked the doll in the shape of a girl who waited next to him.

"No response. Estimated to still be in sleep."

The one who answered him was the demon residing in the doll. Dubbed a parasite at the London conference, it was the pushion information life-form Tatsuya and the others called Pixie.

"We'll just have to wait until tomorrow, then," he said to himself, disappointment creeping into his words.

His face, however, showed no traces of discouragement. He certainly wanted to know where these Parasidolls were, these humanoid magical weapons who would be the main stars of the experiment being plotted for tomorrow. But he hadn't brought Pixie along this time in the hope that he'd actually find them. Besides, if all he was going to do was have her search for the Parasidolls, he wouldn't have needed to go up this high. She was essentially the same type of being, and as long as both she and the Parasidolls were in an active state, they'd be able to detect each other.

Ever since that night Miyuki had lectured him on him staking his life as a magician, Tatsuya had abandoned his thoughts of preemptively stopping the Kudou family's experiment, which could bring grave harm upon the magic high schools' students. This was perhaps just as his mysterious informant wanted, but he'd decided he'd figure out what to do on the day of—in other words tomorrow.

As it was, it was clear that his mystery informant wasn't looking for him to stop the experiment before it happened, given they hadn't sent him any additional information that would aid him in that endeavor.

Instead, Tatsuya had come to look at tomorrow's stage, sunken in darkness as it was, on nothing more than a whim. If pressed, it was to try and distract himself a little from his anger at the Kudou family and the unknown informant for manipulating him. Basically shouting, *You just wait until tomorrow!* Having Pixie search for the Parasidolls had been a mere afterthought.

"Tatsuya."

This observation room wasn't barred to visitors at night. But he was still surprised someone aside from him was curious enough to come visit this top-floor balcony, considering it was the middle of the night, and no lights were on, nor was the air-conditioning.

"Master, here to enjoy the cool air?"

Of course, when it comes to curiosity, Yakumo has me beat by a long shot.

When he'd considered someone aside from him being curious, he hadn't been thinking of *him*.

"Me? Well, something like that. The night breeze feels better than air-conditioning. But I think the young lady over there needs you for something, don't you? I think it's about time you said something to her."

Told to do so, Tatsuya didn't exactly shrug…but let off an air that was similar, before turning away from the balcony.

The figure visible through the dark was a woman older than him but still young by society's standards. She seemed different from usual, because she wasn't wearing the usual affected smile on her beautiful visage but rather a stiff, stressed expression.

"As I thought, that message came from you, Lieutenant?"

Tatsuya addressed her without any preface, almost as though continuing a conversation they'd been having.

The hint of a pained smile loosened Fujibayashi's face a little. "How did you know?"

"Probabilities, ma'am. Out of all my acquaintances, you're the most likely one to wield such advanced technology."

"But maybe it wasn't an acquaintance."

"It wouldn't mean anything to consider that possibility, ma'am."

"I suppose not…"

Though it had slightly loosened, Fujibayashi's face was still drawn back. Was it because of tension or guilt or something entirely different? Tatsuya wasn't yet possessed of the keen insight to see.

It was best to ask about things he didn't know, and it was the only road that led to resolution. And so, without any reservations or hesitation, Tatsuya asked her.

"You sent the warning when I was on the street in front of old Lab Nine, too, right? What were you wanting to make me do, ma'am?"

"What, indeed… What *did* I want you to do…?"

Tatsuya stared lasers through Fujibayashi's eyes. But he couldn't find any signs that she was evading the question.

"Tatsuya, why don't we move somewhere else?"

Whatever the circumstances were, they must have been intricate enough that even magically blocking hidden cameras and bugs wasn't assuring enough.

"If you say so, ma'am…"

Several things about this incident made him unable to declare either Fujibayashi or the Independent Magic Battalion allies. His mind was not absent of concern for traps, but neither was it that serious.

"Would you mind sitting in as well, Master?"

"Sure."

"I wouldn't mind."

"Understood, ma'am. Please lead the way."

With both their acknowledgments in hand, Tatsuya agreed with Fujibayashi's proposal.

The place Fujibayashi brought Tatsuya and Yakumo to was the inside of a vehicle, similar to the camping car Tatsuya was using as a work vehicle. It was parked in a lot a short distance away from the one assigned for Nine School Competition use, and nobody else was inside.

"Master, no communication signals detected."

With the help of Ushiyama and the others, they'd upgraded Pixie as much as her 3H body would allow. Her sensors hadn't picked up on anything suspicious.

"Tatsuya, have a seat. You can feel free to sit down as well, Sensei."

After gesturing for them to sit on a simple sofa, Fujibayashi looked at Pixie thoughtfully but didn't say anything, instead heading into the vehicle's kitchen.

She must have not wanted to take up much of their time. She brought back out three glasses filled with black liquid on a tray. After setting the glasses on the table, she ignored Pixie, who was still standing, and sat down across from the two.

"You want me to explain from the beginning?"

Without urging them to drink, she suddenly spoke up to Tatsuya. Perhaps her casual word choice indicated her stance of speaking to him specifically.

"That would be fine, ma'am. But before we get into any details, I'd like to confirm a few things, if you don't mind."

Without showing any signs of caution, Tatsuya brought the glass to his lips. He'd just been thirsty.

"Sure."

Fujibayashi didn't feel surprise at how he drank the iced coffee without hesitation. She knew he could do component identification on physical matter far more accurately than she could, and besides, poison would *only affect him for a moment.*

"Firstly, I'd like to ask about why you never sent a follow-up leak with more detailed information after that first message, ma'am. Are you under surveillance?"

Starting with the thing I least wanted to be asked, thought Fujibayashi. But that wasn't a reason for her not to answer right now.

"Yes."

"Then secondly, did Major Kazama or possibly General Saeki want you to contact me, ma'am? Or was this something His Excellency Kudou intended?"

"…It was the major's orders. I'm not under watch by my grandfather."

If she wasn't under watch, did that mean she was completely unrelated to the Kudou family in this railroading experiment or that she was so trusted they had no need to?

"May I have a word as well, young lady?"

Before Tatsuya could ask, Yakumo interrupted. Tatsuya, at least, didn't think calling her "young lady" was appropriate. However, Fujibayashi nodded with an unoffended smile, not seeming to have been bothered.

"Please go ahead."

"What sort of position has the Fujibayashi family taken?"

However, she couldn't maintain her poker face at his actual question. She frowned—not because she wished he hadn't asked but because she, too, was concerned about the Fujibayashi's position.

"A neutral one."

"Does that mean you'd rather be in opposition, but you can't publicly go against what the Kudou family does?"

"…"

"The current Fujibayashi head's wife is the current Kudou patriarch's younger sister. With regards to the magicians of Nine and the Traditionalists opposing one another, that relation has led the Fujibayashi to stand on the side of the Nine magicians, despite being of the ancient variety. Were you to part from the Kudou now, the Fujibayashi would be left isolated in Japan's magic world… Is that right?"

Expression had vanished from Fujibayashi's face, probably to prevent him from reading too deep. But her smile was gone, too—and one could only say those efforts had failed.

"But that's not what I want you to tell me. What does the Fujibayashi family think of their use of immortalists from the mainland?"

A sharp light shone from Yakumo's eyes, which were always detached, never displaying any emotion, be it happiness, anger, sadness, or enjoyment.

"I can answer that question—we do not regard it favorably. My father has repeatedly urged Uncle Makoto to reconsider inviting the defecting immortalists into old Lab Nine."

This time, even while she winced under the glow in his eyes, she gave a clear answer. Certainly, the marriage had been why the Fujibayashi treated the Kudou as allies. But the reason they'd chosen a path of opposition against the Traditionalists rather than mediate between them and the Numbers of Nine was because they saw danger in welcoming foreign magicians in too deeply.

"The technology the defectors had was certainly useful. By using the spell they provided, the Parasidolls' psionic consumption had been reduced down to thirty percent at most. But both my father and I still believe the invitation was a mistake."

"Master, I apologize, but let's go in order."

With Tatsuya's short remark, the tension strung between Yakumo and Fujibayashi dissipated. Yakumo's face returned to its normal impassive thin smile.

"Lieutenant Fujibayashi." In exchange, Tatsuya gave her a

constructed, insidious smile, forcing Fujibayashi to experience a different sort of tension.

"I've had to put up with a lot of annoyance and irritation during this incident, ma'am. I knew the gist of it—magical weapon testing was being planned against magic high school students during the competition—but I hadn't the faintest idea what on earth was going on behind the scenes. And to be honest, I still don't. My informant was being quite stingy with information, after all."

"Umm... Tatsuya, that's..."

Fujibayashi's face appeared to draw back ever so slightly.

Calmed by the sight, Tatsuya got rid of his sadistic grin.

"Still, it's not very difficult if you just ignore whatever the puppet masters backstage want."

Miyuki had been the one to make him realize that, but it didn't have anything to do with this, so he didn't note it.

"First, the anti-GAA hard-liners in the JGDF changed the competition events to be more warlike."

Nobody argued with this.

"Next, taking advantage of that, the Kudou family planned to do performance testing on their Parasidolls."

"Though my grandfather was the one who suggested it—my uncle apparently opposed it at first."

"Then was it His Excellency Kudou who decided to use the defecting immortalists, ma'am?"

"...No, that was something my uncle did."

"I see. Let's call the person currying favor with the current Kudou family head and manipulating the defecting immortalists 'X.' X wanted to make the Parasidolls go out of control and fatally wound the competitors. Perhaps they hadn't considered going so far as killing them, but they wanted to deal enough damage to affect their lives as magicians. X's ultimate goal would then be to prematurely end the *supply* of magicians possibly linked to this nation's combat power in the future and, by doing so, create a great obstacle to Japan's national power."

"Yes, we believe so as well. That's why I'm here."

"...To do what, ma'am?"

Fujibayashi didn't look away from Tatsuya's gaze, filled with distrust and suspicion.

"Tatsuya, we hereby request your help in stopping the Parasidolls from going berserk."

Rather than standing and saluting, she remained on the sofa, placing her hands together in her lap and bowing deeply—calling him Tatsuya, not Specialist.

"My help, ma'am?"

"Yes. It isn't an order. What we're asking of you isn't something we can order you to do as a mission. It's a request for help."

After looking up, Fujibayashi stood up from the sofa. Tatsuya followed suit, gathering it to be a wordless command to come with her. She moved to what, depending on your perspective, looked like a coffin, large enough to fit a mature man inside. With Tatsuya watching from the side, she opened its lid.

The hinges must have been spring-loaded, because just a little lift of the "coffin" lid caused it to automatically rise after that. Inside was something ultramarine, something that looked like thick coveralls—a MOVAL suit.

"While unofficial, the Kudou of the Ten Master Clans will be doing the Parasidoll performance testing at the JDF's charge. If we interfere with that, it would equate to internal strife in the JDF, a personal battle between the military and the Ten Master Clans."

"Are you asking me to be an illegal saboteur, ma'am?"

Tatsuya's voice was hard and cold. They were essentially saying that even if his identity was revealed, they wouldn't cover for him, and one could say it was much more serious than that.

"I doubt there's anything I can say that will dissuade you from interpreting it like that."

Tatsuya's glare grew even more severe, but Fujibayashi dauntlessly met his eyes. She may have been feigning confidence, but she didn't seem to be rattled one bit.

"...All right, then."

At the end of their short staredown, Tatsuya was the one who broke first. He'd already been planning to *deal with* the Parasidolls on his own. Frankly, he was grateful he'd be able to use one of the new MOVAL suits with better stealth capabilities.

"Thanks. You can use this vehicle as you see fit. Here's the key."

Tatsuya took the wireless controller from Fujibayashi.

"Press the button here when you're done with it. It'll self-destruct after five minutes but *only on the inside*."

Fujibayashi pointed to one part of the wall, which consisted of what indeed looked like that mechanism—a square box in yellow and black stripes, with a red button prominently sticking out in the middle.

"What about the MOVAL suit, ma'am? I doubt you'd want it to go up in flames when the vehicle self-destructs."

"If you put it back in its box, it'll block the flames entirely. We've tested it."

"Understood, ma'am."

Tatsuya nodded to her, casting a subdued look at the self-destruct button and said, as if to himself, "I'll go along with this because we happen to have a common interest, but I'll ask you to repay this debt one day, ma'am."

Her face going blue at Tatsuya's comment, Fujibayashi said good-bye as though she was running away. She shoved the vehicle and the MOVAL suit alike onto Tatsuya and headed for the hotel. Yakumo was with her, having randomly said, "Just figured." When the big boxy object had fully blended in with the dark, Yakumo spoke to her.

"Young lady, was that really an order from Kazama?"

"...What do you mean by that? Also, would you mind not calling me *young lady?*" responded Fujibayashi, face hard, without looking at him.

"Oh, excuse me. Here's what I'm thinking, Miss Fujibayashi. Maybe you *didn't* need to make Tatsuya do something like that. Just so you don't misunderstand me, I'm referring to how, perhaps, the Parasidolls *won't* go berserk."

"Are you saying I'm lying?"

"Well, it *is* part of your job…" said Yakumo, feigning ignorance, in a way that could be taken as either criticizing or comforting. "All weapons have safeties on them. Retsu Kudou doesn't seem like one who would ever neglect that… By the way, Miss Fujibayashi, here's something you might not know. There exists a technique in esoteric Buddhism, as well, for employing dolls as puppets. Although they are merely imitation doctrine-children used as a replacement by acolytes who can't summon a true doctrine-child for lack of virtue."

"No… I didn't know that, but I can imagine so."

Fujibayashi answered carefully to the sudden change in topic. Though she shot him a sidelong gaze, she couldn't read Yakumo's expression at all. And she knew the dark wasn't the only reason.

"I recently paid a visit to the head temple for the first time in a while. I asked an expert, one versed in the ways, about this. He told me he'd already gotten to the point where he could call down true doctrine-children and that he didn't use imitations anymore."

Yakumo let out a reminiscent smile there, as though there had been trouble.

"But apparently, no caster forgets to define a target to defend and a target to attack. And when the puppet breaks that definition, they punish it. He said they prevent the being moving the puppet from doing anything else bad—and that that sealing technique was included in one big controlling spell."

Yakumo turned around. Empty eyes and a mouth split like a crescent moon. His face was the vision of a doll possessed by a demon, and Fujibayashi nearly cried out—no, she *tried* to shriek and couldn't.

At some point, she had fallen into Yakumo's spell.

"The Parasidolls have a similar spell on them, don't they? One to prevent them from attacking noncombatants, for example. They'd be useless as self-operating weapons otherwise."

"…That's correct."

Fujibayashi hadn't lost her consciousness or her will.

"Even if the immortalists tried to make the Parasidolls attack high school students, the original spell wouldn't allow it. As soon as they tried to go berserk, the control spell would switch to a sealing spell that would stop the parasites."

"That is what I've heard."

But she couldn't hide. She couldn't lie.

"To cause the Parasidolls to go berserk, one would need to undo the spell binding the parasites to their mechanical dolls, then bind the now-free parasite in the mechanical doll once again. While the parasites are bound to their mechanical dolls, they will have no effect."

"I don't know."

"I see… Has testing not made it that far yet?"

Yakumo looked away from Fujibayashi.

She dropped to her knees, exhausted.

He then spoke to the darkness.

"You heard her, Kazama. Did you know that?"

The darkness formed the shape of a man. Kazama appeared under one of the faint streetlights leading from the parking lot to the hotel.

"Know what?"

"That Tatsuya didn't have to cross such a dangerous bridge."

"No, I did not."

Fujibayashi looked up at Kazama's face in shock, perhaps unaware she'd been under direct observation. Without sparing a glance for her, Kazama answered his master's question with—what looked like—a pensive expression.

"You hadn't asked this young lady here?"

"No."

Kazama was an ancient magician himself. He would have known one or two things about puppeteering techniques, at least. He would have *had* to have known about the safeties built into the spells. And if he purposely hadn't asked about that, then…

"Hmm… It looks like you had a reason you wanted Tatsuya to go crazy on them, didn't you?"

"Haven't you kept it quiet from him, too, Master?"

By returning the question with a question, Kazama indirectly affirmed Yakumo's response.

"Not to defend myself, but the commander has no knowledge of this. She is well versed in magic usage but only in modern magic—she's essentially an amateur when it comes to ancient magic."

"Yes, and I'd *thought* that's why she had you as her aide…"

"Why didn't you stop Tatsuya, Master?"

It seemed Kazama planned on not answering things that weren't convenient for him.

"Because it wouldn't have been good to do that."

Yakumo didn't mind that, either. From the start, he hadn't intended to blame Kazama for anything.

"Miss Fujibayashi, returning to our previous conversation."

If Yakumo had felt there would be no danger, he would have said that to Tatsuya.

"That's the general theory. In this very specific case, it's possible things won't go that well."

Yakumo, who had sworn not to meddle in earthly matters, had involved himself in this incident until the end because its effects could possibly reach beyond that.

"…What do you mean?"

"Retsu Kudou probably adheres to the same preconceptions. It isn't just him—perhaps *all* the elderly at old Lab Nine are content with that same 'common' sense."

Yakumo himself was getting to an age where others might start calling him elderly, but he was using the term to refer to the old generation of Nines.

"I'm sure you've gotten detailed reports from Tatsuya regarding the parasites' properties, hmm?"

Kazama and Fujibayashi silently nodded at the question.

"The parasites were attracted here from a dimension not of this world by strongly pure ideas, and they came by passing through a small hole torn in the dimensional fabric. They fused with people who possessed strongly pure ideas and are energized by those strongly pure ideas."

Yakumo repeated the phrase *strongly pure ideas* several times. Fujibayashi was the quicker to realize what it meant.

"Wait... Sensei, you're not saying—?!"

"Strongly pure ideas. And here at the Nine School Competition, with the championship riding on tomorrow's final schedule... Is there any place less brimming with them?"

"Are you saying the spell binding the parasites will malfunction...?" managed Kazama with a groan.

"They may go berserk. They may not. I don't think we can say for sure that they will not, at least."

Yakumo's answer was an awfully irresponsible, incredibly earnest one.

"And the Parasidolls that go berserk will ultimately be destroyed, and the parasites, released from their mechanical bodies, may be drawn to the boys and girls and their strongly pure ideas."

Neither Kazama nor Fujibayashi could argue with the worst-case scenario Yakumo offered. Even if Retsu Kudou had been here, he might have simply gone pale and been unable to object.

"So I think, as a result, giving Tatsuya that combat uniform was the right move. And your judgment, Kazama—that if Tatsuya personally crushes the Parasidolls, it would make the military abandon the foolish use of demons for its own purposes—will probably also go well. Therefore, I will keep this incident to myself for you. In exchange, I'd like you to tell me something."

Yakumo turned to Kazama and demanded he provide information in exchange for not telling Saeki of this cover-up.

"What is it?"

"Who sent the mainland immortalists to the Kudou family?"

Even if Kazama had wanted to answer, he didn't know. The one who did answer was Fujibayashi.

"...A young man named Gongjin Zhou from Yokohama Chinatown."

"Gongjin Zhou from Yokohama Chinatown. I see. I've been hearing that name an awful lot lately."

"You know who he is, Master?" Kazama asked.

Yakumo didn't answer the question. "Anyway, I've asked what I wanted to know, so I'll be on my way. Like I promised, I'll keep this information hiding and the rest of this dodgy business to myself."

Yakumo took a step off the lighted path. And just like that, he was gone.

After Yakumo had left, Fujibayashi finally stood up.

"Commander, I—"

"We're going, Lieutenant. We don't want Tatsuya to see us here."

Cutting off Fujibayashi as she was about to say something, Kazama began walking toward the hotel.

Perhaps fearing criticism from Tatsuya right on the heels of Yakumo, Fujibayashi followed meekly behind her superior officer to what would surely be a punishment.

"Lieutenant."

With his back to her, without checking to see if she was there, he spoke to her.

"Yes, Commander?"

"It seems His Excellency Kudou has fooled you as well."

"What?" Fujibayashi almost tripped while walking.

"There was a possibility the Parasidolls would go out of control. But he told you there was no such possibility. Is that right?"

"Uh, yes, sir."

Though even she couldn't figure out what Kazama was getting at right away, now that he'd said all that, she had a guess.

"You tried to confirm the veracity of that information on your own. Not reporting it immediately was a blunder, but in the end, you brought no false information. As a result, you prevented mistaken orders from being delivered."

Kazama was telling her he'd overlook the fact that she'd been on the Kudou family's side.

"Lieutenant—good work."

"No, I— Thank you, sir."

As Kazama continued to walk without stopping, Fujibayashi paused and bowed to him deeply.

[7]

August 15, day eleven of the Nine School Competition. Tatsuya woke up at the same time he had for the past ten days, ate his breakfast in the First High tent the same, and went through the final checks of the competitors he was assigned to in the same way.

Today's schedule consisted of the women's Cross-Country Steeplechase starting at nine thirty AM and the men's at two PM. Entries into the event had been cut off yesterday at five PM. Some had predicted the schools with lower rankings as of yesterday might not enter, but the result was that every junior and senior eligible to participate had entered, both male and female, and from every school.

Tatsuya was assigned to all the second-year girls as well as Mikihiko for a total of six people. Six may have sounded awful, but excluding the freshman engineers, they had six people to check twenty-four CADs. His assignments were simply concentrated in the morning, and if you averaged it, he didn't have especially many to handle.

He had begun his work at seven thirty and finished tuning everything at nine, and not every minute of that was work. Still, anyone looking in from outside would have seen it as a very difficult workload. Hattori and Isori had asked him, "You okay?" several times, too. So after he'd finished his work and he said he would be taking a break in his room without watching the start of the event, nobody was suspicious of him.

They wouldn't be able to watch anything that happened during the Steeplechase event. Each player was required to have a transmitting device that would check if they left the course, which also made it possible to know where they were all currently running. But even if they'd launched small cameras with flight magic, the trees would block the view, meaning any filming or photography from above was nearly impossible. They could only take pictures of players who got near cameras they'd preinstalled.

The circumstances being what they were, many had decided to watch the races on the local cable television broadcast from inside the venue. Insensitivity was in the minority when it came to the players and staff, of course, so in Tatsuya's case, they'd seen him off with sympathy in their eyes.

Nine twenty AM. Player and visitor eyes alike had focused on the starting line. Twelve female runners per school, totaling 108, were all lined up there. The outdoor women's gear they wore comprised loose vests, sturdy boots, gloves, hats that doubled as simple helmets, goggles to protect their eyes, pads to protect their joints, and all sorts of other unnecessary items, but underneath it all was a one-piece coverall that adhered closely to their bodies. With this many people, it had its own unique beauty.

Without anyone watching him, Tatsuya slipped out of the hotel and walked toward the parking lot. Not to the one released for Nine School Competition use but to the military area.

On the way, he met up with Pixie. She was wearing her usual dress. It had long, loose sleeves and a tight collar, and it wasn't tight at the waist, either, as her skirt went down to her ankles in a style of zero exposure. But fortunately, such clothing was not unusual in midsummer in this day and age.

Tatsuya had summoned her because he'd need her for locating

the Parasidolls. But one more person stood next to her—a girl he hadn't called.

"Minami, what are you doing here?"

Bowing to Tatsuya's voice, Minami answered, "Lady Miyuki ordered me."

"She did?"

Minami had called her not *Big Sister* Miyuki but *Lady* Miyuki. It wasn't a slip of the tongue—her remark clearly had intent behind it. In other words, she was acting not as his underclassman from First High, nor as his false younger cousin, but as a servant of the Yotsuba. Tatsuya understood Minami's intent immediately.

"She said that she could not provide support during the event, but that I should help you in her place."

Minami's expression was sharper than usual. It wasn't the slightly bewildered look she always had, the youthful one befitting a young girl, but the look of a mature magician. Whether or not that was what she desired, this was who she fundamentally was.

Tatsuya immediately discarded the idea of chasing her away. She hoped that her strength would be useful, and in fact, it *would* be. It would be more arrogant to bring her age of fifteen into the equation; after all, Tatsuya himself was still only a boy of seventeen.

"All right. Come with me."

"Right away."

It seemed as though he'd never even remotely considered sending her away.

After changing into the MOVAL suit in the vehicle Fujibayashi had brought with her—Minami had her back turned during the process—he asked Pixie where the Parasidolls were positioned.

"Here."

At the same time as Pixie's thoughts were conveyed to him, sixteen lit-up dots were projected before Tatsuya's eyes along with a map.

Pixie had forwarded the data through the work vehicle's communicator and into the visor monitor fitted into the suit's helmet. He'd already synced Pixie with the work vehicle last night.

The number of lights was the same as Tatsuya had spotted in Nara and Pixie had sensed the other day. That meant she had full understanding of where the Parasidolls were. And currently, they had taken up position in the middle of the course, starting slightly toward the goal line and extending to it. At minimum—or at *worst*—the front-runner, Miyuki (or so Tatsuya assumed) would contact them in about ten minutes.

Then I need to take down the Parasidolls in the front within eight minutes, then clean the rest up within twenty.

Calculating how much of a grace period he had, he turned back to Minami.

"Minami, you stay here and prepare yourself against attackers."

"All right."

At Tatsuya's order, Minami nodded without complaint. Of course, her eyes told him she wasn't happy with it. She'd probably felt that Tatsuya was trying to distance her from the violence. And that was a dangerous misunderstanding.

"Minami, Pixie has a crucial role—she needs to pinpoint the Parasidolls' locations."

"Yes," came the straightforward reply, albeit slightly confused.

"But her searches aren't one-way."

Minami's eyes widened.

"The Parasidolls can detect Pixie here as well. And just like how Pixie knows the dolls can perceive her, those using the dolls will know that I've pinpointed the dolls' positions."

Peering into Minami's eyes, he urged caution, trying to engrave it directly into her mind.

"It's highly likely this vehicle will come under attack."

"I understand." She nodded, her face nervous.

* * *

Nine twenty-nine AM. Descriptive features hidden in the MOVAL suit, Tatsuya left the work vehicle, sending out a signal that would identify him as a member of a—real—unit belonging to the Mount Fuji NCO school, then headed for the training woods where the event was taking place.

Nine thirty AM. At the starting line, atop one of the two-meter-tall scaffoldings erected every hundred meters, a .41 pistol fired a single shot, declaring the beginning of the first Cross-Country Steeplechase.

With most of the throng of runners taking care in their steps as they advanced, the Eighth High group charged straight into the trees. As students from a school that so emphasized outdoors training, they probably felt proud that forests were their home field.

Not wanting to lag behind, a senior from the Third High group jumped out. She was probably impatient to turn the tides against First. Visibly heated up, the female student took off—and fell for the trap.

Tatsuya, having cut off his identification signal, increased his suit's stealth capabilities to their maximum and snuck into the outer area of the training woods, springing toward the Steeplechase course when the pistol sounded.

The Parasidolls were scattered over the second half of the four-kilometer-long course. When he saw this distribution, he felt as though he was being lured in. As though someone were telling him to take down the dolls before the runners got to them—if he could. It seemed to him he was dancing in the palm of someone else's hand.

Cheeky of them to play god like this, but it'll actually make things easier for me.

Even if this guess was correct, he planned to go along with their expectations on purpose. It didn't matter what the wire-puller had in mind. If he neutralized the Parasidolls and reduced the possibility of harm coming to Miyuki to zero, he would fulfill his objective.

Using flight magic at the same time, Tatsuya kept himself low as he dashed toward the nearest doll.

A moment after the race started, sudden laughter went up among the spectators watching on a giant display.

Broadly speaking, the Cross-Country Steeplechase had three rules. One, you couldn't interfere with other players. You'd be disqualified if they spotted intentional interference, but because of the aforementioned poor view, chances they would catch you in the act were slim. If you got caught, you were just unlucky. Thus, this rule was less of a penal regulation and more of a gentleman's agreement.

Two, you couldn't leave the four-kilometer-square course. Each runner had a transmitter working in tandem with the Mount Fuji training grounds' own positioning system; competition HQ could tell where each runner was at all times. Additionally, it was set up so that the runners could tell where they were in the course as well. Along with complying with the entrants' requests and displaying a map and the runner's current position on their goggles, their helmet was fitted to give the runner an alarm when they were about to exit the course.

And three—you couldn't jump higher than the trees. It wouldn't be an obstacle course if you flew above the canopy. It would be like answering the question *What's the fastest way to get through this maze?* with *Can't you just go over the walls?*

The positioning system worked in three dimensions, and the runners could see how far up they'd jumped. But the only way to know if a runner was above the surrounding trees was to check with a long-distance surveillance camera. And so they'd gone with something simpler.

More specifically, they'd strung nets overhead in certain places to serve as obstacles. Which meant that if you accidentally jumped too high, you'd get tangled in the net before breaking out of the trees—exactly what the screen had just shown.

The Third High runner had gotten caught in it. She was the student who'd placed third in Mirage Bat. It was extremely unfortunate for her, having been superimposed like that on the screen, but it was a hit with the crowd. She looked like a butterfly caught in a spider's web, and part of the reason it was a hit was probably that the scene was somehow titillating.

The video wasn't only on venue displays; it was being relayed through cable as well. National broadcast wouldn't have met the JDF's censorship policy, so the cable was local, limited to only the base—but on the other hand, you could get a signal from anywhere on the base, not just at the venue. The video was playing in a high-ranking officers' conference room, too, in a building separate from HQ, on the other side of the training woods from the hotel.

"Unidentified magician infiltration confirmed."

"Can you get it on-screen?"

"Not in real time, sir. We don't have enough cameras."

"A recording is fine. Show me."

"Yes, sir."

The soldiers' attention, however, was not on the female high school student's indecorous state but on someone else.

A different spot in the same training forest came up next to the cable relay broadcast.

It was a short video of a figure in deep blue cutting through the dim forest's trees.

"Can't you make it brighter?"

"Yes, sir, one moment."

After changing the brightness on the video data, he replayed it from the start. Though the outline blurred, the brightened image of the figure was very similar to the flight combat uniforms they had but slightly different.

"That's one of the new MOVAL suits Saeki's been developing."

"Then that intel was correct?"

The Kudou family had been the ones to bring the plan for robotic weapons that used magic.

And the testing of these magical weapons using the Nine School Competition's current event was not a project officially permitted by the JDF but an unofficial, secretive experiment. Interrupting the experiment would never earn even a light official reprimand from General HQ.

It was all too plausible that General Saeki, who was at odds with the Kudou family—with Retsu Kudou in particular—would covertly bring in saboteurs to wreck the experiment; few in this group doubted that information. Still, given the actual sight of someone deciding to outwardly fight with others in the Japanese military and the sense of values therein, they couldn't help but be surprised.

They had no selfish motives. If distinction had been their goal, every one of them could have played things more skillfully.

They were espousing hard-liner philosophies in the knowledge that it would hurt them—harm their chances at promotion—because they simply loved their country. They believed that winning a decisive victory over the GAA would bring about peace for Japan. For that purpose, they needed to persuade those who opposed opening hostilities. If they couldn't persuade them, they were prepared to silence them.

But they needed to realize that process through purely peaceful means. The JDF was supposed to protect Japan's national interests. JDF soldiers bringing war against one another was putting the cart before the horse, injuring national interests, and was ultimately an act of betrayal. No matter how ill-fated the times they lived through, they had decided never to resort to force. They were anti-GAA hard-liners—not hard-liners against their own compatriots. That was their source of pride.

From their point of view, General Saeki's way of doing things, having easily decided to deploy the troop power known as magic in order to defeat this opposing faction, was unbelievable. Certainly, this came with danger. Even in their group, some had said they should avoid the women's event and only run the tests during the men's event.

But they considered the stance of trying to crush the test itself through brute force, even if no human casualties resulted from it, to be intolerable—and vice versa.

"Contact Kudou's engineers. I don't mind if we counterattack but do not kill the saboteur."

"Yes, sir. I'll give instructions not to fatally wound the saboteur."

The hard-liners' leader, Colonel Sakai, was concerned for the life of the magician being used as a pawn. And so even though they were in opposing positions, he ordered care, so they would not lose someone valuable to protecting their national interests.

The current Kudou family head, Makoto Kudou, scowled at the message from the testing site.

"Don't kill the saboteur, he says…"

He had no objection to not killing the magician per se. But if it came to it, would they themselves not throw a magician into the jaws of death only because of what they were? That was why the researchers were developing the Parasidolls. And a magician was trying to stop them from doing that. Makoto couldn't suppress the fury he felt.

"Change the dolls' attack target to the infiltrator. Coordinate and restrain him. I will allow any attacks as long as they don't kill him."

Makoto sent his anger through to the head developer on the other end of his line and, ultimately, to the magician who was trying to get in their way.

"Lord Makoto seems quite upset."

The main developer, after enduring a barrage of angry shouts, turned to his aide, looking like he couldn't care less.

"But he's right—it is an issue."

The screen showed a magician clad in an ultramarine flight combat uniform weaving dangerously between the closely clustered trees, heading straight for a Parasidoll. He seemed to have a way of accurately locating them.

"Set their attack target to the infiltrator. Make capture its ultimate priority. Also—there was a specimen that found our dolls, right? Surely, that's a collaborator of his. Get some people over there to secure it, too."

After ordering the Parasidolls to capture Tatsuya, he commanded the private Kudou soldiers he'd been entrusted with to steal Pixie.

Jumping out from behind the trees and in front of the Parasidoll, Tatsuya stabilized his footing and pointed his CAD at the machine. But an instant later, faster than he could fire his spell, his whole body was hit by an intense impact that sent him flying backward.

This thing is fast!

Careening and falling—a brief, unintended aerial swim. As his mind accelerated and time stretched out, Tatsuya analyzed the reason he'd been hit first.

In that exchange, the Parasidoll's reaction speed was clearly higher than his. No human could follow the speed at which it had visually perceived its opponent and then went into action. It wasn't just that its information processing was fast because it had an electronic brain—it was so fast he could only assume it was a specialized kind made for combat.

At a glance, it had a slender body that seemed a far cry from physically strong. But now he knew that body, clad in a women's outdoor combat uniform in forest camo, contained hidden power and speed that betrayed the eyes.

It wasn't wearing a helmet or a hat, either—because its short hair acted as airflow and water-flow sensors. The reason it wasn't wearing any goggles or protective glasses, either, was because its eyes themselves acted as protective cases over its optical sensors. Its skin was bulletproof synthetic rubber. Its joints were driven directly by spherical servomotors. Having a mask of beautiful features, even more inorganic than Pixie, this gynoid...

It's an F-type mechanical soldier. They are still developing these?

A humanoid robot designed as a combat machine to replace infantry. They were professed to be able to use the same equipment as infantry, and that research had advanced with the goal of having them serve security missions in highly dangerous regions and the like, but Tatsuya had heard they eventually concluded that dropping the sticking point of it being shaped like a person and deploying automatic, self-driving gun emplacements in a nonhumanoid form instead would be more cost-effective, and so development had stopped.

Information-processing capabilities specialized for combat, belonging to a gynoid created for military use. But that couldn't have been the only reason he'd lagged behind how fast it had finished triggering its spell.

The sensation had been on his entire body, not having any specific point of application, and the pressure had been distributed equally, coming from in front of him. It was something he was quite familiar with, having taken acceleration-type spell attacks before. And this speed and the roughness of the information bodies' composition—

A singular acceleration type—no, it's PK!

Tatsuya recovered his stance in midair, preparing for the impact.

His back slammed into the trunk of a Mongolian oak. The impact was lighter than he'd thought, probably thanks to his suit's shock absorption feature. A blunt hit like this wouldn't require Self-Regenerate.

He slid down the tree trunk to the ground, immediately assuming a combat posture. Obeying his gut instinct, he kicked off the ground. There was no time to use magic, no time to flash cast, either—he simply boosted his physical body with psions and jumped to the side with the dash power it gave him.

His decision was rewarded with a successful evasion. A hollow depression had opened up where he'd just been, as though a massive hammer had hit it.

And that's weighting magic. Primitive magic programs—it must be psychokinesis.

One of the parasites he'd fought in winter had had the same tendency. A specimen that used not magic but psychic powers. The powers magicians had abandoned for magic. Overwhelming speed at the cost of versatility, precision, and stability. And Tatsuya could feel that this enemy had taken that even further.

Are the parasite dolls using psychic powers as weapons?!

Perhaps that was a unique trait of this individual. But he couldn't allow himself to be optimistic.

Manipulating his familiar Trident's selector switch, he set it to a Program Dispersion loop cast. It was a dismantling spell that destroyed a magic program's structure and restored it to homogenous psionic noise. Psionic information bodies, their characteristics different from normal activation sequences that assisted in casting, were read into Tatsuya's specialized magic calculation region.

Psionic light fired from the Parasidoll. Tatsuya's eyes didn't perceive the light itself but the structure given form by the light—the magic program.

Information bodies, fired at his legs, having the meaning of "twisting and turning."

Before that meaning could become a phenomenon, Tatsuya's Program Dispersion dismantled the information bodies themselves.

He felt a sense of surprise from the things residing in the doll. Its reaction was strangely slow, as if the doll wasn't the only thing disturbed but its controller as well. Not only did it not follow up on its attack, it didn't even emit the defensive force field it had hit Tatsuya with at the beginning.

He realized this at the same time as he closed in on the mechanical doll. His body moving at the speed of thought, he rammed the heel of his palm into the Parasidoll's chest.

Oscillatory waves of the psions themselves, infiltrating it from his palm. They temporarily loosened the psionic defenses wrapped around the Parasidoll's body, exposing the spell linking the parasite with the gynoid.

Duplication complete.

Tatsuya cleverly used his regeneration spell to copy it.

After gathering itself, the Parasidoll punched at him with the arm strength of a combat robot surpassing normal humans, but having already fulfilled his goal of duplication, Tatsuya sidestepped away from it.

In terms of pure physical ability, the mechanical dolls had humans beat, but humans had hours and hours of skills training.

Surpassing the mechanical with martial arts, twisting down a demon's power with the will of man…

He pulled his left hand next to his waist and clenched his fist, imagining the ultrasmall sphere inside it compressing down even more.

He opened his fist, without closing the distance, then flung his palm toward the Parasidoll from outside his arm's reach, as if to ram the compressed sphere into it.

He fired the anti-parasite psionic bullet into the mechanical doll's electronic brain.

Its psionic defenses torn away, the parasite's pushion information bodies were exposed.

He'd blasted away the spell linking the parasite with the gynoid as well, and the parasite was about to be released.

In human bodies, the psions would never be concentrated in the heart area. And if one lost all their psions, life functions would cease, making it impossible for them to be a parasite host. But the gynoid was a mechanical doll. Its functions would remain unchanged even if it lost its psions, and if a new supply of psions could be had, it could still be a host body for the parasite.

*　*　*

Tatsuya used his regeneration spell.

A spell that duplicated *past* information bodies and used those copied information bodies to overwrite the *present* eidos.

It certainly wasn't limited to information bodies in the sense of physical matter. The spell could copy and overwrite everything, as long as it was psions.

Tatsuya poured a tiny amount of psions into the gynoid; then, with the copied loyalty spell, he relinked the parasite with the gynoid. The magic program's code had been copied wholesale, so the target of loyalty would have still been the Kudou family, but that wouldn't change how the fused parasite wouldn't be able to do anything until it received enough psions.

Tatsuya's prediction turned out to be correct.

The parasite, given the bare minimum necessary psions, didn't turn into a clump of psions and pushions and fly away; instead, it entered a sleep state inside the gynoid.

All the Kudou's personal soldiers chosen to attack the work vehicle Minami and Pixie were inside were users of modern magic that could deliver blunt physical blows rivaling portable infantry missiles.

Old Lab Nine's goal was to develop modern magic that integrated elements of ancient magic. But aside from the three families crowned with the number nine, no old Lab Nine–born magicians possessed within them the casting techniques said to be ancient magic's unique feature. Just as the Traditionalists feared and hated, all those traditional factors had been melted down and absorbed into new spells.

Though they were related to old Lab Nine, they hadn't been

able to gain the number nine. Their abilities were no different from regular modern magicians. But neither were they inferior in any way. Their magic would have been more than enough to take over a single middle-sized vehicle and kidnap the passengers on board.

However, speaking from the result, none of them were able to even touch the work vehicle Pixie was in.

It happened a moment after they showed intent to attack. As though someone had read the signs of their heightened psionic activity that came before magic usage, a powerful magic barrier had covered the vehicle.

Actually, reading pre-magic-activation signs, too, was an advanced trick impossible for anyone but the most veteran. More surprising than that, however, was the strength and precision of the magical barrier deployed along the vehicle's body.

Simply touching the wall didn't cause any pain or shock or injury. It would only repel any force against it.

They tried to apply event alteration to the vehicle, but the barrier spell's influence bounced it back.

They tried to heat all of it, including the barrier, and shake it and put pressure on it—but none of that made it budge.

Even when they tried using hardening magic and self-acceleration magic on themselves before ramming it, the barrier didn't even rock.

In the end, they tried using their guns, knowing it would draw the attention of security forces, but this had no effect, either.

As expected, even with suppressors, they couldn't hide the fact that they'd used guns. The private soldiers got away in the nick of time from the security troops who immediately came running.

The magical barrier that had driven off the personal Kudou soldiers was, needless to say, Minami's.

The Sakura series of boosted, engineered magicians focused on anti-physical barriers. As one of its second generation, she had inherited the first generation's high performance and could now utilize it even more stably than they could.

Minami had gone through combat training at the Yotsuba main residence; for her, detecting the signs of attack-magic activation was a natural skill. After all, the baseline for magicians in service of the Yotsuba was that they naturally hid any signs of casting magic.

And Minami's magical barrier capabilities rivaled or possibly even outclassed those of direct Ten Master Clans descent. She couldn't master the advanced, technical barrier spells of the Juumonji family such as Phalanx, but when it came to singular barriers, she wouldn't even be second to Katsuto's.

This rampart wouldn't break even under tank-gun impacts and missile heat—no small-arms fire from pistols or submachine guns would ever break it.

Tatsuya carefully directed his "eyes" at the fallen mechanical doll and confirmed that it was in complete sleep mode.

This trick was something he'd thought of last night. Listening in on the conversation among Yakumo, Kazama, and Fujibayashi gave him the idea of using Kudou's spell.

His information body perception ability worked on voices as well. Words were engraved on the Idea as information bodies.

Yakumo may have meant for him to hear it all to begin with, but even if not—even if he *had* really been eavesdropping—Tatsuya didn't care at all. His personality wasn't *cute* enough to feel guilt over something that small.

The spell to create the puppet would include the technique to bind it.

In other words, didn't that mean the technique to create it and the one to bind it were fundamentally the same?

He knew, through Pixie, where in the mechanical body the

parasites resided. Whether it was for combat or housework, they needed the same basic structure of a female—or more broadly, a real human form.

Motors in the four limbs, waist, and neck; sensors in the head; fuel cells in each arm; and, if it was human, an electronic brain where the heart would be. The parasites resided in that electronic brain. Which meant the spell linking the parasite to the gynoid would exist there as well.

All of that was guesswork, and he had to try it for real to be sure. But it seemed he'd won his gamble.

"Pixie, where is the closest Parasidoll?"

"Two Parasidolls are inbound to your position from relative four and seven o'clock. Master, please be cautious."

He almost chuckled at the last part. He wasn't appalled—it had warmed him. Pixie had become quite humanlike herself, he felt…or rather, more like Honoka.

A parasite—an independent information body but also a person.

Perhaps they would prove to be the keys that unlocked the mysteries of the mind.

Five minutes after starting. The runners had split into school-separated groups.

The course was already vast, being four kilometers wide, and it was divided into small pieces by the thickly clustered trees. Even if 108 people were all running at equal intervals, they'd quickly lose sight of one another.

And this was a first-time event, a first-time field, and they hadn't learned what sort of obstacles would be here. They'd decided that runners dropping out midway through was a matter of course, and in the beginning, they'd adopted the tactic of supporting the others in their school, which made sense.

The current placements were almost entirely split along school lines. Every school had advanced in a groping manner until now. But having gotten almost a quarter of the way through the four-kilometer course already was due to speed that could only come from magic.

And each school, having gotten used to the course, was about to shift into a higher gear.

"Kanon, you're too far ahead!"

A complaint flew from Tomoko to Kanon, who had increased her pace. But Kanon didn't slow down.

"I have a good sense of the course now! I think the other schools do, too!"

Without turning around, Kanon shouted behind her. Implied in her words was the argument that if they didn't up the pace, they wouldn't win.

"The rest of you don't need to force it!"

Adding that, she pushed her speed even further. With a rapid succession of jumping spells, she avoided tree roots and landed in a spot mostly free of underbrush, then cast an incredibly small-scale Mine Origin. The ground in front of her sunk down, and a mass of sand poured down from the treetops toward the hole.

A pitfall and a torrent of sand. The trap would see any who fell in the hole buried alive. The edges of her lips tugging up proudly, she jumped past it.

When she landed, her right foot sank into mud.

"Gah! Why, you!"

Hastily, Kanon cast another jumping spell, one of which had just ended. Her left foot kicked off the air, and her right foot, buried in the mud, reappeared—with a white string wrapped around her ankle.

Her body completely left the ground.

White strings were drawn taut all over the place. They must have been fixed in place inside the mud.

The string pulled against her body, stopping her in midair.

Because her jumping spell's definition contents became inexecutable, it dissipated. As a result—

"*Wagyah?!*"

—she fell face-first into the pool of mud.

"Chiyoda?!"

Subaru, who had been leading the First High group that had just caught up because of the trap, let out a voice that was mildly amazed at what just happened rather than a shriek at the horrible tragedy.

Kanon slowly got up out of the mud. But she was still buried up to her chest.

She pulled her hands out of the mud. Her right hand was along her left wrist.

The bog exploded.

The mud sprayed several times more magnificently than when she'd fallen in it, emanating from Kanon's body.

Miyuki, sensing magic activation, immediately cast an anti-matter barrier spell. Because of the transparent shield she created, the ten girls avoided being splattered with the mud.

The explosion had come from an acceleration-type spell aptly named Explosion. The user was, needless to say, the one at ground zero—Kanon.

The ground—originally the mud pool—was bored out into the shape of a mortar, and there in the center of it, looking down, was Kanon, squeaky-clean. None of the mud or even the dirt had hit her. The surface of her body and clothes were probably the origin for Explosion, blowing away all the mud and earth and dirt stuck to her. The string wrapped around her ankle was nowhere to be found, either.

It was a dangerous way to use the spell—she could have torn off her body hair and given herself some pretty awful pain, or she could have tragically blown off what she was wearing. But like always, her control was skillful.

Pushing her cleaned goggles up with a hand, Kanon rubbed her eyes. Their goggles were all perfectly sealed, so there shouldn't have been any mud or dirt in her eyes. Still...any teenage girl would have been close to crying if they'd been forced to dive into the mud.

From behind, they could tell that she'd taken a deep breath.

And then.

"This is bullshit! How is this military training?!" she screamed hysterically, shooting out of the crater.

"...We should get going, too," said Subaru to Miyuki, who was standing next to her.

"...Yes."

The two of them, standing at the head of their rear group, resumed their race.

"That's not possible! Is this man even human?!" yelled the head Parasidoll developer in their mobile lab.

Another piece of his confidence put to sleep.

They'd hit him from either side with an oscillatory wave so fast even Ten Master Clans magicians couldn't have kept up. He'd given these two the demon-power of sound. They could both scatter someone's equilibrium with low-frequency waves or destroy their hearing with high-frequency waves. In fact, they had enough demon-power to replicate Phonon Maser, just by firing at full power without regard for operational duration, without an exclusive magic program, just by raising the wavelength.

His adorable dolls' attacks certainly had an effect. They had gone through the shock-absorption defenses of the brand-new combat uniform the military developed and dealt damage to the magician. Staggering and dropping to one knee couldn't possibly have been an act. And yet, this magician had counterattacked instantly after taking the damage.

His first attack was an untyped spell that ancient magic called a farstrike. The developer didn't know the logic behind why that by itself would have damaged the Parasidoll, but he could make a token guess as to what happened. But the next direct attack he made after closing the distance—

"What in blazes did he just do?! What on earth is going on?!"

A simple palm strike. He didn't understand what system could neutralize a Parasidoll with only that. The magician hadn't released the parasite, hadn't destroyed the body—just stopped it from working.

While the skill was uncanny, so too was the physical flesh that had continued to engage in combat as though it had never been hit by the Parasidolls' demon-power attacks.

"Is this guy an immortal...? Are you telling me he's an actual vampire?!"

The surprise in the mobile lab was shared by those in the high-ranking officers' conference room in a separate building from General HQ.

"This magician... What the hell is his body made of? This goes way beyond toughness or tolerance levels."

The surveillance camera's image had switched to one-on-four. Dents in the MOVAL suit were visible even through the wires, in its arms, legs, and back. The attack of a doll that freely launched iron balls directly hit the magician's body, and the ranged attack of a doll that fired out mercury pellets from eighteen spots total bored holes in the MOVAL suit armor.

But a moment later, this magician attacked the Parasidolls as though nothing had happened.

"Maheśvara..." murmured one of their group.

"What?" demanded Colonel Sakai.

"Do you know of the combat magician called Maheśvara by the enemy forces during the Defense of Okinawa four years ago and the Yokohama Incident last year?"

"...Yes, now that you mention it, I have. Someone who wiped out mobile weapons in one strike and would revive an instant after any attack as though nothing had happened… Wait, is it him?!"

"Looking at the situation, it's probable this Maheśvara is a magician with ties to Major Kazama."

"Major Harunobu Kazama, of the 101st Brigade's Independent Magic Battalion?"

A magician clad in a MOVAL suit developed by the 101st Brigade displaying such durability he seemed immortal. The signs all matched up.

"What is a monster like that doing at a high school competition, of all things…?!"

The Nine School Competition may have been an important event for magicians, but for the JDF, it was nothing more than a high school festival. Even if the experiment had casualties, it would only be four or five high schoolers getting injured. It didn't seem plausible for Saeki or Kazama to be worried about actual deaths.

He didn't understand General Saeki's true intentions, but Colonel Sakai had an uncanny premonition about this.

Minami was now in a predicament inside the vehicle with Pixie.

The assault, by the Kudou family's personal soldiers (which was something Minami didn't know), had been driven off by the appearance of security troops from the base. But this time, *those* troops had been trying to get in.

From security's standpoint, the demand was natural. Just like last year, another unidentified group had broken into the JDF base and even discharged firearms. The ones they needed to capture and apprehend were the group that had engaged in violence, but it was a perfectly reasonable response to want to hear what the people getting fired at had to say.

But Minami couldn't accept their demands. Actually, maybe it didn't matter, but she felt like it would be bad if unrelated soldiers were to see them in this vehicle.

"Like I said, we were the victims. I don't believe we have any reason to respond to questioning."

"This is a military base—we have police authority! If you've nothing to hide, then you'll be fine! Undo this barrier and open the door at once!"

They'd been repeating this exchange for some time (incidentally, her voice was being changed as it went through the speaker). At this rate, she could maintain the barrier for about another hour, and she had the completely thought-controlled CAD Tatsuya had given her, so she could instantly change the barrier's properties if they came under sudden magical attack.

But Minami personally didn't want to do anything so dramatic.

Lord Tatsuya, please return soon!

Minami was at a loss, unable to even imagine asking Tatsuya for orders—and getting in the way of his battle.

Fifteen minutes after starting. The runners were no longer sticking with other athletes from their schools to traverse the course; they'd adopted a style of forming first, second, and third groups to go for the goal.

First High's leading group was Kanon, Subaru, and Miyuki. Kanon was in the track-and-field club and ran the three-thousand-meter hurdles. Her magical strengths and weaknesses were secondary—she was used to running while overcoming obstacles. Subaru specialized in jumping magic. Miyuki was avoiding the obstacles by skillfully using flight magic to skim right above the ground.

Their current positions were slightly farther than two kilometers from the starting line; they'd just entered the second half of the course. As Subaru was jumping from tree to tree, kicking off trunks, she suddenly stopped moving and landed on the base of a certain Mongolian oak.

"Subaru, what's wrong?" asked Miyuki, who caught up to Subaru and stopped like she did. The race was still going, but they never knew what sort of obstacles lay in their path in this event. If she'd spotted something concerning, it would be a bad idea to ignore it. That was why they'd split into teams of two or three, never one.

"Look at that."

Looking in the direction Subaru pointed, Miyuki and Kanon frowned. Something in the shape of a human female was on the ground.

"...A combat gynoid."

Kanon announced its identity. She may not have looked like someone good with technology, but she was a daughter of the Chiyoda family, whose field of expertise was combat, even as one of the Hundred. She'd probably seen something similar in the past.

"But it looks like it's not functional."

Miyuki immediately realized it was a Parasidoll and one Tatsuya had taken down. But she didn't let any of that out, instead voicing the result of what she'd seen.

"Looks that way to me, too."

"Perhaps they forgot to retrieve it during previous training?"

That remark was Subaru's. It was a seemingly logical but impossible guess, but Kanon didn't know that.

"...Anyway, if it's not moving, we don't need to bother with it. Could be trying to get us to jump at shadows and slow down."

That was Kanon's decision. If she wanted to think that way, Miyuki didn't need to go out of her way to object.

"Then...?"

"We'll keep moving before we lose any more time."

Answering Miyuki's short question, Kanon began running. Subaru and Miyuki followed suit.

They're tougher than I thought… This is taking more time than I planned. Only about ten minutes left before Miyuki catches up in first place, thought Tatsuya to himself, surrounded by a group of Parasidolls.

Right now, he was quite a bit closer to the goal line than the spot where he'd encountered the first one. He'd silenced all the Parasidolls closer to the starting line. If he caused all sixteen to shut down, this incident would be *for him* resolved.

Psychic powers flew at him from every direction—the Kudou family called them "demon-powers." He advanced, covering only his vital spots—head and heart—then made contact with one of the dolls.

The high-speed type sliced his arm down almost to the bone, but Tatsuya used his other arm to slam the heel of his fist into the doll in front of him.

He went through the parasite sleep process in the blink of an eye.

Getting help from his fully thought-controlled CAD to call up his Program Dispersion assistance activation sequence from his Trident tucked in its holster, he disabled the spell going for his neck. He jumped over the fallen Parasidoll, momentarily escaping their encirclement, then used Regenerate to restore his arm. The spell would make any enemy cry out that he was cheating, but he wasn't all-powerful or invincible by any means.

Regenerate came with pain.

It prevented mental focus and led to an obstruction of magic casting. He was used to the pain, but he couldn't avoid losing a moment to it.

He'd never feel the pain if he was using a full backup for it, but in that case, his entire magic calculation region would be temporarily taken up by the spell, causing *more* than a moment's attack delay.

That was why he was protecting the organs related to life and death. As long as he still had psions, he wouldn't die, even from a fatal wound, but if he *took* a fatal wound, his survival instincts would automatically start using Regenerate with a full backup, and his magical abilities would cease. Against magicians at the very top of the skill ladder and unable to get any allied backup, things would gradually get worse. The Parasidolls were no less than first-class magicians when it came to combat power. Their psychic powers' activation speed outclassed modern magic.

However—the fact that he could consciously complain was actually proof that he had some leeway.

Now that he had a way to defeat them without releasing the parasites, the Parasidolls were no match for him.

The reason parasites possessing humans had been such difficult opponents was because if he killed the host, it would release the parasite, and Tatsuya didn't have a way to destroy its main body.

But the Parasidolls' hosts were gynoids storing accumulated psions. They could break but never die. And if he made sure a tiny amount of psions was still left in the machine, the parasite's main body would go into a sleep state to prevent exhausting itself.

Even while peppered with wounds from the concentrated psychic cross fire, he overcame his own blood loss and agony and forced the twelfth Parasidoll into a sleep state.

Four to go... There!

"Four Parasidolls remaining!"

The report came up from his subordinate like a cry, and the main researcher on the Parasidoll testing team bit his lip so hard it might bleed. He didn't know Tatsuya's—no, Maheśvara's—worth. If a single magician took down all sixteen Parasidolls, he knew this test and the entire Parasidoll development project itself would be stamped as a failure.

"But these last four... You won't be able to handle the Prime Four like the rest...!" muttered the lead developer to himself while gazing at the Parasidoll monitoring screen.

It sounded like an empty threat or perhaps like frustration at having lost, and the subordinate sitting next to him peered into his face with a look of concern.

As soon as Tatsuya sensed the presence of the four Parasidolls, a fist-sized cannonball came flying at him *before he could fire a spell.* It flew faster than the eye could see; Tatsuya only "saw" it with his ability to perceive information bodies. Diameter of twelve centimeters, mass of five kilograms, velocity of four hundred kilometers per hour. It was far from a bullet's speed, but its mass was orders of magnitude higher.

Tatsuya thrust out his right hand and stopped the cannonball. When it touched his hand, the sphere, made of packed earth, shattered. It hadn't merely broken—small particles had radially sprayed out. It was a result of dismantling the cannonball's movement vector, on the level of the earth composing it.

He'd defeated the preemptive attack with his signature move, but he didn't have a chance to breathe. A subtle, threadlike force field came into existence, about to shoot out at him. The repulsive force acting in both vertical directions relative to the direction of motion had the same principle as the weighting-type spell Pressure Cut. The force field was accurately divided, without a blade or wire to act as the reference line, perhaps because of mechanical, digital precision.

Once again, Tatsuya had no choice but to prioritize defense. With a Program Dispersion, he nullified the Parasidoll's Pressure Cut. In that time, another individual had closed into punching and kicking range.

It held weapons in both hands—large knives with blades about thirty centimeters long. Those weren't any threat to Tatsuya by themselves. The issue was the speed at which the Parasidoll swung them.

It's fast—

In terms of pure speed, it rivaled Erika's self-acceleration spell.

—however!

It didn't have the *technique* that she did. Its movements were precise and without waste, but that was all. In fact, the more precise it was, the easier it was to predict. Tatsuya dodged the two slashes from left and right, then triggered Program Dispersion. The accelerated spell lost its effect, and the doll's movements decreased to *human* speed.

That was one, he thought, about to ram his right fist into it. However.

"What?!"

A repulsive wall emerged in front of the knife-wielding Parasidoll. It didn't belong to the one who had used Pressure Cut. The fourth Parasidoll had deployed this magical barrier.

As it repelled Tatsuya backward, the knife-wielding one retreated as well. Now together, the four Parasidolls assumed a diamond formation. In front was the high-speed close combat type, on the right was the one that fired cannonballs made of packed earth, on the left was the ranged Pressure Cut user, and in the back was the one that created the repulsive barrier.

A cannonball flew at Tatsuya as he collected himself. Tatsuya jumped to the side out of its way with help from flight magic, but the cleaving blade followed him, closing in. After he dismantled the magic blade, two knives were there to greet Tatsuya. And an invisible wall to act as a shield.

These things have good coordination!

As though one brain was controlling four bodies, their combination was sharply distinct from the twelve he'd already put to sleep. And this trick was so good it didn't give Tatsuya a chance to attack.

"Yes, that's it, Prime Four. That's the way, my pretties!"

In the Kudou mobile lab, the main Parasidoll development researcher was now in a heat haze as he watched the screen.

"Right there! Cut him in half!"

A subordinate spoke in a reserved manner to his excited chief. "Chief, weren't we ordered not to kill him?"

"What?! Are we watching the same thing here? That magician has advanced self-regeneration abilities. Severing a limb or two won't kill him," answered the man, as though the idea wasn't even worth talking about, his eyes still fixed to the screen—and filled with lunacy.

"Master, to the right!"

Obeying the active telepathy ringing in his head, Tatsuya immediately tilted himself to the left. The earthen cannonball grazed his right shoulder and flew behind him.

"Fifty seconds until reload. Slash from the left—please dodge one meter to the right."

He dodged as he was told, and sure enough, the flying Pressure Cut blade passed by thirty centimeters to his left.

"Pixie, you know how they'll attack?" asked Tatsuya into his comm unit, using the armor built into his glove to handle the high-mobility type's knives.

"Cannonball incoming. Aiming for the head! ...Yes, Master. I can hear what these girls are saying."

"Saying? They aren't acting independently?"

With a deft duck, he dodged the cannonball, then nullified the self-acceleration spell at the same time. He tried to ram his right hand, fitted with the series of function-stopping spells, but a barrier blocked him at the last moment.

"Those four are constantly exchanging thoughts as they act."

The response came back from Pixie as the barrier's repulsion forced Tatsuya to take distance. He found himself deeply convinced by that answer; it wasn't *as though* one brain was controlling four bodies—they *were* being controlled by one mind, physically separated in four.

And Pixie could intercept the Parasidolls' *conversation*. Which meant countering them would be easy.

"Pixie, relay their conversation to me."

"Right away."

"Oh no! What's happening now?!" shouted the chief researcher. This time, his subordinates could sympathize.

The first four Parasidolls they'd created at old Lab Nine, the Prime Four—suddenly their attacks had stopped working.

He used his palm to block the clumps of earthen cannonballs and even dodged the G-Daggers—*G* for gravity—which was what they called the flying Pressure Cut blades. He handled the high-mobility type's attacks as though he'd been waiting for them; when the repulsion shield came up, the enemy was the one to retreat. Their side had no damage, but the other guy was clearly predicting the Prime Four's movements.

The MOVAL suit–wearing magician took the initiative for the first time. Altering the pattern thus far, they first aimed for his legs with two consecutive G-Daggers. But they dissipated before firing.

Neither the chief nor his subordinates could tell what was going on. But though they may have stopped thinking, the Parasidolls wouldn't. Once ordered, the automatic weapons would continue carrying out their mission unless their instructions changed or they were commanded to stop.

On the screen, the high-mobility type engaged the enemy. Behind that one, the artillery type readied itself, its hands wrapped around a cannonball. The knife type was bait—the cannonball was the main attack. But the MOVAL suit magician slipped right past the knife user as if he already knew that.

Repulsion shield information bodies formed—and then vanished into the sea of information.

The MOVAL suit magician appeared before the artillery type and touched the cannonball with his right hand. It went to dust and fell from the Parasidoll's hands.

The artillery type stood there, seeming dumbfounded...like a *human* would be.

The magician struck its chest with his left hand.

"Impossible...?!"

The researchers cried out. They couldn't believe it—or rather, they didn't *want* to believe it. Nonetheless, the instrument monitoring the Prime Four's artillery-type specimen signaled that its functions had stopped.

A perfectly coordinated attack by four Parasidolls. But their combination was so perfect that missing one weakened the move overall.

"Slashes to right hand, right leg, left leg."

Tatsuya was aware of those attacks without having to wait for Pixie's advice. The artillery type's role was to harass him with ranged physical attacks. Now that it was gone, that meant he could focus on dealing with the magic.

Tatsuya dismantled the Pressure Cuts with Program Dispersion. Then he charged for the Parasidoll readying its knives. After disabling the barrier that formed in front of him, he reached for a knife. For the Parasidoll, this was unexpected—a movement pattern that hadn't been input into its electronic brain. Had the machine delayed or had the demon?

Tatsuya's hand grabbed the knife.

The neo-Damascus steel knives—a synthetic carbon nanotube–based steel—turned into tiny particles and crumbled down. This didn't only affect the blade he'd grabbed, but hit the other knife he hadn't touched as well.

He'd crushed them with magic, so he hadn't needed to physically touch them to begin with, but the sight of it was strange and mysterious.

Of course, it wouldn't confuse Tatsuya, the one who caused the phenomenon. He stepped toward the defensive Parasidoll waiting in the back rather than the weaponless one. Without any assistance from the MOVAL suit, he closed the five-meter gap in one step.

A repulsion-field barrier deployed. It was faster than Tatsuya, but the speed of psychic powers *didn't care* about versatility.

But Tatsuya had the skills to nullify not only in-construction spells but completed ones as well, so the ability to merely create a barrier didn't mean much. Without the offensive ability to go along, it couldn't threaten him.

The defender went to sleep.

The close combat, high-mobility type and the long-ranged non-contact combat type remained. And these *girls* were already nothing more than Tatsuya's prey.

"Master, congratulations!"

Minami almost dropped her magical barrier upon hearing Pixie's sudden telepathic shout. The release of passionate emotion, which didn't make sense coming from a nonhuman, made Minami mutter "Another one..." without realizing it.

The next thing she had to say was this:

"Pixie, has Lord Tatsuya destroyed all the Parasidolls?"

The request for confirmation had too little worry in it to imply she was concerned for his safety.

"Yes. Master has caused all of them to enter a state of hibernation," answered Pixie with her voice after that big whoop.

"I hope he comes back soon..." Minami murmured.

But that was when she realized that if he came back now, the situation could get even worse.

The security forces were still surrounding the vehicle. If someone of unknown affiliation, identity hidden by a combat uniform, ran right into those soldiers, wouldn't that lead to an extremely unpeaceful ending...?

And then her portable terminal informed her of an incoming voice message.

Wondering who it was, she looked at the sender. She wasn't hopeful, assuming it wouldn't be displayed, but contrary to her expectations, it showed the name Fumiya Kuroba.

"Yes?"

Confused as to why he knew her call number, she picked up, while still maintaining her magical barrier.

"This is Fumiya Kuroba. Am I speaking to Miss Minami Sakurai?"

"Yes, but...?"

"I'm glad I got through. I apologize for looking up your number without asking. Anyway, I wanted to check something."

"No, I don't mind you knowing my number, Lord Fumiya—but what is it you wanted to check?"

"Miss Sakurai, you're the one currently holding up the barrier in the car surrounded by security guards, right?"

"Please call me Minami... As for your question, my answer is yes."

A slightly perplexed feeling came through the terminal, but the conversation resumed a moment later.

"...Miss Minami, you weren't trying to be a decoy by doing this or anything, were you? In other words, you don't need to keep the security troops there for some reason, right?"

"No, and in fact it's quite a lot of trouble... Also, Lord Fumiya, please call me Minami and not Miss Minami, if you please."

"...We can discuss that at a later date. More importantly, I'm about to knock all the security troops unconscious. Please maintain the barrier until then."

"Understood. I'll leave it up to you... And also, please try your best to call me Minami, as I am but a maid and you are a candidate for next head of the family."

"...*Okay, I'll get started. Probably won't even take five minutes.*"

At the end, Fumiya's tone had gotten much more casual.

It was not clear whether Minami thought *I won...!* at this time.

Looking toward familiar psionic wave motion, he'd seen a fairly powerful magic barrier. Fumiya had a hunch and confirmed that the caster was indeed one of the Sakura series connected to the Yotsuba—Minami, who was staying with Tatsuya.

Fumiya had a feeling he knew what was going on. His beloved "big brother" Tatsuya was out wrecking the Parasidoll experiment, so he'd probably needed the vehicle for something. Which meant he couldn't allow the security guards to see inside it. And he certainly couldn't leave more unnecessary work on Tatsuya's plate.

You were just unlucky.

Fumiya took out his well-used knuckle duster–shaped CAD. He was in a normal male high school uniform right now, but he couldn't let them spot him. Still, he decided the situation didn't call for *disguising* himself.

Twenty meters between him and the vehicle. Direct Pain would actually reach perfectly fine at this range. Getting as close as he could was an adjustment so that he wouldn't deal *too* much damage to them.

You really were unlucky, he said to himself, an excuse to the soldiers, before slamming a mercilessly powerful Direct Pain into the security troops swarming the vehicle.

By the time Tatsuya got back to the vehicle, he was naturally surprised by the security forces lying around the parking lot. It took a moment before the black-suited men and women under Fumiya's command ran to the scene after he'd contacted them about it.

Checking to make sure nobody was watching, he went inside the vehicle. As directed, he returned the MOVAL suit to the "coffin," pressed the self-destruct button, and fled the scene with Minami and Pixie.

Just like Fujibayashi said, none of the security guards lying around the vehicle seemed unduly harmed.

Tatsuya didn't stick around to make sure.

The biggest difference between the Cross-Country Steeplechase and normal track-and-field events was that nobody knew how the other runners were doing. Even in normal cross-country races, where participants also didn't have a good view of their rivals, the running courses were preset, and it was possible to get a feel for everyone's current positions by overtaking or being overtaken by others. But the Steeplechase essentially had no course, and vision was obscured by the trees, so all the runners wouldn't be able to tell how anyone else was doing, aside from the group they were in.

However, they could gain information on whether any runners had completed the track and how many from the information terminal in the glasses-shaped goggles.

The number of people who had finished, shown in the corner of the map displayed on the goggles, was zero.

Two hundred meters until the goal line.

Miyuki was now sure they were in the lead.

Kanon, running next to her, was too.

Suddenly, Kanon increased her pitch. Subaru, too, gave a burst of speed so she wouldn't fall behind.

Miyuki wavered. She wasn't exactly going easy on them with her current pace. This was as fast as she could go while still being careful of traps. If she accelerated any more, she could overlook one. Should she keep her careful eye out or risk it and go for the gold?

"Kyaa!" "Whoa?!"

Just as she thought that, two cries went up in sequence.

A volley of paint pellets, fired from several automatic gun emplacements, had hit Kanon, sending her careening to the side. The pellets couldn't penetrate anything, but in exchange, the kinetic energy was all converted into impact. A string of them hitting her from waist to leg had knocked her sideways; she couldn't dig in, and it was all she could do to adopt a defensive posture so she wouldn't get hurt when she hit the ground.

Subaru got caught in a net-bullet and fell to the ground, entangled. The magic she'd used was jump, not flight, so her spell reduced her falling inertia. Therefore, though the direct impact was lighter compared to Kanon, struggling while tangled up in a net like that might have been even more embarrassing for a young girl.

"Ugh… They didn't need to go all military on us *now*…"

Kanon groaned bitterly, but whether it was a complaint or a witty remark, it seemed fairly relaxed. Deciding they'd be okay, Miyuki said, "Please excuse me. I'll be going on ahead."

She got no answer from the other two. Though she did get the full brunt of their mental cries of *You're heartless!*

Still, the Steeplechase was an individual competitor event. They might have been from the same school, but on the track, they were enemies. It was simply a convenient tactic to form teams, that was all. Sticking to her cold, unfeeling decision—though it wasn't *that* dramatic—she faced the goal line again and resumed the race.

She glanced at her navigation map to check.

The number of runners who had finished was still zero.

Miyuki continued through the goal line in the lead. Kanon rallied and got back into the race, taking a beautiful second place, while Subaru took time to get free of the net and came in eighth. The other two First High runners, Honoka and Shizuku, came in at a friendly fifth and sixth.

[8]

In haste, Colonel Sakai and his group exited the HQ branch building. They knew that, logically, the chances of the magician in the flight combat suit, Maheśvara, coming after them were zero. But they had undeniably taken a supportive position in the Parasidoll experiment. It wasn't logic but an instinctual fear that had driven them out.

After exiting the building and arriving in the parking lot, they noticed that for some reason, the sky suddenly clouded.

Looking up, Sakai realized that the sky hadn't gotten cloudy.

A dark fog had swept through them.

"What is this…?"

"Gas?"

"No, sir, this is magic!"

The magician serving Colonel Sakai correctly pinpointed the black fog's identity.

But all he knew was that it was magic. He had no way to discern its effects nor cancel it out.

"Colonel Sakai and company—I have come to invite you all."

They turned toward the theatrical voice and saw an older man wearing a suit, despite it being midsummer, a soft hat that lay crooked on his head, bowing to them in an affected manner.

"To invite you to the world of your dreams."

That was last thing Sakai heard before his consciousness faded to black.

First place in the Cross-Country Steeplechase went to Miyuki in the women's and Masaki in the men's.

Once again, the overall victory went to First High this year. Since it had been a struggle until partway through, the First High team was even more excited than last year.

However, since at the very, very end Masaki had won first prize, the Third High competitors attended the nighttime after-party with satisfaction in their faces. Maybe they felt that with how well Masaki had done, they were sure to take it all next year.

Another school that stood out was Fourth High, which had won the rookie competition Monolith Code and Mirage Bat. The lovely twins responsible, despite not looking the part, adopted an unashamed attitude, granting a sense of realism to *the rumors.*

And not only the competitors but the adults as well were raising their glasses in a toast...

Retsu Kudou, currently surrounded by the former heads of the Kuki and Kuzumi and their clans who still followed him, smiled as he tipped back his sake cup.

It wasn't a satisfied smile exactly. It had a remorsefulness about it. Both Mamoru Kuki and the former Kuzumi head knew what was on Retsu's mind. They didn't ask him—but in exchange, they had taken several turns pouring his drink for him.

"I'd like to thank everybody for your hard work."

Eventually, Retsu began to naturally show his gratitude.

"On the surface, the Parasidoll experiment met with unfortunate results, but we gave the Maheśvara a very difficult fight. I'm sure it left a strong impression on those who want to use magic for military purposes."

Applause went up from all those present, indicating their approval.

"Those plotting the enlistment of young magicians will see their downfall as early as tomorrow, along with the Traditionalists. Allow me to say that that is a major achievement as well."

"No, it won't be tomorrow."

But suddenly, a voice interrupted him from the other side of the door.

"Who is it?!"

The one seated farthest back stood up and opened the door.

However, Retsu knew from the voice who had produced it before seeing them. "Kazama... And General Saeki."

But Kazama, the one who had made the rude interjection, was not the only one there.

"It has been quite a while, Your Excellency."

Everyone seated had fallen silent. Nobody offered Saeki a seat, either—and Saeki didn't seem to mind.

"Why the sudden visit? This is a personal gathering. Unfortunately, we haven't the means to entertain you."

"I'm deeply aware this was an unexpected visit. Once you've accepted a souvenir, we will depart at once."

"A souvenir?"

Saeki's tone was clearly unfriendly. Even under normal circumstances, she was thought of poorly by the Nine faction; a vixen who would dare disobey Retsu.

As the hostility silently grew, Saeki gave Kazama a signal.

"...I am Colonel Sakai from the JGDF General Headquarters. I have colluded with Makoto Kudou, current head of the Kudou, to promote the automatic magic weapons experiment during the Nine School Competition..."

Everyone, save for Retsu, stood up with a clatter.

The recording from the device in Kazama's hand was both a

confession and a repentance of having joined hands with the Kudou family and forcing the weapons test to be with high school students.

"…So Colonel Sakai has fallen into your hands."

"Yes, but we weren't the ones who captured him."

"…Would you mind telling me who was?"

"We received this recording from the Yotsuba."

The guests, stiff and still standing, all gasped.

"Maya… I see the Yotsuba will never permit any to harm their family." Retsu nodded, his tone sounding oddly convinced.

"Not so."

But Saeki denied it.

"What do you mean?"

"When Lady Yotsuba provided this recording, she did so under the condition that we not make the data public."

Retsu frowned dubiously. He didn't know what Maya's goal would be with that.

"Lady Yotsuba's objective is the purging of the Sakai group and the so-called anti-GAA hard-liners. We received this voice data from Lady Maya under the condition that we not distribute it while cleaning up after the fact."

"I see… Sakai and the others must have touched a nerve," murmured Retsu, voice firm. But he still didn't understand everything. "And what did you want to obtain that data for?"

"Your Excellency, the JDF will no longer force magicians to act as weapons."

"…"

"You may bet the gray hairs on my head if you wish. Magicians will never be sent to a battlefield against their own volition. Including your granddaughter and *him*."

"Are you…telling me to retire?"

"The Parasidolls will certainly become effective weapons—as long as we don't misuse them. Ten years ago, General, you wouldn't have made such a mistake."

"Watch your mouth, General Saeki!"

"Stop."

After Mamoru Kuki broke free of his chains and exploded, Retsu waved him down.

"Conducting magic weapon experiments on underage magicians. No matter how you try to smooth it over, you cannot call that *proper usage*."

Next to Saeki, Kazama butted in. His voice was like magma, seething with anger.

"Major Kazama, stand down."

"Yes, ma'am, my apologies!"

This time, Saeki chided Kazama.

She gazed straight into Retsu's eyes. "You can leave the rights of military magicians to those of us still in active service. We will not allow you to do anything concerning, Your Excellency," she stated outright.

"I see," answered Retsu, shoulders drooping—but seeming somehow happy.

Night, August 16, 2096.

A quiet bustle was going through Yokohama Chinatown.

"The target is headed for the west gate."

"He has the terrain advantage. Make sure you have at least three people when you corner him."

The group darted about in the darkness, exchanging only soft whispers—a unit led by Mitsugu Kuroba.

"Target spot— *Gah!*"

"What happened?!"

"It's like a dog or something…!"

"Be careful. Gongjin Zhou uses immortalist arts different from both Dahan and the GAA."

Mitsugu's confidant, waiting next to him, murmured, "He's tougher than we thought, boss."

"He's one of those most responsible for disrupting the nation from the inside. He'd need individual strength, too," answered Mitsugu, his voice calm. It didn't contain even a shard of unrest.

The confidant continued, his tone sounding reassured. "The lady has said she would dispatch Tatsuya Shiba, didn't she?"

"We'll secure Gongjin Zhou before he gets here."

But after hearing what his subordinate had just said, Mitsugu suddenly let his irritation bubble to the surface as though his previous calm attitude had only been a front.

"...Should we not wait for Lord Fumiya and Tatsuya Shiba?"

"What could Maya be thinking?"

Mitsugu seemed to have completely lost his cool, and despite being in front of a subordinate, he called her simply Maya.

"We shouldn't use *that* here. *It* was never something we should have let out. *It's* the crystallization of all the Yotsuba's sins. Locking *it* up in the Yotsuba is the only way we can possibly repent."

Mitsugu, realizing his confidant was watching him dumbfound-edly, loudly cleared his throat.

"I'll go. You take command."

"Yes, boss."

Mitsugu melted into the dark.

That, thought the confidant, would settle things—they didn't need to wait for Tatsuya's arrival.

"End of the line, Gongjin Zhou."

A few minutes later, Mitsugu was confronting Zhou.

"My, my... To think an even greater Yotsuba darkness, the head of the Kuroba, would personally make an appearance for my humble self. It seems you think too highly of me."

"I don't think it's an overestimation. Blanche's insurrection, No-Head Dragon's secret dealings, guiding the GAA special unit

here, arranging to smuggle in the parasites… It's amazing you pulled all that off by yourself."

"I simply lent a helping hand. It all would have happened eventually even without my involvement."

"You're a nuisance—turning that *eventually* into a *right now*."

"Delays solve nothing, don't you think?"

"I don't understand what's so bad about putting all that off until later."

Mitsugu inched closer.

"At this range, you can't escape using your vaunted *Qimen Dujia*. Give up, Zhou."

"Indeed… With you being so close, *dujia* techniques won't be of much help."

Even as Zhou admitted his special skill had been sealed, he hadn't become any less relaxed.

"Instead, I ask that you please excuse the slight pain—*ji, Xiao Tian Quan!*"

Mitsugu didn't even have time to gasp before a four-legged shadow dropped out of the night sky.

The giant doglike silhouette leaped for Mitsugu—and bit off one of his arms.

"Guh…"

Mitsugu bent over without a word. The black beast was already nowhere in sight.

"Well. It took me ten years to create that. Still, in exchange for an arm of Mitsugu Kuroba, I can't call it disproportionate."

Leaving only those words behind, Gongjin Zhou's figure faded into the shadows.

"Dad!"

The moment Fumiya, who had gone to get Tatsuya, saw Mitsugu, he pushed through the wall of black suits, his face utterly pale, and ran to him.

"Who could have…? That's right! Tatsuya!"

Remembering the extraordinary abilities of his venerated second cousin whom he'd brought along, Fumiya looked at him, eyes practically clinging. In response, Tatsuya took out a handgun-shaped CAD with his left hand.

"Stop… I will not take favors from you."

"Dad, what are you saying?!" Fumiya began to violently shake the heavily wounded man.

"Fumiya," said Tatsuya to stop his young cousin before turning his left hand to Mitsugu. "You may not like it, but Fumiya and Ayako would both be saddened if I left you like this."

Tatsuya cast Regenerate. Bitten off and gone to places unknown, *Mitsugu's* right arm appeared from nowhere, aligned with the wound, and connected itself.

Unconsciously holding his *own* right arm, Tatsuya said under his breath, "I was right to leave Miyuki and Ayako behind. Still, I can't believe someone would wound you this badly, Mr. Kuroba… What kind of spell could Zhou possibly have used?"

Mitsugu was looking at his own arm in frustration. Not meeting Tatsuya's eyes, he shook his head.

"I don't know. He said *Xiao Tian Quan*—'barking heaven dog'—but there must be more to it than that."

"It refers to a myth, after all… Perhaps it's a type of compound-form spell. That does present an issue…"

Tatsuya didn't ask where Zhou had escaped to.

He knew that was something he'd have to figure out himself—at any cost.

(To be continued)

Afterword

The Irregular at Magic High School has made it to Volume 13. Did you enjoy the Steeplechase arc?

I indirectly touched on this in the story as well, but a *steeplechase* is a word for an obstacle course. It isn't just about the event on the Nine School Competition's final day. The initial concept was that the main character would have to overcome all sorts of obstacles to uncover the conspiracy against them, almost like running through an obstacle course. But once it was all finished, it ended up feeling more like going back and forth in a labyrinth with a lot of dead ends than it did an obstacle course. Maybe having this volume's subtitle be "Wandering Arc" would have fit the story better. Although then it would have seemed like even the runners would have been wandering aimlessly through the Cross-Country Steeplechase course.

The story this time wasn't about the Nine School Competition itself but the conspiracy surrounding the Parasidolls. The focus of that is on the Cross-Country Steeplechase, so I cut out most of the other athletes' competitions. All kinds of little stories developed not only during the matches but in the off-time between them, offering some glimpses of it, but loading the story up with those sub-episodes would have been compositionally impossible.

To that end, I've gotten approval to write about the smaller episodes happening alongside the Steeplechase arc as a short story. We haven't currently decided how many there will be or what kind of form they'll take, but I believe we'll be able to announce it on the official Twitter in the coming days.

Speaking of the coming days, by the time this book reaches the readers' hands, I think the anime will have started its broadcast. Please go and enjoy that as well. The anime Blu-rays will come with extras where I write about magic high school characters never before introduced, so please look forward to that.

Now then, I hope we'll meet again for the next volume—the Ancient City Civil War arc. I ask for your humble patronage not only in that regard but with the comics and anime as well.

I hope you'll continue to read *The Irregular at Magic High School* in the future.

Tsutomu Sato